DEADLY KISS

The Immortal Reign 1

ARIEL MARIE

WARNING

Due to the explicit language and graphic sexual scenes, this book is intended for mature (18 years +) readers only. If things of this nature offend you, this book would not be for you. If you like a good action story with hot steamy scenes with lesbian vampires and their human mates, then you have chosen wisely…

CHAPTER ONE

"Two oh seven!" a harsh voice called out.

She had been reduced to a number.

Quinn Hogan sat in the sterile waiting room and glanced up to see a man of about thirty walk over to the check-in desk. He conversed with the woman who had called his number.

An orderly arrived and escorted the man away.

Quinn swallowed hard and peered down at the number in her hand. Wrapping her arms around herself, she sat back, afraid of what was to come.

Today was the day her name had been drawn.

She had been called down to the government lab to donate a blood sample for the draft.

She had made it to age of thirty-five without having to submit to the orders of the government. She had prayed this day never came...but here it was.

A shiver passed through Quinn at the thought of what they were demanding the humans to do.

As much as she wanted to run away, there would be nowhere for her to hide.

At the turn of the new millennium, vampires had revealed themselves to the world. Mankind had long assumed they were the only ones inhabiting this planet.

For the first time ever, every human on the face of this earth banded together to fight a new enemy —the vampires.

Humans had not wanted to bend to the will of the bloodsuckers. The ego of mankind could not stand the thought that they were no longer the top of the food chain.

The war commenced with the armies of every nation working together with a common cause.

Unfortunately, it was a war the humans lost.

The number of vampires living among them had been staggering to discover.

The vampires swept through this world, destroying everything that was ever considered normal.

Quinn looked around the room at the other poor souls who were subjected to give a blood sample. Each day, names were chosen, and people were to report to their local government lab.

Cold plastic chairs lined the room, and almost every single one of them were occupied. They tried to soften the decor with plants, warm colors, and light music playing, but they didn't fool anyone.

The air was full of tension. No one knew if they would be matched after their sample was submitted.

To be chosen would result in being uprooted from one's current life and sent to live with a vampire.

As their mate.

The vampires believed in fated mates. Someone destined for them. Even though there were countless amounts of them spread out throughout the world, they claimed their numbers were declining. Per their decree, they needed their fated mate to procreate and continue on their bloodline.

Quinn had never personally confirmed the myths and legends she had heard about vampires. She tried to stay as far away from them as possible.

She not only hated them, but she also feared them.

The war had taken everything from her.

Her parents had been drafted in the war to fight, and neither of them had made it home. They were not soldiers, but the American government hadn't cared. They needed bodies to fight these monsters.

Any healthy person was put in fatigues, given weapons, and marched to war. Age hadn't been a factor. There hadn't even been time to train the unexperienced soldiers. The second a gun was put in their hands, they were sent off to fight.

Her brother, Lane, she hadn't seen him in years. For the longest it had been the two of them. He was older than her by a few years. They had stayed together, and he had been her protector. Ten years ago, he'd disappeared. She had tried to do everything she could to find him, but not having money meant that her search would be a dead end.

No one cared about a missing human.

She had gone to the police who had basically told her he was probably claimed by a vampire and for her to stop looking.

When she had the extra funds, she hired private

detectives to start searching for him, but they all came back with the same outcome.

No traces of Lane anywhere.

Quinn sighed and closed her eyes, trying to will the tears that had formed to go away.

She didn't want to be paired with a vampire. A tremor snuck through her at the thought of sharp fangs piercing her skin.

"Two ten," the voice rang out.

Quinn froze. She opened up her balled fist, her gaze dropping to the slip of paper in her hand.

Two hundred and ten.

It was her number.

Quinn pushed up and stood to her full height. There was no use in trying to stall. She hefted her purse on her shoulder. There wasn't much in there, but it gave her something to hold on to.

It was a struggle to get her feet to move toward the desk. All she wanted to do was hightail it out of there and just run.

Her gaze landed on the entrance and took in the guard standing outside.

She wouldn't get far.

Quinn exhaled and pushed forward.

"Hi." She paused to clear her throat. "You just called my number. Two ten."

"Name?" The woman didn't look up from her computer.

Quinn studied her and determined that she was human. She had a tan which wouldn't exist on a vampire. They were highly allergic to sunrays.

"Quinn Hogan."

"Age?"

"Thirty-five." Quinn answered her other questions. Address. Place of work. Family status. Height. Weight.

"Did you bring your birth record?" It was then the woman switched her focus to Quinn.

Quinn nodded. She reached inside her bag and brought out her birth certificate and identification card. She handed them over to the woman. She watched her scan them into her computer before passing the documents back to Quinn.

"Please stand over there so we may take your photo."

Quinn moved over to where the woman pointed. She stared into the camera, waiting for the woman to finish. The flash went off twice, then she was done.

The same orderly who had escorted the man away earlier arrived at the desk. He too appeared to be human.

Quinn tried to keep the expression on her face neutral. How could these people work at a place like this? The results of these labs would totally destroy someone's life.

Not that the war hadn't done enough of that already.

But forcing humans to comply with this felt almost as if they were traitors to their own kind.

"Anthony will escort you to the back where you will donate your sample." The woman motioned to the orderly.

He offered her a small smile, but Quinn was in no mood to even draw one up. His smile faltered when she didn't return one.

"Follow me, ma'am." He waved her on.

She walked past the desk and trailed behind him. He led her down the stark white hall of the medical facility. The scent of antiseptic filled her nostrils.

At least they kept the place clean.

When imagining the facility she was to report to, she had thought it would be some dark, drab monstrosity that wouldn't meet any health codes.

By the looks of it, the lab had to be funded by vampires. Thanks to the war, the government didn't have any extra money to spare.

Gripping the strap of her bag, she attempted to will her heart to slow down. Quinn was trying not to panic. She knew she would give her sample and then be able to leave.

"Here you go." Anthony gestured to an open door. He placed some paperwork in a folder posted on the wall.

"Thank you." She entered a room that resembled a doctor's office. She sat in the chair and exhaled a shaky breath.

"They should be with you in a moment." He gave a nod and pulled the door closed halfway.

Quinn took in the supplies resting on the table by her. A few vials for her blood to go in along with the tools they needed to draw it. Gloves, Band-Aids, alcohol pads.

If she wanted, Quinn could pretend she was at a normal doctor's appointment and getting blood drawn to check her health.

The door was pushed open, and a pretty woman dressed in scrubs entered.

This woman was a vampire.

There was no doubt about it.

She was pale, beautiful, and everything about her seemed perfect.

"Quinn Hogan?" The woman glanced down at

the papers in her hand, dropping them on the table next to Quinn.

"Yes." Quinn tried to act normal, but she was failing. It wasn't often she was near vampires. This one gave off a calming sense for some reason. Quinn's fear increased at the thought of how the woman would react once she began drawing the blood needed.

"My name is Asha, and I'll be obtaining your sample." The woman must have picked on Quinn's anxiety. "Have no fear. This will be quick and painless."

"I don't like needles," Quinn muttered. She didn't want to insult someone to their face. Especially not a vampire. Humans, she could handle.

"I understand. Please push up your sleeve." Asha began preparing the things she needed.

Quinn sat up and pushed up her sleeve on her left arm, exposing it.

Asha cleaned off the area with an alcohol swab and within seconds had a small needle in the crook of her arm. Quinn watched her dark-crimson blood flow into the tubing and enter the vial.

Three vials, and Asha was done. She withdrew the needle and placed a small bandage on the insertion site, wrapping it up with soft tape.

"You can take this off in about twenty minutes," Asha instructed. "I don't scent any diseases in you that would cause you to bleed excessively."

Well, that confirmed what Quinn assumed. Asha was a vampire.

Quinn nodded as she pulled her sleeve down.

"Thank you." She didn't know why she was thanking the woman. Asha had been correct that the blood draw was painless. She'd barely felt the needle prick her skin.

"I'm not sure if you know, but I'm obligated to explain this process to you." Asha placed the vials in a clear bag and closed it, turning her attention back to Quinn. "We will run your blood and enter it into our computer database. It will notify us if you match with anyone. Each evening the positive matched drawings are announced on public television. If you are paired, an armed guard will pick you up and escort you to your mate."

Dread pooled in the pit of Quinn's stomach at the thought of being matched with someone and forced to be with them.

"What are the chances of me being matched with someone?" Quinn asked.

"I'm told it's around one in a million."

Quinn relaxed slightly. Hearing those odds made her feel slightly better.

"If there are no other questions, you are free to go." Asha handed her some papers. "Here is some general information they give out about the draft and a number you can call if you want to know your blood type and anything else found in your samples."

"Really? You run other tests on us?" Quinn took the papers and stood. She hadn't heard of that before.

"Of course. We need to ensure any potential mate is healthy so the vampire is aware of it before the claiming."

Quinn didn't want to think what would happen if someone was in the beginning stage of cancer.

Their vampire would probably just eliminate them and moved on.

Quinn spun around and left the room. She followed the exit signs and tried to not think of being matched. She couldn't have that bad of luck.

She wasn't sure why, but the sense of dread was still there.

* * *

"Shit, shit!" Quinn speed-walked toward her job. After she had left the lab earlier, she had gone home and taken a nap. It was rare for her to do so, but she was just too anxious about the results. The moment her head had hit the pillow, she was out like a light.

Now, she had a few minutes to get to work before she would be late.

She had grown up in a small town, but after Lane's disappearance, she had moved to the nearest city, figuring it was better for her to be amongst more humans. Her hometown had been run over by vampires who brutalized humans. If she had stayed, she was certain a vampire would have captured her and drained her.

So she'd moved to Stramford. The town was not what it used to be before the war. No city was.

To make a living for herself, she worked odd jobs here and there. There weren't that many opportunities for employment, so Quinn could not afford to lose this job.

The economy was in the toilet. Many buildings that used to be thriving were now boarded up. The area she lived in was a run-down part of Stramford, but it was full of hard workers trying to survive.

Finally, she arrived at The Diner with two minutes to spare. Flinging open the door, she burst inside and headed straight for the bar.

"There she is!" Sara called out.

"I'm here." Quinn stuffed her bag in one of the little cubbyholes behind the bar. She spun around to grab an apron off the hook on the wall.

The Diner was a small restaurant located in downtown Stramford. It gave off old-school vibes, decorated in early twentieth-century decor. It wasn't much, and the food was decent and cheap. The bar was for single patrons who may not want a table. A couple of guys were eating their supper while eyeing the television on the wall.

The place wasn't that big, but it always had a steady flow of traffic due to it being one of the only respectable places to get a good hot meal.

That's why Quinn couldn't afford to lose this position. She was easily replaceable by anyone dying to have a steady job.

She was to work the evening shift, and there were a few people sitting in some booths. It was still early. Soon the place would be packed with the dinner rush.

She eyed a couple who was just seated in her

area. She grabbed a notepad, pen, and stuffed her apron with straws, heading over to them.

"Hello," she greeted them with a smile. One thing that hadn't changed since the war was the service industry depending upon tips for their salary. Quinn ensured her customers always got top-notch service. "Welcome to The Diner. I'm Quinn and I'll be your server today."

She quickly took their order of drinks. She fell into the rhythm of work and tried to push her adventure to the lab to the back of her mind. She didn't want to think about that now.

A few more guests began to file in, and she threw herself into taking care of her tables with time escaping her.

"Shush! The draft is about to come on," Sara called out.

Quinn was in the middle of busing her emptied table and froze in place. She turned around to see Sara fiddling with the television.

Sara and Quinn had become somewhat friends when she'd started working at the diner. It was no secret that Sara was dying to enter the draft. Quinn couldn't believe her friend was a vampire enthusi-ast. She wanted to be claimed by one of them. Quinn didn't know why her friend lived in a fantasy world. Didn't she know what vampires were known for?

Why couldn't they just take the people who wanted to be paired with vampires? Let them volunteer?

But that wouldn't work for vampires. They wanted the true mates of their species.

Quinn shuddered and glanced around the diner. Everyone's attention was drawn to the television.

Quinn would rather die than be mated to a vampire.

They were known to be cruel, powerful, and used humans as a food source.

It was no way to live.

The show that had been on was now interrupted by the draft. A beautiful brunette sat at a desk, as if this was the regular nightly news. It was apparent she was one of them.

Her tiny fangs peeked from underneath her top lip painted red with lipstick. She smiled, and the full sight of her fangs came into view.

"Good evening, America. Here are your nightly draft picks," she announced.

Quinn studied her and felt insignificant to the vampire. Why would they want humans? Quinn was definitely the opposite of the woman on the screen. She wasn't tall, was plus-sized, and brown-skinned with short curly hair. Quinn chose to keep her natural hair close to her scalp for it was easier to care for.

She glanced back up and tuned back in to the announcements. A woman's name and picture appeared on the screen. It must have been the photo they'd taken of her at the lab.

Quinn's mouth grew dry watching another name and photo appear on television. They continued revealing other names of humans were who matched.

Her heart pounded while she sent up a prayer that her name would be not chosen. She blinked and froze in place.

Quinn Hogan.

Her photo appeared.

"It can't be," she whispered. Fear accosted her.

No.

She couldn't have been chosen.

The odds were one in a million.

She swallowed hard, feeling sympathetic gazes land on her from the patrons.

"Quinn!" Sara exclaimed. She turned around with a grin that immediately died. She must have seen the horrified expression on Quinn's face.

"It's going to be okay." Sara flew over to her side. Her wide blue eyes locked with Quinn's. Her friend was a pretty blonde who was more optimistic than Quinn.

"No, it won't." Quinn shook her head.

Sara wrapped her arms around her and drew her in for a tight hug.

"It won't be as bad as you think," Sara whispered. She pulled back and cupped Quinn's face. "Whoever is your mate will be lucky to have you."

Her friend was truly delusional.

The bell over the door sounded. Quinn and Sara jumped, turning to look at the newcomers.

Two of the largest men Quinn had ever seen entered the building. Both were dressed in dark uniforms with an insignia on the chest. The first one had long blond hair while the other was dark-skinned and bald.

Vampires.

"Quinn Hogan?" The bald one's voice was a deep baritone that brought goosebumps to her skin. No man's voice should be that low.

"Yes?" Quinn's voice shook. She stepped away from Sara with one final glance. This was probably the last time she'd see her friend and this diner.

"You are to come with us. We are your escort," Blondie said.

As much as her first instinct screamed for her to run, she knew she wouldn't make it far. These men were deadly vampires with weapons adorning their body.

She untied her apron and walked over to the bar. She refused to meet at anyone's gazes for she didn't want to see the pity in their eyes. She hung up the apron and grabbed her purse. She stood up straight, waiting.

"Come with us." Baldy motioned for her to walk with them.

She exited the building with them and was escorted to a large SUV. They drove her to her apartment building that was located five blocks away.

They followed behind her as she entered her tiny apartment. It wasn't much. An efficiency with everything in one room along with a bathroom. This had been her home for years.

"Pack one bag with anything of value to you." Blondie walked over to the window and peered out of it.

Nodding, she threw together a bag with the few items of clothing she owned. Quinn peeked over her shoulder at the two vampires speaking in hushed tones. She reached underneath her pillow and drew out a small knife she kept hidden. A girl living alone could never be too careful.

She hid it in her bag, burying it inside one of her sweatshirts. This would be her get-out-of-jail-free card. She refused to bend to the will of vampires.

Quinn walked over to her dresser and picked up the one picture she had of her family. She stared at her parents, her brother, and herself. This picture had been taken a few months before her parents were forced to fight in the war.

They all appeared happy.

Her vision blurred with tears. Blinking them back, she turned and gently placed the picture in the bag with her belongings.

Taking one last glance around her drab place, she faced the vampire guards.

"I'm ready."

Blondie gave a nod and stalked over to her, hefting up her bag. Her gaze flew to it, her heart skipping a beat.

She kept her mouth shut and followed them out of her apartment. They got into the waiting vehicle.

They sped away from her building. Quinn

glanced back at it, until it was no longer able to be seen.

She spun back around in her seat and bit back a sob.

Vampires had taken everything from her.

Now her freedom, and probably her life.

CHAPTER TWO

"Your Grace."

Velika ignored the warrior vying for her attention. She gave a shout and swung her sword. It clashed with that of her opponent's.

His blue eyes flashed, his fangs on display. He didn't back down and he was a worthy vampire who was just as competitive as Velika.

She growled, spinning around and sending her weapon toward Luther's. The force of his weapon knocked hers from her hand.

This was how she trained.

As if her life depended upon it.

She dodged his advances. His sword came at her, but she used her vampiric reflexes to spin out of the way. Luther swore, too slow for her. She lashed her foot out, landing a powerful kick to his back. He stumbled for a second then caught himself.

Velika Riskel was a highly experienced vampire warrior. She was the youngest daughter of the vampire king and warden of Northwest America.

Luther, her second-in-command, had trained with her for years. She had never been beaten by him or anyone else when it came to hand-to-hand battling. Not that she thought Luther would lose on purpose.

No, Velika was just that good.

They met daily for sparring. Velika wanted to ensure she was in top shape. Those who wore her family's crest on their chest, were loyal and willing to die for them, had to follow a leader who was willing to fight alongside them.

Her warriors had to know they followed a female who was hard to defeat. It gave them confidence and helped the morale of vampires to know their leader would die for them.

That was how she'd got the title she held. It

wasn't because of her father. It was because of her aggressive nature to conquer.

Luther's fist came within a hair's breadth of her face. She drew back just in time. It would have hurt like a son of a bitch had he connected.

Velika was tall, lithe, and fit. She was a hard opponent when it came to fighting. She wasn't one of those small vampires who only cared about wealth and status.

She was a warrior princess who fought for the good of vampires everywhere.

Luther gave a yell and charged at her. He wrapped her up in his arms, squeezing the breath out of her.

She grinned. He had made a lethal mistake.

Getting too close to her.

She braced herself and brought her knee up sharply, catching him in his nether region. The air was knocked out of him, and she took advantage. Her elbow connected with his face, and when he released her, he bent down in agony. Velika brought her knee up, connecting it with his chin. He jerked back, falling to the floor.

She took out a dagger from the sheath on her waist and fell on top of him, resting her knee on his sternum and her knife at his throat.

"Do you yield?" she growled.

They were both breathing hard, covered in sweat and a little blood. Tendrils of her blonde hair escaped her high bun and fell into her face.

"Yield," Luther breathed. His head fell back against the floor.

Quinn barked a laugh and stood. She replaced the weapon on her hip then offered her hand out to Luther and assisted him from the floor. The training room was where warriors could come to spar. It was a large room with different mats for sparring; weapons lined the walls that allowed them to practice.

Velika pushed for her warriors to be the best.

"I only yielded because the poor chap looks as if he's going to shit bricks if you don't answer him." Luther nodded to the young lad standing off to the side.

Quinn turned and finally focused on him. He barely had hair on his chin. A young trainee. She narrowed her gaze on him, pissed that someone would send him to interrupt her.

"Well? What do you want?" she snapped. She rested her hands on her waist and waited.

"The queen is requesting your presence via

holograph." He swallowed hard and waited to be dismissed.

"Tell them I shall be there in a minute." She waved him off.

She didn't miss the relief that crossed his face. He gave her the standard salute of a fist over his heart and bowed. Then he spun around on his heel and practically sprinted from the training room.

"You are too hard on the young ones," Luther murmured. He tossed her a bottle of water.

She caught it with one hand.

"If I'm not tough on them, they die." She twisted off the cap and took a long pull.

"And that is why they follow you." Luther winked at her. He leaned down and snagged his towel from the floor and wiped his face. His dark hair stood up on end. He was a handsome vampire, and women all over always practically threw themselves at him. It was a wonder he wasn't mated off.

"Let me go see what my dear mother wants." She flung the empty bottle to him and stalked past him. His laughter filled the air behind her. She knew what he was hinting at.

She, a big bad warrior, still had to answer to her mother.

Velika snorted. She would like to see someone

ignore her mother. People called her and her sisters ruthless.

They needed to meet their mother.

There was a reason Mira Riskel was the queen of the American vampires, and it wasn't because of she had a pretty face.

Velika left their training room. Her feet ate up the distance. She was irritated that she was being called away from training.

She refused to change before speaking with her mother. The queen should understand that she put defending the vampires as top priority. She proudly wore her leathers and weapons.

Her skin was still damp with sweat, and she was sure she looked a mess.

Apparently, whatever the queen wanted, it had to be important. The queen was never to be ignored. If Velika didn't take her mother's call, the woman just might show up.

It didn't matter that she was a vicious fighter for their race. Neither her nor her sisters would ever ignore their mother. Her sisters were spread out across North America, defending the continent in the name of their father, the king.

When vampires conquered the planet, the seven kingdoms were officially revealed. It was decided vampires would no longer live off the grid and underground. No longer would they hide in the shadows. It was time for vampires to showcase who they were and their power.

The humans gave pushback.

Their arrogance led to an all-out war. The humans believed they would be able to eradicate vampires, and it was the vampires who had to prove just who was the more superior race.

Which was such a shame.

But it was either kill or be killed.

Now that the dust had settled, the vampires were trying to help integrate life with the humans. Some still fought back.

Their government finally broke down and agreed to the terms set by the vampires.

Velika never understood how humans were ignorant to the fact that they were not alone on the planet.

Velika's father, Niall Riskel, was the king of all of the North America continent and had been for centuries. Vampires were blessed with slow aging and could live for centuries.

They weren't immortal, for a vampire could be killed.

Velika arrived at the communications room. A

few techs were working at the bank of monitors. They glanced up when she entered the room. They immediately stood and bowed to her with their fists over their hearts.

"I'll take my mother's call in the conference room," she barked out.

"Yes, Your Grace," one replied.

She marched into the smaller room and shut the door. A table and chairs were in the center. A small black box rested in the middle of the table. A series of lights lit up, and within seconds her mother's figure appeared, standing at the head of the table.

The clarity of the image was amazing. Had Velika not known she was speaking with her mother virtually, she would assume the queen was physically in the room.

"Mother." Velika gave her the customary bow as a show of respect.

"Oh, please, Velika. You are my child. I do not want you to bow to me," Mira snapped.

Velika raised her eyes to look at her mother. She was beautiful. All her daughters resembled her. She had long blonde hair that was styled into a regal high bun, her makeup was light, and her royal crimson robes touched the floor. The woman was five hundred and eighty years old and didn't appear a day over fifty.

"Well, I figured since you interrupted me during training, this must be official royal business." Velika stood to her full height and folded her hands behind her back.

"Watch your tone, young lady." Her mother's image ambled over to her. A smirk was on her lips. "You have always been a smart-ass just like your father."

Her parents were one of the lucky couples. They were true mates and had found each other through an accidental meeting. They would spend all of eternity with each other.

"How is the old man?" Velika relaxed and smiled at her mother. There was something about being the youngest of three children. It didn't matter how old she or her siblings got, Velika was the one who always got away with murder when it came to their parents.

"Your father is busy as ever with political issues and demands to kill everyone. You know, the usual." Mira smiled. She sighed and stared at Velika. "It's been a while since I've seen you in person. When are you coming to visit?"

"Soon, Mother. You know it's been busy here,

too." There were always rebels and protests that Velika had to deal with. Humans and vampires protested the war. The threat of rogue vampires was always on the horizon, there was always the threat of human radical militia groups who despised everything vampire, and now the lycans were creating mischief.

"How is the Northwest?" her mother asked. Her figure sat in the chair at the front of the table.

Velika chose a seat near her. It always amazed her how lifelike figures were through the hologram.

"Dreary, just how I like it." Velika loved Washington state. The town of Ensfield did not experience much sunshine.

Not having too much sun was better for her kind. She could move freely around during the day as much as she wanted. The thick clouds always held the dreadful sun away.

"I still don't understand why you choose to go out during the day." The queen visibly shuddered. "It's just not normal. Our kind are nocturnal and belong out during the nighttime."

"Well, Mother, those who are conspiring against vampires walk around during the day and night. A good warrior is always prepared." Velika sat back. She didn't want to try to argue with her mother.

She did not want the queen's wrath upon her. She may be a seasoned warrior and commander of an army, but she was no idiot.

No one crossed the queen.

Not even the king himself.

"I guess you have a point. It's no wonder your father appointed you as a warden." Pride appeared in Mira's eyes. She crossed her legs and sighed. "I am sure you are curious as to the nature of my call. As much as I would love to catch up, I have to tell you that there is a certain matter that I have taken into my hands."

Velika wearily stared at her mother.

This wasn't good at all.

"If there was an issue that needed to be taken care of, Mother, my sisters and I would have handled it."

"I have been demanding this of you and your sisters, and you all ignored me." Mira rolled her eyes in the most un-queen-like fashion. "Well, no more. Now we will do this my way."

Dread filled Velika. She jumped up from her chair and rested her hands on her hips.

What the hell had her mother done?

"I'm not following you. Will you please stop talking in a code," she growled.

Mira slowly pushed up from her chair, a devilish gleam in her eyes. Velika remained cool and collected.

A nagging feeling at the back of her mind alerted her that she wasn't going to be happy with what her mother was about to say.

"I have entered you and your sisters into the draft. It is time for the three of you to take mates."

"What have you done?" Velika demanded. She wasn't ready to take a mate. She was in the prime of her life.

She was fighting for her father, securing her area of their kingdom. She didn't have time to take a mate. Her prime focus in life was protecting all that vampires stood for.

The draft was something that all vampires were familiar with. It was a system the seven kings had created with her father leading. As the years passed and vampires hid underground, the chances of finding their fated mates were slim.

Only fated mates would produce offspring. With the number of true mates declining, the number of vampire births were dwindling.

It was discovered that humans and vampires were compatible when it came to mating. After the war, the draft went into effect.

This allowed them to further the reach of finding mates for vampires.

"Withdraw my name," Velika demanded. Desperation filled her. This couldn't be happening. She had her life planned out and didn't need her mother meddling.

Neither of her sisters would want this either.

"It is too late."

An icy chill slithered through Velika. She shook her head, not wanting to believe that she could not withdraw. She began thinking of who was on the council she could contact to bend the rules. Being the daughter of the king had to amount to something.

"It can't be. Call them and tell them it was a mistake. You are the queen." She stepped near her mother. Anger filled her at the thought of being forced to do something. Her gums stretched and burned as her fangs descended.

She was going to hurt something.

The moment the call with her mother was over, she'd go hunting.

"The other reason why I'm calling you is to notify you that a match has been made with a female." Mira smiled, clapping her hands. "A human one."

"Mother—"

"It will do good for the world to see that the royal family is not above finding their mate through the blood match. This person is perfect for you in every way."

"I don't want a mate!" she shouted, her voice echoing through the room. Her hands balled into tight fists.

"I cannot undo what is done, my dear. She is already on her way to you."

Fuck, they sure worked fast. It was common knowledge that they quickly secured the human before they had a chance to run.

Velika stalked away from her mother and rested her hands on the table.

This just couldn't be. Maybe she was having a dream and this was turning into a nightmare. She closed her eyes, sliding her tongue over her sharp fangs until she nicked it slightly. The taste of copper filled her mouth.

No, this was not a dream.

"Mother, you don't know what you have done." Her chest was rising and falling fast. Velika lifted her head and looked at her mother.

"I know I have help bring the other half of my daughter's soul to her." Mira's eyes were sincere, and Velika knew her mother meant well in her own way, but this was going too far. "You must teach her our ways and claim her so that she may join you in all eternity."

Velika shook her head. She wouldn't do it. She didn't have time to concentrate on a mate. If what her mother said was true and a human showed up, she would let her go. She refused to tie a person to her whom she would neglect.

Hell, Velika was sure the human probably didn't even want to be entered in the draft. There were plenty who protested that it took away human rights.

Velika bit back a snort.

What about vampire rights?

"Mother—"

"You must do this, Velika." An angry storm rolled onto her mother's face. She moved to stand next to Velika. "Once you've won her over, then we can be certain that your line won't die out anytime soon."

Velika's balled fists tightened. She could feel the pain of her nails digging into her skin.

What would she do with a human?

They were too delicate and weren't built for the life of a vampire's mate.

She didn't care what her mother wanted.

Velika would release the human.

"I have alerted your staff to prepare a room for her when you were training with Luther." Her mother walked away from her and stood near her abandoned chair. She had calmed down and presented as the regal queen again. "A mate is a blessing from the goddess above. You should be happy and thankful there is someone you will be able to spend the rest of your life with. A lifetime of loneliness is not worth it. Take this gift and cherish her."

Her mother's figure disappeared.

Velika grabbed the nearest chair to her and threw it at the wall with all her strength. It splintered into pieces and fell to the floor.

She glared at the mess. It didn't fix anything, but it did calm her a little. She knew what would make her feel better.

Hunting.

A knock sounded at the door.

"Who is it?" She growled. She faced it as it opened.

Luther and her personal advisor, Petra, entered. Luther's eyebrows rose sharply at the sight of the broken chair while Petra shook her head.

"Everything good in here?" Luther asked.

Velika ignored his question and turned her attention to Petra.

"I'm going to assume your mother told you the news," Petra said. She folded her hands together, meeting Velika's gaze head-on. They were longtime friends, and Petra was always allowed to speak her mind. "I have just received word that the human will be here within the hour."

CHAPTER THREE

Quinn sat frozen in the SUV while her vampire escorts drove her to her destination. She had only been given the name of the vampire she would now belong to.

Velika Riskel.

The guards hadn't said much to her other than to answer that question.

She had much preferred it.

The shock of the vampire she was matched with had rendered her speechless. How did she get matched with royalty?

A vampire princess. Commander of the Northwest territory.

One of the most ruthless vampires in the country.

Fear gripped Quinn. The Riskel royals were known for their fierceness and ruthlessness. Everyone knew of King Riskel, the ruler of the North American continent. The human government had basically rolled over and showed their belly. The king ruled the lands. The United States and Canada all answered to the king.

There was no way Quinn would be able to survive whatever Velika had in store for her. She was already planning to run the moment she got the chance.

She would be willing to risk the wrath of the princess.

The commander's skills with weapons and fighting were always being covered on the news. Quinn was sure the princess had some weird deadly fetish for humans that would lead to her being drained dry.

She swallowed hard, not wanting to imagine what would happen to her.

Vampires claimed they were protecting the humans, but Quinn had heard otherwise. Terror overtook her at the thought of what the vampire would probably do to her. She had heard about people who were drafted, never returned to their homes and never seen again.

When she was a little girl, her mother would always tell her she shouldn't listen to what she heard through the grapevine.

Nothing ever good came out of gossip.

If Quinn closed her eyes, she could hear her mother's voice.

The rest of the trip was completed in silence. She had been uprooted from her home and swept away to a town in Washington. She settled pack in her seat, trying to come up with a plan of escape. She'd have to wait until she arrived at her destination to see what she'd be up against.

Quinn must have dozed off. She opened her eyes and found her head resting on the door. She jerked to a sitting position and looked around. The interior of the vehicle was still dark and silent. The two vampire guards remained in the front, not speaking.

She glanced out the window and watched the dark scenery fly past. The road became winding, curving up the side of a steep hill. Quinn grew curious and pressed her face against the window to try to catch sight of anything that could help her later.

Finally, the thick trees that lined the road gave way. A large castle came into view. It was nothing like she'd ever seen.

Her eyes grew wide. She knew the royal vampire family was filthy rich, but a freaking castle? She had imagined a mansion of some sort. While the rest of the country suffered and was barely making ends meet, the vampires prospered. They lived lavish lives, and by the looks of this castle, Velika Riskel was no exception.

Who could escape from something like this? It appeared like a fortress that was impenetrable. They drew closer to the building, and the sight of guards walking along the perimeter became visible.

Any hope of escaping was slowly dwindling.

The vehicle finally drew to a halt in front of the building.

She stared at the structure. This was where she would live out the rest of her days as the vampire's slave and blood source.

Images of her being tied up and bled daily to feed the princess came to mind. She cringed.

Maybe she shouldn't have listened to the gossip mill. But everything she'd heard wasn't all entirely false. Word how vampires treated their humans back home traveled around. That was why so many humans hoped to avoid being matched with a vampire. If humans ran from their vampires, if caught, they were turned back over to their vampires for punishment.

She shivered at the thought of what some humans may have suffered.

Her gaze landed on the front door that opened. A man in a suit stood, waiting.

A butler.

The two guards exited the SUV.

Her door opened, and Baldy stood waiting for her step out. She cautiously got out, and her eyes were immediately drawn to the building again. Her feet automatically took a step toward it. Had the circumstances been any different, she would have admired the structure. It was breathtakingly beautiful. Even in the darkness she was captivated.

In the daytime, she was sure it was magnificent.

"I will take that." Baldy took her bag from her before she even had a moment to object.

She bit back a protest and followed him over to the front steps.

"Miss Hogan," Baldy announced.

Quinn stood behind him and peeked around

him. The butler regarded her with such disdain. His lip curled up as if she stank and was filthy.

Quinn resisted the urge to smell herself. She glanced down at the outfit she had put on for work. Her heavily distressed jeans and soft t-shirt with sandals were clean and decent. It was one of her favorite outfits.

She was completely out of her league.

That was very apparent.

"Follow me, please, Miss Hogan." He didn't even bother to introduce himself.

Quinn didn't see any sight of Baldy or her bag. She walked inside and froze.

The butler peered over his shoulder and must have seen the expression on her face. "Don't touch anything, miss. My name is Mortas. I have been the butler for this home for years."

Holy cannoli.

She wouldn't be shocked if she looked down to see her mouth dragging on the floor. The foyer reminded her of something one would see in those fantasy movies from before the millennium. She'd seen a few old movies, and the wealth that was on display in this house was out of this world.

The massive crystal chandelier was the star of the room. Her eyes were drawn to the ceiling. The molding along the walls appeared to be hand-crafted. The dark wood was a direct contrast to the light paint.

She continued slowly behind the butler, trying to take it all in.

Expensive paintings were on display, crisp white marble floors, and even the scent permeating the air was fancy.

"I'm sure after your long trip, you will want to freshen up," Mortas said. He led her over to a wide winding staircase. "The princess will want to meet you, and we should have you outfitted in something more appropriate."

"Where is my bag?" she asked.

"It has been taken up to your room." Mortas sniffed. He looked as if he would have rather burned her bag than have it anywhere in the castle. He started up the stairs without checking to see if she was behind him.

She took a few steps then paused, growing bold.

"Why didn't she meet me when I arrived?" Quinn asked.

"Excuse me?" Mortas swung around and glared at her. The air around them lowered several degrees. It was obvious he didn't particularly like humans, or maybe it was just her. "Princess Velika does not answer the door for anyone. That is my job."

"I'm her mate." Quinn couldn't believe those words were uttered from her lips, but it was the truth. According to the vampire laws, this match was proof of fate or whatever crap they believed in. "Doesn't that count for anything?"

The fact Velika was not waiting for her proved she had been correct. She was no more than a slave, or servant who the princess would just use as a blood source.

"Now come," he barked, not answering her. He spun back around and headed upstairs.

Quinn sighed and followed him. They walked along confusing hallways until they came upon a room with a ten-foot-tall wooden door. Mortas opened it and waved her in.

"Thanks," she muttered, entering the room. She spun on her heel. "Where are my—?"

The door slammed shut in her face. A click sounded, alerting her he had locked her inside.

This treatment didn't appear to be what the mate of a princess should be. Quinn exhaled and turned back around to take in her surroundings.

The room was fit for royalty. That she would have to admit. It wasn't for a servant or slave. This room was luxury at its finest. She quietly walked around and assessed it. A massive round bed stood on one side of the room, with a large fireplace near it. A roaring fire was burning bright.

Soft drapes decorated the windows, and there was a walk-in closet that was bigger than her old apartment.

Her gaze landed on her small bag resting on a high-backed chair. She rushed over to it and unzipped it. She riffled through it, finding every-thing still in it. Comfort filled her when her hand wrapped around her weapon. She would keep this close to her for any moment she would need it.

She continued on into the attached bathroom with marble flooring and a standalone shower with a separate bath.

Quinn giggled uncontrollably, feeling as if she had lost her mind. She had never experienced this type of luxury before. She blinked back the tears that threatened to fall. Now was not the time to lose it.

This vampire was obviously loaded.

But Quinn wouldn't get used to it.

She slowly sobered at the thought.

No matter what, the princess was a vampire, and she would take what she wanted from Quinn.

No longer was she her own person, she now belonged to someone.

She was going to make a run for it, the first chance she got.

Quinn left the bathroom and went back into her bedroom. She went over to the window and pushed aside the drapes.

Her heart sank at the view that met her. They were high up and on a cliff. There would be no climbing out of her window, she'd certainly fall to her death.

She grimaced, not wanting to die that way.

A knock sounded at the door. Quinn turned around when the door opened, and a tiny woman breezed through. She was dressed in a gray uniform dress with a white apron on.

"Good evening, Miss Hogan. My name is Delia, and I have been assigned to attend to your needs." She gave a curtsey then stood to her full height.

"Attend my needs?" Quinn echoed. "What does that mean?"

"I am to assist you with getting dressed." She walked across the room, and it was then that Quinn noticed the woman had something in her hand. "I have the perfect outfit for you to wear to meet the princess tonight."

"What's wrong with the clothing I have on?" Quinn pulled at her shirt and looked down at herself. Why did they have to make a big deal about what she had on? It wasn't like she was born rich. She was a woman who had worked hard for the little she had. It wasn't much, but dammit, she had busted her butt to get it.

"I would suggest you burn them." She nodded toward the fireplace. She spread something out on the bed, standing back from it. "You are the mate to Princess Velika, and you should want to look your best when you first meet."

"I do not come from money. I may be poor, but I have my pride."

"Well, now that you are here, Her Grace will take care of you." Delia stalked to the bathroom, ignoring the glare Quinn threw at her. "Bath or shower?"

"I don't need your help. I'm capable of running my own water." Quinn rolled her eyes. These people apparently thought she was an invalid. She was poor and human, not an idiot.

"Miss Hogan, I am assigned to see to your needs. Please allow me to do my job." Delia paused by the door and eyed Quinn over her shoulder.

"Fine. Bath." Quinn didn't know why she was

taking her anger out on the poor servant. It wasn't her fault Quinn was drafted and sent here.

Delia gave a nod then disappeared into the bathroom.

Quinn glanced around the room, anger inside her exploding. Tears blinded her. She leaned back against the windowsill and let them fall.

What had she done to warrant such a life? To be snatched from everything she knew and brought to be the property of a vampire?

She must have really done something horrible in her former life and this was her punishment.

She reached up and rubbed her eyes with the palms of her hands. She inhaled sharply and tried to beat down all her emotions that were swirling around inside her. She didn't know what to do now.

She ambled into the bathroom and stopped inside the doorway. The scent of fresh-cut roses met her. It wasn't a scent she was used to. Back home, no one dared to waste money on buying flowers that would only die a few days later. As beautiful as they were, money was better spent on something else.

"I hope the water temperature is to your liking." Delia knelt on the floor by the tub. It was built into the floor with a few stone stairs that descended into it.

Quinn stared at the high mountains of bubbles in the water. She couldn't remember if she'd ever had a bubble bath. Her old apartment had rules of five-minute showers to ensure everyone would have hot water. Whenever she bathed, she had to be quick due to the time limit.

Life had been hard, and there weren't too many luxuries she could indulge in. One thing she ensured she had was chocolate.

She couldn't live without it and would put aside money to buy her favorite chocolates.

"I'm sure it will be fine." She gave a halfhearted smile and walked over to the tub. The aroma of the roses grew stronger.

Quinn practically tore her clothing off, not caring that Delia was still in the room. The tub was large enough to house at least seven full-grown adults.

And she had it all to herself.

She walked down the stairs and submerged herself in the water. A moan slipped from her at the wonderful sensation of the warm liquid lapping at her skin. The bubbles tickled her chin, and the scent overcame her.

"Oh God, yes."

This was one new luxury she didn't think she would want to give up. The water was deep, and her body slowly floated along to the center of the tub. Her feet barely touched the bottom. She could swim from edge to edge if she needed to. She basked in the sensation of the warmth licking her skin.

"Let me help you." Delia still knelt by the tub.

Quinn took in the woman's stubborn expression. She wasn't going to take no for an answer. Quinn relented and slid over to Delia and presented her back to her.

A soft sponge slid down her spine. Quinn closed her eyes and allowed Delia to bathe her. She had to admit it was the best damn bath she had ever had.

"Are you one of them?" Quinn asked softly.

"Them?" Delia questioned.

Quinn closed her eyes and inhaled, opening her eyes. She looked over her shoulder and met Delia's gaze.

"A vampire. Are you one of them?"

"I am." Delia tilted her chin up slightly in a show of pride.

"Do you have a problem with your princess taking a human for a mate?" she asked. Quinn was curious if all vampires were accepting of the draft.

"It is not my place to say." Delia shrugged. "Whatever makes the princess happy."

Quinn turned back around and didn't say a word. She was scrubbed until her skin tingled. Her short hair was washed, and once Delia was finished, Quinn felt like a new woman.

She stood from the tub and found Delia waiting with a fluffy towel. She wrapped it around her and was a little embarrassed by the color of the water. The bubbles had dissipated, and it looked as if she hadn't bathed in weeks.

If Delia noticed the water's hue, she didn't make it known. She turned and exited the room. Quinn stepped over to the counter and stared at her reflection in the mirror. Her brown skin was vibrant and refreshed. Her dark hair was curled tight and close to her scalp.

Quinn would have to admit she felt amazing after the bath. She backed away and realized her clothes were missing.

Spinning on her heel, she rushed into the bedroom to find Delia opening the dresser drawers and pulling some items out.

"Where is my clothing?" she demanded.

"They are burning in the fireplace." Delia walked casually over to the bed and placed something on it.

"Those were my clothes. Who do you think you are?"

"Please allow me to assist you in getting dressed." Delia nodded and folded her hands together in front of her.

"Ugh!" Quinn pinched the bridge of her nose. She didn't have that many clothes left and now she was down one outfit.

Dammit, those had been her favorite jeans. They were so comfy, and she'd had them a long time. She'd had to save money just to purchase them.

"Please, ma'am. You don't want to be late meeting the princess."

Quinn stared at the garment on the bed. There were lotions and perfumes set out on it for her to try. The dress was black and molded to her upper body with a tie at the side. The skirt flowed around her and had two high slits that allowed her legs to come into full view.

She glanced at her bag, disappointment filling her that she wouldn't be able to strap her knife onto her leg. It would be easily seen, and she wouldn't risk it being found.

To Quinn's surprise, Delia had products for her hair. Her curls shined bright after being worked with the leave-in conditioners and oils. Delia applied light makeup to her face.

Delia had worked her magic. Quinn almost didn't recognize herself. She had never worn makeup before.

Delia stepped back away from Quinn, pleased by her own handiwork.

"Thank you," Quinn murmured.

A knock sounded at the door. Delia scurried over and opened it. Two guards stood waiting.

"We are to escort Miss Hogan to the princess."

A tremor snuck its way through Quinn. She wasn't sure if she was ready to meet the princess. Reality was setting in.

She was going to finally see the vampire who would own her.

"Come, Miss Hogan. It is time." Delia motioned for her to go with the guards.

Quinn stood from her chair and walked out of the room.

It was almost as if she were moving in slow motion. Her heart pounded as fear encompassed her.

Quinn gave a strained smile at the guards. She would try to appear relaxed, but she felt anything but on the inside. They flanked her sides, and they began the trek down the hall.

Tremors snuck through her body.

At least she would die clean, having experienced a little piece of heaven in the bubble bath.

She stole a peek at the guards. Her shoulders slumped, feeling the overwhelming sense this was her final walk before death.

CHAPTER FOUR

"She had no business sticking her nose into matters that don't concern her." Velika rested her hands on the balcony. She glared out at the large moon, and the dark desire to hunt consumed her. It was building inside her, and she could easily go into town and compel a human.

It wouldn't take long at all. Her powers were strong, and humans fell easily under her command when she put her mind to it. Just the thought of consuming the warm, delicious copper liquid had her fangs descending. Her gums burned and stretched as the sharp canines pushed forth.

The dark sky was clear of clouds. The moon was bright and high, its light shining down all around them. Her castle looked down on the town of Ensfield. It was a beautiful area that was home to humans and vampires. Anyone who called Ensfield home was under her protection, even if they were against her.

She defended her area and refused to allow anyone to invade and try to do harm to anyone.

The town was founded centuries ago. Vampires had been living amongst the humans in secret. The town had been in an uproar at the turn of the new millennia. Many humans ran scared once they discovered who the vampires were.

Over the years, the town had finally settled after the war. There were those who remained, and the relationship between the vampires and humans was strained.

Not all vampires were for living in harmony with the humans. If they had their way, they would have enslaved the humans and did as they chose with them.

This had caused a divide amongst vampires.

Velika refused to turn her head and meet the gaze of her very close friend and personal advisor. Petra Orsova was her right-hand woman. No decisions were ever made without her. To Velika, she was the calm sense of reason that Velika wasn't born with.

Petra's low chuckle filled the air.

"First off, she's the queen and your mother. Both of those titles give her the right to do what she wants." Petra rested her hand on Velika's for a moment. "You should be lucky you have been matched with a mate. Some vampires are still looking for the one person they can spend their entire lives with."

Velika sighed but pushed down the small sense of guilt. Petra, as always, was right. She glanced over at her friend who was silently watching her. There was as slight sense of envy on Petra's face.

Velika stood to her full height and turned back to stare out at the beautiful landscape before them.

"I know I sound ungrateful, but I have a lot of work to attend to with the rogues conspiring against us, the human protestors, and protecting all who are loyal to the vampire nation. Where does that leave room for a mate?"

"You will make time." Petra shrugged as if the notion was very simple. It was much easier said than done.

"A human mate is delicate and needs to be watched all of the time."

"That is not necessarily true. Humans are stronger than you give them credit for. You will need to claim your mate with the bite to ensure her aging will match yours. You will then have a partner to share your life with."

"I have you." Velika folded her arms and leaned against the bannister.

"I am not your mate." Petra smirked. She shook her head and sighed. "We may be best friends, but there are still some things we do not share."

Velika rolled her eyes. Why couldn't they be fated mates? Petra was one of the few vampires she trusted with her life.

Fate had to have sick sense of humor.

Why couldn't her mate be a vampire?

"Biting her and sharing my blood with her will not make her tougher. Humans are another breed I don't understand."

"Well, you've never really put yourself around many to get to know them," Petra pointed out. "Get to know her. Speak with her. She's your mate, she can't be that bad."

Velika shot her a glare, but all it did was make her friend giggle.

Velika's glare was known to make many soldiers tremble in their boots, but not Petra. She could see right through Velika.

"How do we really know the lab tests performed are correct? How do I know they just didn't pick a random human and assign her to me?"

"Not this again." Petra's smiled disappeared. She pinched the bridge of her nose. "How many times have we discussed the testing that is done on the humans and our blood samples are one hundred percent accurate? Stop trying to find a fault with the system and believe in what your father discovered."

"Fine, a test is done to find a mate for me." Velika paced back and forth in the small area. "But who is confirming the actual results? How do I know the test was performed correctly? There are a lot of vampires' lifelines at stake if this was to go wrong. What if the woman who is on her way here is someone else's mate and there was a mix-up of blood?"

"Oh, please. Stop it," Petra warned. She was the only one who would dare to speak to Velika the way she did. They had been friends for over two hundred years. They had met when they both were youngsters. "It is time to meet your mate. She's already here."

Velika stared at Petra and knew she was right. But that didn't keep her from wanting something to be wrong with the testing and the draft. Velika's father and his people were the ones who were testing the theory that humans could be the mates of vampires.

And they had been correct.

There had been humans who had known about vampires all along. Even some who had mated with them already.

Because of this, her father and his council studied the link between vampires and humans.

Now, because of their research and success, the draft was created. There were humans who were against it and then some all for it.

She didn't know which human she'd got but she prayed for the latter.

There were some human extremist groups who wanted to find their vampire mates. They were about everything vampire.

Velika shouldn't be picky, but if she had to choose, she'd just want a human who was open to the possibility.

"Fine. Let's go."

They walked back into the building, entering Velika's office. She had spent most of the day in virtual meetings with vampire commanders from around the world, training, and now she would have to go meet her mate.

"They are going to bring her to your private suite," Petra announced.

Velika paused, having thought they would meet here.

"Why my private living quarters?" She raised an eyebrow at the notion.

"Just in case you two hit it off." Petra grinned.

"Whatever. Let's get this over with." Velika stalked to the door.

They exited her office and headed toward the secluded area of the castle that was for Velika. A private detail of guards trailed behind them. Two of her warriors were always near her. Even though she was in her own home, with the size of the place, one could never be too sure the enemy would not try to attack.

If she and her mate had chemistry, maybe she would claim her then later they could talk about what it meant.

She was getting pulled into a million directions

and would go through this to appease her mother and Petra.

"And you don't want to change your clothes?" Petra murmured, eyeing Velika's choice of clothing.

"What's wrong with what I have on?"

"Fighting leathers? Can you be any more menacing?"

"I am a commander for my father's army, warden of the Northwest. There is no telling when I will be called for battle." Velika scowled. Her leathers were practical, as were the weapons lining her body. She was a deadly vampire and had a reputation to uphold. She had at least taken a shower after she'd spoken with her mother and put on fresh clothing.

She and her sisters were known as the deadly princesses. They each were commanders, guarding a portion of her father's territory.

When together, the three of them were fierce, unbeatable, and extremely deadly.

"You are going to meet your mate for the first time, and you look like you are about to go off to war with all of those weapons. You will probably scare the poor thing to death."

"That would take care of my problem." Velika

shrugged. If that were to happen, then Velika would have to believe the gods were on her side.

"Your Grace," Petra gasped. If she were using Velika's title, that meant she had gone too far.

"It was a joke." Velika grimaced.

They arrived at a wide winding staircase that took them to the second floor. The castle had been under Velika's control for the last hundred years. The prior vampire commander had conspired against the king, and it was Velika who was sent to deal with him.

She'd successfully removed him from his station and taken his place.

The town's coven was now hers.

Petra was not a fighter. Velika had taught her enough self-defense to protect herself, but she was not one to rush off to war. Her position as advisor to Velika was to help her with non-combat situations. Such as dealings with the humans which were delicate and needed to be handled with kid gloves.

"Taking a human mate will help solidify the relationship with humans and vampires," Petra announced.

They arrived at the large double doors of Velika's private quarters. Her guard, Keir, opened the door.

Velika and Petra entered the suite. The light was low with a fire roaring in the hearth. The sitting area was where Velika could relax with a couch, a chaise, and two large high-backed chairs near the hearth.

Sconces were placed around the room with candles burning. It was such a homey feeling that it was where Velika enjoyed spending time. French doors led to the balcony that stretched around her entire suite. Her bedroom was located through a set of doors that were left open. Her servants must have come in to clean and prepare the room for her arrival.

"You sound just like my mother," Velika muttered. She walked over to one of the high-backed chairs and took a seat. She gazed into the flames that were scorching high. The heat caressed Velika, warming the room. Living in the north was usually cold, but the temperatures were currently low now. The weather was fickle but tolerable.

Petra moved to her side without saying a word. They remained silent, enjoying the show of the flames.

"Do you think my mother was right?" Velika broke the silence. The war that raged inside her about this mating business was confusing. Deep inside, she would love to have a mate, but then yet, this world was in such a turmoil. She had so much resting on her shoulders that she didn't think she could be a worthy mate to anyone. Her parents were the prime example of how mates should be.

Velika didn't know if she could be the vampire a human would need.

"I know your mother was right."

Velika closed her eyes and nodded.

Goddess, give me strength.

Velika's eyes flew open at the sensation of Petra's soft hands covering hers. She knelt before Velika in a sign of fealty. She kissed the back of Velika's hand. It was the ultimate show of respect to a superior vampire.

"Don't scare her away." Her friend glanced up at her with pleading eyes. She rose to her feet at the sound of a knock on the door.

Anticipation filled Velika. She wondered what the woman would look like. The hairs on the back of her neck stood to attention.

Petra gave her a nod and faced the door.

"You may enter," Petra called out.

The door opened with Keir coming forth.

"The human," he announced.

Velika motioned for them to come forward. She

would admit her curiosity was getting the better of her.

Another guard came into the room, stopping to give her the standard salute of the fist under his heart.

"Your Grace, we are here to present to you the human female," he declared.

"This meeting between the two of you shall be private," Petra whispered. She leaned down and kissed both of Velika's cheeks, then retreated from the room.

Velika's attention was drawn to the small female who was dressed like a Greek goddess.

Velika sat up higher in her chair.

The woman was tiny and curvy with warm brown skin and dark ringlet hair that was kept close to her scalp. The material floated around her legs as if she glided into the room.

Her eyes were cast down to the floor.

Velika instantly reacted to this female. A possessive feeling exploded inside her chest. A light, sweet scent wafted through the air, teasing Velika. She wanted to get a close hit of it.

Velika narrowed her eyes on the woman who stopped in front of the guards. She kept her hands folded together and didn't make a sound.

By the gods, the draft was correct.

This was her mate.

Her arousal for this woman was intense, taking over her. Her blood blazed through her like molten lava.

This short, curvy woman was her true mate, and she had been brought to her.

The sweet aroma surrounding her was quickly transforming. Now it was tinted with the sour hint of fear.

Velika stood abruptly, the need to protect this human consuming her.

"Leave us."

The guards bowed then removed themselves from the room. The only sound was the crackle of the fire burning near her and the click of the door closing.

Velika stared at her mate.

She would claim her.

CHAPTER FIVE

Terrified couldn't even begin to describe what Quinn was feeling. Vampires surrounded her. The fear of the unknown was upon her.

What would happen to her?

She stood behind the vampire who had announced her presence. Not once had they used her name. She was just 'the human.'

She couldn't keep her hands from shaking. She folded them before her to not show her terror.

The room was like the halls, low light. Candles flickered in their contraptions on the wall while the massive-sized fire burning illuminated the room.

A woman in a long flowing dress brushed past her on the way out. Quinn didn't get a glimpse of her, but her attention was drawn to the long leather-covered legs of the woman sitting in the chair near the hearth.

The guard gave her a nudge from behind, pushing her forward. The servant assigned to her was out in the halls waiting to see if she were needed. Quinn almost wanted to ask to have her by her side. Delia had been the only person to speak with her. Not that they were friends, but at least this person was a little friendly.

She stumbled forward and paused.

The woman in the chair stood.

"Leave us."

The voice was deep and husky, eliciting a chill down Quinn's spine. She wasn't sure what this reaction was, but she tried to ignore it.

A deep sense of need washed over her. She clenched her eyes tight, not wanting the sensation to overcome her.

What was this?

Quinn exhaled, trying to calm herself down. Her body still trembled, but now she wasn't sure why.

She must be going crazy. Maybe some people went mad before death claimed them. She just prayed her death as swift.

Unable to resist looking at the vampire, she peeked at her. Her eyes widened at the sight before her. The woman stood tall and lean. Her body was encased in all leather, and from where Quinn was standing, she took in the weapons adorning her body. Her blonde hair was pulled away from her face in a low ponytail. She had on boots that were laced up around her shins.

She had pale, flawless skin which was a wonder since she was a warrior. Quinn would have assumed a someone who was known to fight battles and wars would have scarring on her face.

But no, this woman walking toward her was breathtakingly beautiful.

There was no need for introductions. This was Velika Riskel, the youngest daughter of the vampire king and queen. There were stories of her that would give any person nightmares.

A known killer.

A vampire.

Quinn swallowed hard.

Quiet footsteps drew close to her. Her fear came

rushing back. Was this it? Was this how her life would end? Would she bleed her dry or take what she wanted, then end it with one of the daggers strapped to her waist?

Quinn stared at the floor, not wanting to do anything to upset the vampire.

Velika stopped in front of Quinn. There was barely any room between them.

Quinn tried to remember everything she knew of vampires, but at the moment, her mind was drawing a blank. The only thing she could remember were sharp fangs and inhuman strength.

A chilled finger tipped Quinn's chin up.

"Look at me," she commanded.

Quinn quivered at the order. She blinked and raised her eyes to meet the vampire's gaze. Her face was void of any expressions, and Quinn was unable to read her.

Quinn's heart skipped a beat as she stared into the icy, hard blue eyes.

"Why are you scared?" Velika asked. Her fingers cupped Quinn's chin to hold her in place.

"I am not." Quinn tried to keep her voice steady. She didn't want to admit her fear of the woman before her.

"You are lying. You stink of fear. Did someone harm you?"

"No."

"Threaten you?"

"No." Quinn gave a slight shake of her head.

She tightened the grip on her hand, not wanting to admit the truth. But there was a fleeting appearance of anger that passed on Velika's face. The glare was sure to stop anyone in their tracks.

"Then what is it?" Velika asked her. This time she softened her voice slightly. "There is no one here but you and me. You may speak truthfully."

Quinn swallowed hard, contemplating if she should tell the truth. She sighed and tried to look anywhere but at Velika.

"I'm afraid of you," Quinn admitted. She held her breath, unsure of the retaliation she would receive.

"Me?" Velika released her and took a step back. Her eyebrows shot up high. "You have nothing to fear from me. You are my mate, and it is my responsibility to protect you."

Quinn stood there in disbelief.

Protect her?

She couldn't have heard her right.

"Protect me? But you don't even know me. Why

would you want to protect me? Because a test says I'm your mate?"

Velika's lip curved up in a smirk. She closed the gap between them again and this time she cupped Quinn's face.

"I, too, didn't believe in that wretched draft until this moment."

"Why?" Quinn's voice came out in a whisper. She was completely captivated by this vampire. Was she working her over? Was she using compulsion to make Quinn have this strong reaction to her? The second Velika was near her, Quinn had the sudden urge to rip her dress off and beg the woman to fuck her.

Her pussy became wet from the slightest touch. Her breasts grew heavy while her nipples drew into tight buds. The soft material of the dress brushed against them. Quinn had to bite back a groan from the intense sensations coursing through her.

"Because the moment I saw you and breathed in your seductive scent, I knew you were mine."

Quinn blinked. She took a step away from Velika and shook off her hold. Putting a little distance between them allowed Quinn to get some of her bearings and think.

"But you don't even know my name, do you?"

she challenged. She didn't know if this was going to rile the vampire. If it did, it would allow Quinn to see her true nature. She ran her hand along her chin and cheeks as if to wipe off traces of Velika's touch.

Velika paused and stared at her.

Quinn's breath caught in her throat.

Maybe she shouldn't have said anything. She should have just remained the docile human and waited to see what her future held.

"Human, you are right." Velika stalked toward her.

Quinn scrambled and walked backward, trying to escape Velika's advances. The vampire's smile grew, and an unfamiliar glint appeared in her eyes. Quinn had the sudden feeling that she was being hunted down by the vampire. Quinn backed into a piece of furniture, unable to move anywhere.

Velika crowded her space. She stared down at Quinn with the hint of her fangs peeking from underneath her lip. "Tell me your name. Please."

Quinn had the distinct feeling that it was rare for the vampire to use the word please.

"Quinn. Quinn Hogan." She found her name tumbling out of her mouth before she could even think about it.

Yes, she had to be under a spell.

"And what is my name, Quinn Hogan?" Velika reached out a hand and tugged on the tie of Quinn's dress.

"Princess Velika Riskel," she whispered, unable to look away from the vampire's intriguing eyes.

"I'm sure you have heard that when a vampire sets their eyes on something they want, they take it."

The soft material of her dress floated to the floor, leaving her naked.

The sharp intake of breath escaped Velika. Her gaze roamed Quinn's body.

Quinn, already in an intense state of arousal, shook from the pure heat of desire that burned in Velika's eyes.

Any self-doubt that Quinn may have had before was erased by Velika's heated assessment.

Velika's calloused hand gripped her face tight just as her lips covered Quinn's. Initially, her lips were cool to the touch but soon warmed up, gliding over Quinn's.

Quinn froze at first.

Velika's free hand rested on her shoulder then blazed a trail down her body. Her hand cupped Quinn's aching breast. She gasped, and Velika took full advantage of it.

Warmth rushed through Quinn's body.

Velika's tongue slipped inside and met Quinn's. The vampire grew bolder with her kiss, demanding Quinn return it.

Quinn relaxed and kissed her back. She felt the pointy tips of Velika's fangs and shivered, thinking of them piercing her flesh.

Velika tilted her head, still holding on to Quinn's face while she deepened the kiss. In all of Quinn's thirty-five years, she had never experienced a kiss so passionate and erotic.

Velika teased Quinn's nipple, pinching and twisting it hard. A cry stole from Quinn's lips, but it was captured by Velika's kiss.

Velika trailed kisses over her cheeks and moved to her neck. Quinn stiffened to begin with.

Was this where she bit and claimed her?

But the only sensation was the scraping of Velika's fangs on her skin. Quinn trembled, her core growing wetter. A trail of her juices slipped down her inner thighs.

"I can smell your arousal, Quinn Hogan," Velika mumbled, her lips brushing the crook of Quinn's neck. She nipped at the sensitive area, not hard enough to break the skin, but enough to get her point across.

She continued to leave hot kisses on Quinn's body, heading down to her breasts. She cupped both of them, looking her fill, leaning down and encircling one with her tongue. A growl slipped from Velika that was so inhuman, but it fed Quinn's arousal.

She never would have thought she would be standing in place with a vampire taking advantage of her. Tears burned her eyes for the deep betrayal of her body. Velika nipped her taut bud, and Quinn gasped. The pain was slight, but it was erotic at the same time.

Velika moved to the other one, bathing it with her warm tongue then suckling the nipple into her mouth.

Quinn moaned, unable to hold it in. She reached back and rested her hands on the back of the chaise while Velika had her way with her body.

"Your body is fully awake for me." Velika slipped a finger between Quinn's drenched folds. She drew it through Quinn's slit and pulled it out. She held it up where they both could see it coated in Quinn's wetness. Velika licked her finger clean. A growl vibrated from her chest. The blueness of her eyes enhanced and almost appeared translucent.

There was a raw hunger in her face and voice. "You are mine, and I'm taking what I want from you."

She yanked Quinn to her and claimed her mouth again. This time, the kiss was anything but gentle. It was heated and raw. Velika's tongue fucked Quinn's mouth with savagery.

Then Velika tore her mouth from Quinn then gave her a slight shove.

Quinn cried out as she fell back and flipped over onto the chaise. In a blur, Velika was there to guide her down.

Her eyes widened in surprise at how fast Velika was able to move. She adjusted Quinn on the sofa and peppered kisses over her body.

She sucked and nipped at Quinn's soft belly and continued her journey.

The crackle of the burning timber near them was the only other sound in the room. The warmth of the flames reached Quinn, but at the moment, she wasn't cold. Her body was heated, and a slight film of sweat covered her.

She gasped when Velika parted her legs.

Quinn squeezed her eyes shut, unable to voice the word no. She should be screaming it and pushing the vampire off her. This wasn't right. She hadn't wanted to be drafted and matched to the princess or any vampire.

Quinn opened her mouth to shout, but the only things escaping her lips were moans and gasps.

Deep inside she wanted this.

Needed this.

She'd never had anyone make her body feel the way it was now.

Velika was a vampire, and she had to keep remembering that.

"Your body deserves to be worshipped for all eternity," Velika murmured, pressing a kiss to Quinn's inner thigh. Her tongue slid over the sensitive area. She drew it back up and repeated the motions on the other leg.

Quinn tried to fight whatever hold was on her.

She reached out a hand to force Velika away but somehow found her fingers threaded through Velika's thick blonde hair and pulling her face to her center.

Velika kissed her labia, then parted them with her fingers, exposing her swollen clit. She flicked her tongue over Quinn's bundle of nerves.

A cry escaped Quinn. She tightened her hold on Velika's hair. She opened her legs fully to ensure Velika could reach every aspect of her core.

Velika didn't need any coaching. She encircled Quinn's clit and suckled it. Her core clenched, pleasure building inside her.

Velika sank two fingers deep inside Quinn's pussy. She fucked her with them while she continued to tease Quinn with her tongue, stroking her bud.

Quinn writhed on the chaise. She had never imagined that sex could be so good. None of her previous lovers, not that there were many, could hold a candle to the princess. Her prior lovers had been very selfish and didn't take the time to ensure she had received pleasure. It had turned her off of sex, and she had been content with being single.

Velika continued to thrust her fingers inside Quinn's slick core. She twisted them round and hit the right spot, drawing Quinn closer to her orgasm.

Velika worked Quinn's body as if she had secret instructions on what made her tick. Quinn no longer had control over her limbs. Velika took her to the point of no return. Her body trembled with need until she could no longer take any more. Intense pleasure washed over her, and she careened into her climax.

There was nothing else she could do but

scream. She was unable to help how loud she had become while being fucked.

It was surprising no one raced into the room in alarm.

Her body arched off the chaise. Velika's strong grip held on to her legs while she continued to suck on Quinn's clit.

The waves of ecstasy rippled through her. Her muscles grew taut until she flopped down onto the chaise. Her body was limp and useless. Quinn had to focus on breathing. The force of her orgasm had taken every bit of strength from her.

She opened her eyes and watched Velika stand.

She whimpered, knowing, this had only been the beginning.

Velika stood and undressed. She dropped her daggers on the floor near the chaise just in case she would need to reach for them in a split second. Her leather tunic followed, as did the rest of her clothes and boots.

She stood in all her glory and took in her mate. Quinn.

It was a beautiful name that matched her exquisite mate.

The sounds of her pleasure filling the air flamed the desire inside her. It was one of the best sounds she had ever heard.

Velika licked her lips, enjoying the taste of her mate. It was a taste she would want to experience every day. She could have spent an eternity buried between Quinn's thighs. Her sweet nectar was a gift from the gods alone.

Quinn's brown skin was soft and tantalizing. She was mesmerized by the look of utter sexual satisfaction gracing Quinn's face.

Her human.

She had thought to fight it before, but now that she'd tasted what was hers, she would never let this woman go. She would claim her and keep her at her side for all eternity.

Velika inhaled, breathing in the sweet aroma of Quinn's arousal. It coated her thighs and Velika's face.

Velika crawled back onto the chaise and braced herself over Quinn. Her hands rested on each side of the girl's head. She stared down at her, memorizing every facet of her mate's face.

She was still shocked that the test had been correct.

She had a mate.

Velika turned Quinn's face to hers so she could look deep into her eyes.

"You are mine, Quinn Hogan."

Quinn's breaths were increasing. Her chest rose and fell swiftly. Velika ghosted a finger down her sternum, lingering between her beautiful breasts. They were full, round, and her areolas were a darker shade of brown than her skin.

Velika breathed in the thickening scent of Quinn's arousal.

She was pleased at how responsive her mate was to her touch. Velika sensed the wetness between her own thighs. Her clit pulsed with need. Her release was already building. Licking and drinking in all of Quinn's essence had left her at a heightened state of arousal.

She was nowhere done with her human. For now, she needed to take the edge off the coursing desire to claim her. She didn't want to hurt Quinn. She had already shared with her that she was to protect her.

It was ingrained in her genes that she never hurt her mate. She would never allow one strand of hair on this woman to come to harm. Velika would do what she must to shield Quinn away from her enemies.

Velika's eyes stray to the delicious mounds of Quinn's breasts. She burned with the desire to take this woman. She reached out and spread Quinn's legs open. She straddled the human, holding her one leg close.

She reached down between them and spread Quinn's labia open and settled down onto her where their clits brushed each other.

A moan slipped from Quinn while a growl escaped from Velika.

"No matter what you are thinking in that head of yours…" Velika paused. She rotated her hips to rub herself against Quinn. Her fingers gripped Quinn's leg, raising it higher to allow her to grind down on top of her. "Your body has proved it knows who it belongs to."

"Ah…" Quinn cried out.

Velika set a rhythm. Quinn swayed her hips in tandem with Velika. Their juices flowed, allowing them to slide effortlessly with one another. Quinn's breasts rocked with each motion. Velika couldn't resist capturing one with her free hand. She massaged and caressed it.

She yearned to capture it with her lips. Instead, she pinched it and tugged on it. Quinn threw back her head, her moans filling the air.

Velika leaned over her, increasing her pace.

They were moving as one.

Velika tried to push down her need, but it grew. She didn't want to turn savage on her mate. She had to fight to control herself. The sound of Quinn's blood rushing through her arteries was hard to ignore. She ached to sink her fangs into the crook of Quinn's neck and drink her fill, but she resisted.

"Oh God," Quinn gasped.

"Your god cannot help you." Velika arched her back to slam her pussy against Quinn. She thrust harder, increasing both of their pleasure.

There was nothing else but the two of them. Velika only wanted to hear her name on her mate's lips. The human god had nothing to do with what was going on now.

The scent of Quinn and the taste of her sent Velika to the edge of no return. Their movements were hard and fast.

Velika watched Quinn's facial expressions. Her human was so delicate but so full of passion. Velika was caught off guard when her climax hit her. A cry from the depths of her soul came erupting out of her mouth.

Quinn joined her, another scream echoing through the room.

Velika fell forward. Their bodies were a tangled mess on the chaise, but Velika didn't care.

Quinn belonged to her, and she belonged to her precious little human. Nothing was going to get between them.

CHAPTER SIX

Quinn opened her eyes and stared at the ceiling. She pulled the sheets over her naked body and turned over onto her side. She took in the empty spot that should have held a certain vampire.

She strained to listen to hear if she was alone.

Nothing.

She slowly sat up in bed and rested back against the pillows. She wasn't sure what time it was. The windows had a black steel covering that had come down at some point in the night.

Memories of last night flooded her. She bit her

lips, her cheeks warming at what had commenced between her and the vampire.

Her clit was still deliciously tender from having been the center of Velika's attention. Her nipples were sore and aching. They were still drawn into tight buds. The silky sheets brushed against them, alerting her to how sensitive they were.

Her throat was slightly sore from all the screaming she had done. Last night she had been thoroughly fucked.

There was no other way to describe it.

Velika had done as she said and took what she wanted and in return rewarded Quinn with out-of-this-world orgasms.

Her vision blurred from the unshed tears. She had lost her freedom and belonged to Velika. The way her body reacted to Velika, it had to be a spell. She had never behaved in such a way and allowed anyone to use her as Velika had.

She had to get away.

Last night Velika had not bitten her, but that wasn't to say it wouldn't happen today. Quinn shuddered with the thought of those large fangs sinking into her skin. The sensation of them teasing her had been erotic.

She grimaced, trying not to recall everything Velika had done to her.

Footsteps padding into the bedroom drew her attention. She glanced up and found Delia standing with a silky material in her hand.

"Good morning, mistress." Delia bowed her head. She came to stand by the bed.

"Morning." Quinn cleared her throat. Her cheeks grew hot again thinking of what she may look like. Just yesterday she had been brought to the castle, and already she had fucked the princess. She was sure the room smelled of sex. From Velika mentioning her being able to scent things on Quinn, that led her to believe Delia would also have a sensitive nose.

She just wanted to cover her face and dive underneath the sheets and hide forever.

"I am here to collect you, ma'am." She held up a black silk robe for Quinn.

Quinn nodded and slipped from the bed. She stood and allowed Delia to assist with putting it on. She secured the ties and faced Delia who motioned for her to follow her.

"Where is Vel—the princess?" she asked, trailing behind the vampire servant.

They exited the suite and were met by the same

two guards who had collected Quinn from her room last night. She avoided their eyes, not wanting to see their expressions and any judgement.

"The princess has much work to attend to. She's a very busy woman," Delia replied.

They walked next to each other while the guards were behind them. Quinn glanced over her shoulder and wondered if they had been outside Velika's room the entire night.

If so, she was sure they'd got an earful.

"Oh." At that moment, her stomach made itself know. She rested her hand over it, unsure of when the last time she had consumed any food.

"Once you have cleaned up and dressed, the guards will escort you to breakfast."

They arrived at Quinn's room. The guards resumed their post outside her door while she and Delia went inside. She was ushered straight into the bathroom where Delia assisted her with washing.

If the vampire was embarrassed by the love marks that marred Quinn's skin, she didn't say a word. She had another beautiful outfit waiting for Quinn.

"Who purchased all of these clothes for me?" she asked, twirling around in front of the long mirror. This dress showcased her neck and shoulders. It closed with a simple tie. The edge of it brushed her knees. The sandals that were provided were also a perfect fit.

Quinn stared at herself, barely recognizing the woman in the reflection. She had never had clothes this expensive. All of them were purchased used and well-worn.

If she just imagined slightly, she would say she looked beautiful.

Her brown skin was practically glowing, her dark hair was washed and curled close to her scalp.

Who was this person?

Don't get used to it, she chastised herself.

"When you registered for the draft, if you remember they took your measurements. Once you were matched with the princess, the queen herself took the liberties of ensuring you had decent clothes to wear."

Quinn's eyebrows jerked up in surprise. The queen had ordered and purchased her clothing.

"The king and queen know about me?"

"Of course. There isn't much the princess or her sisters can do without the king and queen knowing." Delia picked up the towels Quinn had used after her bath. "From what I heard, it was the queen who entered the princess into the draft."

"So, the princess was not looking for a mate and didn't enter herself?" Quinn wasn't sure why that saddened her. Velika had not been searching for her? It had all been because of her mother.

"No, mistress." Delia walked away from the laundry chute that was in the corner of the room. Her face softened, and a small smile played on her lips. She was starting to open more to Quinn and become friendly. "But believe me, the princess will care for you, protect you, and cherish you."

"How do you know this?" Quinn grew skeptical. Everything she had heard about vampire claiming was the complete opposite. They were brutal, vicious, and used up their vampire mates.

"Because that is our way."

Quinn wanted to believe her, but she still couldn't shake everything she had been led to believe for years.

But was Velika cruel last night? a voice at the back of her mind asked.

"Will I see the princess today?" she asked abruptly. She and the princess hadn't really discussed much. After their initial conversation, the rest was full of moans, grunts, and screams until morning.

What did a vampire commander do when not at war?

"I'm sure the princess will make some time for her mate." Delia looked confident at her words. She turned and walked to the door. "Come. Let's get you something to eat. We have a human chef on staff."

"Really? I thought vampires only drank blood for nourishment." Quinn rushed after her.

They exited the room. Her guards fell in line behind them without saying a word.

Did she really have to have a vampire guard no matter if she were in the castle? She was going to think of a plan on how she could escape without them noticing.

"That is true, but there are a few humans employed by the royal family, and they must eat."

Humans working for vampires?

This was something Quinn would love to see. She even wanted to talk with them.

Her stomach rumbled again.

She'd ask Delia about the other humans, but first, she needed to eat.

"**O**h my. This is wonderful," Quinn gushed. She took another healthy bite of the homemade flaky biscuits and closed her eyes. Butter and honey coated the warm bread.

Quinn was in heaven.

It had been a long time since she had eaten such fresh and delicious food.

"I'm glad you enjoy them." Timbi tossed her a wink. The older African-American was a pleasant woman who was quickly becoming one of her favorite people.

Anyone who could cook this good was an automatic friend in her book.

"I am." Quinn took another bite and groaned. She swallowed the tasty morsel and took a sip of her coffee. Something else that was amazing. The coffee they served at the diner was entirely watered down and was nothing more than brown water. "How long have you worked here?"

"About ten years." Timbi moved over to the stove and stirred something in a large silver pot.

Quinn didn't know what was in it, but the aromas floating around the kitchen were mouthwatering.

When she had first arrived to eat, they were going to have her sit alone in the dining room, but Quinn refused. She didn't want to eat alone, and Timbi appeared kind and didn't mind if she sat at the island.

Quinn's guards remained at the doorway, not saying a word. Delia had left having stated she had other chores to attend to, but she would be back later.

"And you enjoy it?" Quinn was amazed and tried not to let it show, but Timbi must have heard something in her voice to cause her to glance at her over her shoulder.

Timbi ambled back to the island and rested her forearms against it. Her dark-brown eyes locked on Quinn.

"What do you really want to ask me, girl?" The cheerful woman was now gone, replaced by a guarded individual.

Quinn peeked at the guards who were staring off into space. She sighed and played with her napkin.

"You know who I am, right?" she asked carefully. She wasn't sure if the entire castle had been alerted to her arrival last night.

"Word gets around." Timbi shrugged. "You, my

dear, were matched to Princess Velika and you want to know if she goes around biting all of us poor humans who work for her."

Quinn grimaced. Honestly, that would have been one of her questions. Her shoulders slumped.

"I need to know what I'm in for. Who is she, and do I have to fear for my life?" she admitted honestly.

Timbi stared at her, sighing and standing to her full height. She slid her hands into the pockets of her chef's uniform.

"Velika Riskel is one of the most honorable vampires you will ever meet. She's stubborn and a little rough around the edges. You would be as well if you grew up fighting to survive your entire life." Timbi leaned her hip against the counter. "Yes, I've worked for her for ten years. I replaced the last chef who had worked for her for fifty years. Unfortunately, we humans don't live as long as they do. The humans who work here are all paid and treated fairly. Should you fear for your life? Yes, you should." She turned somber eyes to Quinn whose mouth was probably on the floor.

"I should?" she squeaked. Panic filled her. If Timbi were speaking the truth, then—

"I didn't say you should fear the princess."

Timbi held her hand up. She nodded to the guards. "You won't ever have to fear the princess. It is her enemies who will come for you."

Quinn glanced over at the vampires and found both the guards eyeing her. She had thought this entire time they were there to make sure she didn't run.

In the end, it was to make sure someone didn't come and kill her?

"What... What are your names?" she asked the guards.

"Mistress, my name is Keir." The first one stepped forward and bowed to her.

"I am Sabien, mistress." The second did the same motion.

Both of them slapped their fist just beneath their heart.

"And you are assigned to protect me? I thought it was so I wouldn't try to leave." She spun around on her stool to face them. She was just a human; why would her life be worth two vampires keeping an eye on her?

"Yes, mistress. We are to guard you with our lives," Keir replied.

Quinn's mouth flapped open and closed. She didn't know what to say to that. She, a lowly human, would never have been considered worth more than a vampire.

What is going on?

"The smells from this kitchen are divine. I always envy those who are able to consume what Timbi cooks." A woman with dark hair breezed into the room. Her pale skin was flawless, and she wore a black dress that hugged her every curve, and high heels. This woman screamed vampire. Her blue eyes locked on Quinn. She immediately headed for her.

"Ms. Orsova, how are you this morning?" Timbi asked.

"I'm doing well. Tired and about to crash." The woman had a friendly smile. She stopped in front of Quinn. She leaned in and kissed both of Quinn's cheeks. "It is so nice to officially meet you. I'm Petra Orsova." She stepped back and held out her hand.

"Um, hello. I'm Quinn."

"You must forgive me for scurrying out of Velika's room last night when you arrived."

Quinn sat stunned. This was the woman who was with Velika when she was escorted in. She hadn't caught sight of her when she'd brushed past her. She grew uncomfortable, not knowing what her relationship was with Velika.

"Ms. Orsova is an important woman around here," Timbi said. She came around the corner and shared a hug with the vampire. "She is the official advisor to the princess."

"Oh." Quinn pushed aside all thoughts that this was a woman she had replaced in the princess's bed.

"Oh, will you look at her. I bet you thought there was something between me and Velika." The woman threw her head back and laughed. Sharp, pointy fangs peeked from underneath her lips. She shook her head and moved closer to Velika. She took her hand and patted the back of it. "Did Velika not speak with you about members of her council, or what will be expected of you or the town?"

Quinn shook her head. She found her cheeks warming again. This had been the most she'd ever been embarrassed. She just wanted to crawl into a little hole and hide.

"Isn't that like Velika." Petra tsked. She released Quinn's hand and sat on the stool next to Velika. She motioned to the fridge. "Timbi, dear. Would you be so kind to warm me up my favorite?"

"Of course, Ms. Orsova." Timbi smiled.

"Now, I'm sure you have so many questions. I

will try to catch you up on some things, but Velika will have to do the rest." Petra smiled and motioned to her food. "Please continue. Don't stop on my account."

Quinn's appetite had disappeared. Instead, she took a sip of her coffee and kept the mug in her hand.

"Well, I'm not sure of anything. One minute I was at work, and then I was being ushered to my home to pack up one bag, and then here I am." She waved a hand in the air.

"You poor dear." Petra had very kind eyes. It almost distracted Quinn from the fangs that peeked out from beneath her lips. "We'll help you get settled in. You will find this castle is an amazing place to live. It's been here for centuries. There have been some updates, but we are trying to keep the old-world charm to it."

"We?" Maybe there was more to Petra and Velika besides what she'd admitted to. She didn't know why jealousy reared its ugly green self. Quinn had no right to tell Velika who she could sleep with.

Hell, she'd just got here last night.

"Velika and I have been friends since we were kids. We are as close as sisters, and I've been on Velika to update this place. She claimed these lands about a hundred years ago. She finally listened to me when it came to the castle."

"Here you go, Ms. Orsova." Timbi sat a goblet down in front of her. "Just as you like."

The slight hint of copper filled the air.

Quinn's eyes locked on Petra as she took a healthy gulp of her drink. She sniffed, recognizing the smell.

"Is that blood?" Quinn whispered, feeling queasy.

Petra sat her mug down and nodded. "What did you expect? Me walk over to Timbi here and demand she give me her blood?" She leveled her gaze on her.

"I don't know, um…" Quinn stumbled. She just couldn't say anything right. Might as well take her foot and put it in her mouth.

"I'm just messing with you." Petra motioned to the drink. "Vampires own quite a few blood banks around this country. Even before we presented ourselves to the world, we had processing centers where we could offer clean, safe blood to all vampires. This allowed us to consume what we needed to survive without drawing attention to ourselves."

"So vampires never drank directly from

humans?" Quinn found her hand resting on her neck. She must have unconsciously started rubbing at the mention of blood-drinking.

"I never said that. There is nothing better than drinking fresh from the source." Petra's blue eyes grew eerily iridescent. "A good vampire will compel a human, take just what they need, then leave the human with no memory of the transaction."

"But that's assault. You are taking their blood without their permission." Quinn gasped. She jumped down from her seat, fear creeping into her. She glanced at Timbi who froze in place with a knowing expression on her face.

Quinn's breaths increased at the thought of being surrounded by vampires. Her gaze flickered to the guards standing near the kitchen's exit. She turned back to find Petra staring at her with a peculiar look.

I have to get out of here.

"Quinn, what is it?" Petra asked, slowly standing from her chair. She held her hands up and moved toward Quinn as if trying not to spook her.

But it was too late.

To think that she could have been one of those humans who was unknowingly used by a vampire for their pleasure was frightening.

She rubbed her arms, her darting gaze moving to the other door. She swallowed hard. The pounding beat of her heart filled her ears. She couldn't think, she couldn't breathe.

This was too much.

"Calm down, Quinn. It will be okay," Petra's voice softened.

"Quinn," Timbi's voice was stronger. The older woman moved into Quinn's eyeline. She came around the counter and stood before her. "Breathe."

Quinn tried to imitate the woman, but she couldn't get her body to respond.

The urge to flee was strong.

Tears blurred her vision.

All the people who were used against their will.

None of this was right.

Flashes of vampire attacks she had heard in alleyways when she was rushing home from work came to mind. She cringed. The sounds of the cries still haunted her to this day.

Run.

That was her basic instinct.

"Quinn." Timbi's hands rested on her shoulders, bringing her out of her reprieve. She glanced at her and found the older woman staring at her with an intense look. "They won't hurt you."

Quinn blinked. She glanced around the room and found Petra and the guards staring at her.

"Breathe, honey. You are safe here. Remember?" Timbi gripped her tight. She brought Quinn close to her and wrapped her arms around her. "There is nothing to fear from anyone in this room. Do you hear me?"

Quinn nodded and gripped the woman tight. She didn't know how long they stood there, but finally her heart rate decreased and she was able to breathe.

She had to be strong.

Dig deep, Quinn.

They are different, a voice whispered. Memories of her night with Velika surfaced. The way the woman was with her should have erased all doubts about her, but unfortunately this fear she had was too embedded in her.

She pulled back from Timbi and wiped her face.

"I'm so sorry, Quinn," Petra whispered. Her wide eyes were filled with sympathy. "This is all new for you, and it was very callous for me to speak of things without taking into consideration what you may have experienced or witnessed."

Quinn nodded, unable to speak. She gave an appreciative smile to Timbi. Had it not been for her, she would have gone into a full-blown panic attack.

"Are you okay?" Petra asked.

"I don't know." She sighed. "Where I come from, humans are attacked frequently. You hear about it constantly, and it's brutal. Some of them die from being drained. You learn to live in fear, always looking over your shoulder and knowing that one day it could be you."

She shivered at the horrific memories. Some of her customers would just disappear. Rumors were always that they were killed by vampires, or they ran from town to get away from the monsters.

Most people in her town tried not to go out after dark unless they were in groups. Humans would be an open target if they were out alone at night.

"Oh my." Petra appeared to grow even paler. "Attacking humans and brutalizing them is illegal and against vampire laws."

"Vampire laws?" Quinn snorted. Yeah, like any of the vampires back home abided by rules.

"Come with me, Quinn?" Petra asked.

Quinn eyed her warily. She may have appeared nice, but she wasn't sure she could trust her.

Petra must have sensed her hesitation. "I want to take you to the library. If you are to mate with a vampire, then you will have to learn the coven laws that all vampires are to abide by."

"And if they don't?" Quinn folded her arms in front of her.

"Then they will have to answer to Velika. She is the judge and jury."

CHAPTER SEVEN

"We are already being stretched thin." Velika stared at the vampire sitting across from her. She had a headache that was growing in intensity. She rubbed her temples and tried to will the pain to go away.

Meetings with the town's council could be grueling. Today's demands were not anything she hadn't heard, but they had every right to be voiced. The tension in the conference room was thick.

"The lycan numbers are growing." Niles James' fist pounded the table.

The other two council members sitting alongside him nodded.

"Remember who you are speaking to," Arad said. He was a captain in her army and was one of her most trusted warriors. He sat forward in his chair, brandishing his fangs. Velika knew the captain wouldn't have any problems putting a council member in place. "You will show the daughter of your king respect."

The small council represented members of their coven. They were a thorn in Velika's side, but their sole purpose was for the good of the vampires who were under Velika's protection.

Velika held up a hand to which Arad responded. He nodded to her, thumping his fist underneath his heart. He had been made a captain in her army fifty years ago. His dedication, loyalty, and battle experience were something she admired and rewarded him the position. He was a large vampire, standing almost six and a half feet tall. His long blond hair was braided in an intricate design, a homage to his ancestors of Estonia who had migrated to America centuries ago.

"My apologies, Your Grace." Niles bowed his head. He raised it and met Velika's gaze. "You must understand, my loyalty is to the vampires we serve, and I am passionate about protecting them."

"I understand, and no need to apologize for your loyalty to our people." Velika hated playing the political game, but she understood that as a member of the royal family, she could not escape it. She sat up higher and eyed all three of the council members. "What proof do you have about the lycans?"

"They aren't as organized. They have been in hiding for centuries," Luther interjected.

He sat beside Velika, and she was thankful for his presence at the moment. She eyed the empty chair where Petra usually sat and wondered where her advisor was.

The lycans were scattered throughout the world. They had been living underground for centuries just as the vampires had done. They weren't as organized and had been at war amongst each other for years.

Velika and her sisters had kept their ears to the ground to try to stay ahead of the situation.

She winced from the throbbing pain in her head. She just wanted to leave this cursed meeting and go find her mate. It had taken everything she had to slide from underneath the covers and leave her very naked mate. The need for blood was causing this wretched pain. If she didn't take from her mate soon, she would need to get blood from another source.

Quinn's body had been her playground. She had tasted every inch of the human and she currently craved more. Her fangs were descended, and she had wanted to sink them deep into Quinn and drink her sweet-smelling blood.

Instead, she had found herself downing a warm glass of B-positive blood after leaving her private quarters.

It wasn't what she wanted, but it had curbed her thirst.

Quinn's cries of ecstasy still echoed in her head. She wasn't sure how much longer she would last in this meeting.

Luther could handle the council.

"I am hearing that they are planning a revolt. They have a new leader now," Councilman Tobias Christoff said. He leveled his icy gaze on Luther. "We are demanding that someone look into this problem. We cannot afford to have those beasts running wild."

Lycans and vampires had been at odds for centuries. Over two millennia ago, the lycans were used by the vampires as guards. They had been the guardians of the vampires while they slept through the daytime. They revolted against the vampires, no longer wanted to be used as their slaves.

The vampires who were much stronger and had more in numbers, hunted the wolves down until their numbers barely existed.

For years now, Velika had received word that they were growing.

She really didn't need this at the moment.

They were already dealing with the humans, and now it would appear they would have to investigate this lycan issue.

"Fine," Velika growled. She was done with this meeting. "Luther, I am putting you in charge of investigating this claim. The council is right. We must investigate it—"

"But, Your Grace," Luther sputtered.

She held up a hand and gave him a firm glare.

"I am not asking for you to take a full army and go off trotting into the woods. Put together a small team that could discreetly look into this matter." She caught sight of the council members nodding. Compromising would save them headaches. She didn't want to sit here and argue. "I want a full report on their findings in two weeks' time."

"Yes, Your Grace," Luther said.

"Council, we are dealing with a lot now, and I

ask for your patience with this matter, but I assure you, we will investigate.

"And that is all that we ask." Niles appeared satisfied.

"Is there anything else we would need to discuss?" she asked the room.

"Your Grace, there is the matter of your mate. We heard that you were matched with a human," Iona Dawn, the single woman on the council, spoke up. She was an older vampire with long white hair and bright-blue eyes who Velika considered the most sensible of the three. She came from a strong line of vampires, and her family had had a seat on practically every council for centuries. "Congratulations."

"Thank you." Velika gave her a tight smile. She was ready for this meeting to be over so she could find said mate.

"Be that you are now a mated woman, we must have a celebration." Iona smiled.

"That is not needed—"

"Oh, but I insist. You are the first of the Riskel daughters to find your mate. This is something we must celebrate."

Velika held back a growl. She didn't want to have to deal with all the aristocrats who would swoop down on Ensfield just so they could have a see at her mate.

This wasn't something she would be able to avoid.

"I'll arrange a little soirée just so that our coven can meet the mate of their commander." Iona stood from her chair, and the men followed. "Nothing too fancy."

Velika stood and held back a snort. She had known Iona for years, and nothing was ever little. Vampires loved to mingle and throw lavish parties.

Announcing that Velika had a mate was going to greatly put Quinn in danger. She already had a guard assigned to her. Once word got out, Velika was going to have to increase the security around the castle. The royal family had plenty of enemies who would love to get their hands on the mate of the princess.

"I'm sure you will do fine arranging every-thing," Velika said. The council bowed to her and exited the room, leaving her alone with Luther and Arad. "You two stay. Please shut the door."

The guard on the outside closed it.

"It is true?" Arad asked, his eyebrows rising high. "You were matched with a human for a mate?"

"Yes, and that is why I have asked for you to stay behind." She motioned for them to take their seat.

"What is it, Your Grace?" Luther asked.

"My mate is here in this castle. My mother seemed to think that me taking a human mate will appease the humans. It will show we can live in peace and harmony," she began. She looked at both of them. A light of awareness appeared in Luther's eyes. Before she even said anything, he already knew where she was going with this. It was one of the reasons why she had made him her second. "You as well as I know, not every vampire will be happy with royalty taking a human mate."

Arad grunted.

Some of these same vampires they were fighting now who wanted to rule the world and take the humans as slaves would not agree to royalty mating with a human.

To some, it was unheard of.

Humans were their food, their property, and should be treated as such.

Velika vowed to never let Quinn see that side of her people.

"You alrcady know any vampire who follows you will die to protect your mate," Luther said.

"And if they don't agree with who fate had chosen to be your mate, then they will die by my hand."

"Or mine," Arad snapped.

"I'm glad you are loyal to me," she said. "I want security upped in the castle and when she leaves. My mate is not a prisoner. We will welcome her to Ensfield and to our coven. I want her to feel at home."

"We will ensure no harm will come to your mate." Arad thumped his chest again.

Velika knew she would be able to trust these two men. Loyalty was apparent in both of their eyes.

"We are entering a new era. I was at first resistant to the idea of taking a mate, but now that I have met her, I wouldn't trade her for anything in the world."

Velika stalked toward the library having searched all over for her human. She was surprised to hear Petra had taken Quinn there.

Her heels echoed on the marble floors. She was tired of the back-to-back meetings and just wanted to see Quinn.

The political side of her job was draining. She turned the corner and saw Petra coming out of the library. The two guards who were assigned to Quinn were standing outside the doors. Petra's gaze landed on her.

Instantly, Velika knew something was wrong.

Her fangs burst through her gums. Her hand hovered over her dagger on her hip.

"What is it?" Velika demanded. Her eyes flickered to the door and back to Petra.

"Come." Petra motioned for her to follow.

"But I was coming to see Quinn." Velika stood in place. She didn't have time to visit with her friend. She just wanted a little break between all of the craziness to see Quinn. She needed to hold her in her arms and breathe in her wonderful scent.

Holding Quinn in her arms all night had helped her sleep.

Usually, Velika only slept for a few hours before she was up again. It had to be the mating bond that was forming. Velika would have to claim her mate soon. Just the thought of it had her wanting to go to her now.

"We need to talk before you go in there." Petra waved for her again.

Velika sighed and followed her down the hall.

Petra paused at the end of the hall near a window. Steel shutters covered it, blocking out any sunlight.

Velika was thrown off by the time. She had been working so much, she hadn't realized that it was still daylight.

"What is it?" She scowled. She rested back against the wall and stared at her friend. This better not take long. She had more pressing matters to attend to—her mate.

"Did you and Quinn talk at all yesterday?" Petra asked.

"Of course we spoke." Velika sighed, unsure where her friend was going with her question.

"Do you know of her background? Where she comes from? The town she lived in before she came to you?"

Velika stiffened. No. They hadn't had that kind of conversation. Something about Quinn being afraid of her had her wanting to prove she was not a bad vampire. The desire and the scent of her arousal had been too tempting.

"No." Velika cleared her throat. "We didn't do much talking."

Petra rubbed a hand on her face and turned her icy-blue eyes on Velika.

"Did she mention how much she was terrified of vampires?"

Velika paused, then released a curse.

"She mentioned she was afraid of me," Velika admitted quietly.

"And what did you say or do when you heard that?"

You have nothing to fear from me. You are my mate, and it is my responsibility to protect you.

Velika grimaced. She had been overrun by her basic instinct to claim her mate's body. She had been so driven by her desires that she'd overlooked what her mate had been saying.

"What has she told you?" Velika asked, ignoring her question.

"She's from a small town called Stramford, Oklahoma, where vampires are not ruled by anyone. They hunt, attack, and kill humans without recourse. She's absolutely terrified of our people."

Velika stared at Petra without saying a word.

She blinked and looked away from her friend.

"Do we know that to be true?" she asked. Velika was already planning to speak with her sister, Hegna, who oversaw Oklahoma. How was a small town in her sister's territory being overrun with rogue vampires and no one knew it?

"I was waiting to speak with you first before sending word to your sister." Petra stood to her full height. This was not her friend at the moment. Standing before her was the princess's personal advisor.

"What will you have me do?" Velika whispered. This was where she would need the assistance of her friend. Velika only knew of the way of vampires.

Take, mate, and cherish.

Her hands balled into tiny fists. If her elder sister could not control vampires in her area, then maybe she would pay a personal visit to the small town.

"Get to know her. Talk with her. Teach her our ways. If she is going be the mate of this coven's leader, then she has to trust us," Petra said.

Her words rang true.

Not just assume to know of vampires but trust them.

Trust her.

Velika closed her eyes and sent up a prayer to the goddess above that Quinn would give her a chance. She couldn't risk losing her mate. She would need to consummate the mating bond soon to complete her claim on her mate.

Once the bond was sealed, Quinn would be able to spend her entire life with Velika.

"And then what?" Velika asked. Her friend was wise beyond their age, and she trusted her judgement.

"Only once you've gained her trust, then claim her."

"Iona is wanting to throw a welcoming party for Quinn. She wants my mate to be introduced to the entire coven."

"She's not ready for that." Petra shook her head fiercely. "You know what happens at those types of parties. The things she will see will not be good for someone who already fears our kind."

"I don't have a choice." Velika glanced down the hall to ensure the guards weren't listening to their conversation. "What will it look like if I refuse to have anyone meet her?"

Petra bit her lip. Velika could practically see the gears turning in her head while she was thinking. She reached up and tucked a strand of her hair behind her ear.

"Then you need to hurry and get her to trust you. If you do, then we can deal with the others later."

Velika spun on her heel, up for the challenge.

CHAPTER EIGHT

Quinn walked around the stuffy room. The library of the castle was full of leather-bound books. She had never seen so many in one place.

Libraries had come to their demise after the war. Many were burned by looters, and it was very hard to get so many replaced.

Not that she didn't know how to read.

Her mother had introduced books to her at a young age.

Quinn strolled along one shelf, allowing her fingers to caress the books, trying to decide on another one to browse through.

Petra had given her a short lesson on vampirism. She had tried to calm Quinn's fears and suggested she try to learn about them.

Some of the books she had chosen were written in an odd language she was unable to decipher. According to Petra, some of them were dated back to the seventh century.

She stopped in front of a book resting on a shelf. It was in pristine condition but appeared old. She reached for it and took it over to a table. It was extremely heavy, and the binding was beautiful. The cover was made of a dark leather.

She pulled out the chair and took a seat. She breathed in the scent of old leather and found it to be pleasant.

She closed her eyes and exhaled. It had been a long day here in the library. She had discovered artifacts, photos, and other mementos of vampires.

Opening her eyes, she flipped the book open.

Book of Sânge.

She didn't know what the word sânge meant, but she would have to look it up.

Her gaze skimmed the old paper. She ran a finger down it then turned the page.

A slight click sounded through the air. She

returned her attention to the door and found Velika staring at her.

Quinn sat up higher, taking in Velika. She was dressed in a black leather tunic with matching pants. Her knee-high boots had a large platform heel, giving her at least another three inches. Her daggers adorned her hips while her long blonde hair was braided in intricate designs.

She was a badass warrior.

The sight of her took Quinn's breath away.

Quinn found herself unable to break eye contact with Velika.

"Afternoon, *miere*." Velika drew closer to Quinn, stopping near her chair.

"Hi." Quinn's voice squeaked. It had been hours since she had seen the princess. Memories of those last moments before she'd fallen into a restful sleep came to mind.

"What are you reading?" Velika arched a perfectly sculpted eyebrow as she peered down at the book on the table.

"Well, I just picked it up and sat down. I'm not sure what this book is yet," Quinn admitted. She rubbed her hands on her legs. "Petra recommended I read up on vampires to learn more about you."

"Why read about them when you have one

standing right here." Velika held her arms out. "Why not just ask me anything you want to know. I shall answer you truthfully."

"Um, okay." Seemed fair enough. She could only read English, so if more of the books were in a different language, then she wouldn't be able to discover anything.

"I only ask one thing in return." Velika took the chair opposite Quinn. She sat and brought her feet up onto the table and crossed her ankles.

"What might that be?" Quinn asked, curious.

Velika's intense blue eyes sent a shiver down her spine.

Dammit.

There went her body again, reacting to this woman.

"You answer a question about you."

Quinn nodded, unable to speak. It was a fair request.

"Good."

Velika smiled, and Quinn's breath was immediately snatched from her lungs. She had known the princess was beautiful before, but seeing her fully smiling, she was breathtaking.

"Go ahead. Ask away."

Quinn paused and tried to think of a question.

"Were you born a vampire?" she asked and gripped her hands together in her lap. She didn't know why she was so nervous around Velika. It wasn't like she hadn't spent all night in her bed doing things that grown folks did with each other.

"I was. I am what some would call a pureblood. My ancestors can be traced back over a few millennia, if not farther."

"Oh, wow. That is amazing." Quinn sat frozen in place. She unfortunately couldn't trace her family that far back. She knew the names of her parents and grandparents, but that was as far back as she could go. "What do you want to ask?"

"Tell me about your family."

Quinn stiffened. She glanced away from Velika, the question touching a sensitive nerve in her body. Her gaze roamed the room, taking in the decor while she tried to blink back the tears. She turned back to Velika to find her patiently waiting.

"My parents are both deceased. They were peaceful people who were forced to fight in the war. I never saw them after they were sent off to fight. My brother, I haven't seen him in over ten years." Her voice ended on a sob. She inhaled and tried to will the tears away but was unsuccessful. They burned a warm trail down her cheeks.

How she missed Lane.

The years after their parents' death was only made better by having him with her. Ever since he went missing, she had felt as if she had lost her last piece to her parents and the happiness that once was before the war.

"Pain is unavoidable in this life," Velika said. "Embrace it. Push through it and you will come out better for it. That is all we can do in this world. It is a cruel one, and we must learn how to deal with it."

Quinn wiped her face with the backs of her hands. She sniffed and cleared her throat. Velika's words were shockingly deep. What she'd said was true. The world was cruel, and it was harsh. She had learned from an early age to make the most of it.

Another question popped into her mind, but it was too silly to ask. She had heard a rumor when she was younger, but she didn't know any vampires to ask these questions. She opened her mouth then closed it.

She couldn't ask such a question.

"What is it?" Velika tilted her head to the side. She studied Quinn carefully.

"Are you able to see your reflection in a mirror?" she blurted out. She slapped her hand over her mouth, unable to believe she had asked such a stupid thing.

"Come." Velika stood abruptly from the table and ambled over to her side. She held out a hand to Quinn.

She glanced down at it before slowly sliding her hand inside it. Velika assisted her up and tugged her behind her. They strolled through the library, passing rows of shelving to a corner where a little seating area was set up with a couple of oversized plush chairs. On the wall was a floor-length mirror.

Quinn took the time to study the vampire. She was tall, toned, with hard muscles. Weapons adorned her body. Her braids ended just in the midst of her back.

Quinn felt short and plump in comparison to Velika.

"Tell me what you see." Velika guided Quinn in front of her, and they walked to the mirror and paused. Velika stood behind her and wrapped her arms around her.

Quinn gasped at the sensation of Velika's warm frame. She bent down and rested her chin on Quinn's shoulder.

In the mirror it was just the two of them.

That rumor was now confirmed to be false.

Velika nuzzled Quinn's neck. Her eyes fluttered closed at the sensation of Velika's fangs scraping against her skin.

"I see us," Quinn breathed. Her body rested back fully against Velika. She bit her lip, enjoying the feeling of Velika's hands skating over her stomach to cup her breast.

"Petra told me of your home and what happens there," Velika murmured. Her lips brushed Quinn's neck.

Quinn stiffened, her eyes flying open. Just the mention of her home brought her reality crashing back to her.

Vampires.

She was the property of a powerful one.

Quinn stepped forward, but Velika's arms tightened around her and held her in place. Fear crept up inside her, almost choking her.

"You do not need to fear me. I can scent it on you," Velika growled. Her lips swept up Quinn's ear. "I would never hurt you or let anyone harm you. This I promise with all of my honor." She turned Quinn around, staring deep into her eyes.

Quinn swallowed hard. "You tell me that, but then I have to fear for my life because I am your property, and someone may want to hurt me because of you."

"They can try to get their hands on you," Velika snarled. Her fangs peeked from underneath her lip. She cupped Quinn's cheek, gently stroking it with her finger. "You are not property, Quinn. You are my mate."

"What's the difference? I didn't come here of my own free will but taken and presented to you like I'm a prized possession." Quinn's eyes blurred with tears. She blinked them back, refusing to cry in front of the commander.

"Property is something I don't care about. Something I can sell or give away to anyone who would want you," Velika rasped. Her eyes became translucent in color. She closed the tiny gap between them. "My mate is someone I would not hesitate to kill for, protect until there is no more breath in my body and will cherish for all eternity."

Wow.

Quinn shook her head. She found her body automatically leaning into Velika's.

"I am only human. You won't have eternity with me. What happens if you shall tire of me, or I grow old, and you no longer desire me?"

Velika's hand slid down her throat. She offered

a wide grin, putting her fangs on full display. Quinn didn't know if the shiver that rippled its way through her was from fear or from arousal.

"When it is time, you will beg for me to claim you. You will want my bite," she whispered.

Quinn's body trembled uncontrollably. Velika's warm fingers caressed her skin every so softly. Quinn couldn't tear her eyes away from Velika's.

"My teeth will sink here, I'll taste your pure sweetness and then, you will consume my blood. Only then will you be able to live through time with me. By my side."

Live together for centuries? Quinn didn't have anyone she would miss. If only she could find her brother. What if he were still alive? If they never found each other then she'd outlive him, and she didn't know if she could deal with him dying.

She paused and wondered if she should share her troubles with Velika.

Would she be able to help in searching for Lane?

"I don't know," she replied. What did she say to all of that?

Give her a chance, a voice whispered.

"It will happen." Velika released her and took a step back. The woman exuded confidence. She glanced around the room and back at Quinn. "Petra was right. You need to learn more about vampire society and our culture."

"What?"

"You will need to become well-versed on vampires if you are to sit at my side and rule my territory. Petra will oversee your schooling." Velika smirked. She turned on her heel and waved. "Come."

"Where are we going?" Quinn scurried behind her. She almost crashed into Velika who spun back suddenly.

"We are going shopping. My coven will be throwing a gathering in your honor."

"What? Why would they do that?"

"Why, to welcome you, of course." Velika took Quinn's hand and towed her behind her. "My coven will be welcoming you with open arms."

"Are you sure?" Quinn asked. She had to run to keep up with Velika's fast pace. "What if they don't?"

There was no way these vampires would take to a human sitting alongside their princess. She was already fearful that she was going to have to be extra careful due to certain vampires wanting her dead just to hurt Velika.

Now she was going to be expected to socialize with an entire coven of vampires?

Velika stopped at the door with her hand on the handle. She glanced at Quinn. Her expression was one that chilled Quinn to the bone.

This was the true princess.

The fierce warrior.

"Then they will answer to me."

Nighttime was falling, and Velika had been up all day, unable to grab an ounce of sleep. She stood by the front door of the castle with Mortas by her side.

"How long shall you be gone, Your Grace?" he asked.

"However long it takes for my mate to find a suitable dress for the upcoming event." She eyed the servant who was serving Quinn. The female assisted Quinn with a long flowing cape. It flowed down toward Quinn's feet and would provide her some warmth.

"But of course, Your Grace. I shall await your return." He nodded and walked away, disappearing down the main hallway.

The temperature was dropping, and she didn't want to chance her mate getting cold. This time of year, the temperatures fell drastically. Velika would be fine, but with Quinn being a human, she would not be able to tolerate the temperatures.

Petra may have reservations about Quinn and the vampires of their coven, but Velika would not be able to deny her coven. Not allowing them to meet with her mate could cause big issues she'd rather not deal with.

Velika would gain her mate's trust and would not leave her side at the party.

With them leaving the castle, there would be tight security. Word had been spread that Velika had been matched with her mate. There were too many enemies of the Riskel family that Velika would not chance anything disturbing them on their outing.

Heeled footsteps made their way to them.

"Why didn't you tell me we were going shopping?" Petra coasted in beside Velika.

"Because it was to be Quinn and me," Velika retorted.

"What do you know about shopping?" Petra snorted. She tugged her purse up higher on her shoulder. "While you were off learning how to kill, I was perfecting wheeling and dealing when it came to the art of shopping."

Velika rolled her eyes at her friend.

She was right.

Velika only wore fighting leathers and couldn't even remember the last time she had donned a dress.

"I'm ready," Quinn announced. She walked over to join Petra and Velika. Excitement was apparent in her eyes. Her warm brown skin practically glowed. Her short hair, big brown eyes, and luscious lips almost had Velika cancelling the trip. The thought crossed her mind to drag Quinn back to her sleeping quarters and take her again.

But she resisted.

Velika was pleased her mate was looking forward to their outing. It would be good for her to see that she was not property but an equal. Once she got used to her new situation and learned about vampire mating, she would be able to relax and get over her fears.

"Come, *miere.*" Velika took her hand and ushered her out the door.

The guards assisted them into the secured SUVs. Velika and Quinn settled in the second row, while Sabien and Keir got in the driver and passenger seats. Within a few minutes they were on their way to town.

"Quinn, darling. I will show you the best shops to get good deals," Petra offered from the third row.

"Oh, okay." Quinn gave her a smile.

"Price does not matter, Petra," Velika reminded her. She and her family were well-off, and money had never been an issue. Their wealth extended generations.

"Well, you know how people are. When they see royalty, people love to inflate the cost of things," Petra said. "I wouldn't want you to be taken advantage of."

They rode in a comfortable silence.

Velika couldn't take her eyes off Quinn. She sat with her face smashed against the window.

"It's so beautiful here," Quinn murmured.

"You should see it when we get a light snowfall," Petra said.

Velika reached over and took Quinn's hand. Quinn jerked around and stared at her. Velika brought her hand to her lips and placed a small kiss on her warm skin.

"You will love Ensfield." Velika decided she would take her mate around the world if it pleased her. From what it sounded, she'd had a hard life growing up, and Velika wanted to bring nothing but pleasure to her mate.

"Do humans live here, too, aside from the ones who work for you?" Quinn settled back and turned slightly toward Velika.

"They do." Velika nodded imperceptibly. "Everyone who is in my territory is under my protection."

"Does everyone get along?" Quinn asked.

"Of course not." Velika vowed to always be honest with her mate. "I don't know of any place where everyone lives in complete peace. Even those humans who hate vampires fall under my jurisdiction."

"But if they don't want you to, why do you still protect them?" Quinn's fingers tightened around Velika's.

"There is more than just vampires they have to worry about." Velika covered Quinn's hand with her other one. "I guard the territory against all enemies. Believe me when I say, they are better off with us."

Quinn shivered but didn't say a word.

"Our ETA is three minutes," Sabien announced.

They were going to one of the finer shopping

establishments. There was an open market with plenty of vendors, human or vampire. Everything that could be thought of was sold there.

"We can stop at Adele's. I'm sure we will find something wonderful there," Petra said.

Sabien drove up to the front of the building. Keir opened the door and aided them out. The other guards were in the SUV behind them. They walked over to them. They made a formidable sight, decked out in guns, knives, and swords. Her security team would ensure they were uninterrupted tonight.

The safety of her mate was of the utmost importance. Quinn would come to trust that Velika would not allow any harm to come to her.

Quinn's eyes widened as she watched the vampire guards stand before them.

"Now, *miere*. Let's take you shopping."

CHAPTER NINE

All eyes had been on them from the moment they had entered the shopping complex. Quinn thought the guards would flank them the entire time, but they hadn't. The guards had spread out. Some of them she couldn't see anymore. Keir, he stayed a few feet behind them to give them space.

Quinn glanced around the expensive showroom of the store. Adele's was something she had never experienced before. In her small town, they didn't have clothing stores like this.

Most of the stores were low-end and had larger secondary clothing sections. All of Quinn's clothing she owned were thrift finds. She couldn't afford to pay full price for anything.

"I think this would look gorgeous on you." Petra held up a black lace dress.

Quinn wasn't sure what to say. The few items she had touched held prices she couldn't fathom paying for. All her monthly bills didn't amount to some of the dresses Petra had showed her.

"It looks pretty," Quinn said.

"It may be a little long on you, but we can have a seamstress take it up for you." Petra walked over to her with a few dresses in her hand.

"I can take that for you, ma'am." Furia, a saleswoman who was assigned to aid them, stood by waiting.

Petra handed her the items.

"I'll go ahead and open a fitting room for you." Furia gave a slight bow then walked away.

She must be vampire. Quinn hadn't seen any humans bowing to Velika when she passed. It was a dead giveaway for the vampires.

"Do you see anything that catches your eye?" Velika asked. She rested a hand on the small of Quinn's back.

Quinn was entirely out of her league, but there was one dress that drew her attention. She gave a nod and went over to a white one that took her breath away. It was an off-the-shoulder gown, the back dipping down low with a sheer lace covering.

"This is beautiful." Quinn ran her hands over it. She couldn't believe she was touching something so expensive. There were plenty of humans out there starving or struggling to make ends meet, and here she was, shopping for an outfit for a party she didn't want to attend.

But the softness of the material had her wanting to feel it against her skin.

"Then you shall try this one on as well." Velika lifted the dress from the rack. She took Quinn's hand and pulled her behind her as she made her way in the direction where the saleswoman had disappeared.

"I don't know, Velika. It's expensive—"

"Stop checking the price tag." Velika swung to her with a fiery look in her eyes. "If it makes you happy, then I will purchase it."

Quinn jerked her head in a nod. They entered the fitting room. There was a large waiting area with oversized couches and mirrors. A woman stood, waiting in the corner. Furia exited a room with a bright smile.

"Found something else?"

"Yes, she will try on all of them," Velika announced. "Ms. Orsova is searching for accessories."

"Please go help her." Furia snapped her fingers to the other who scurried off out the room. The saleswoman turned to them and waved for Quinn to enter. "Please, ma'am. Allow me to help you."

Velika gave her a nod and a little nudge.

Quinn ambled over and entered the fitting room. The door closed behind her with the woman instructing her to call for assistance.

She glanced at herself in the mirror. She was dressed in clothing that had been provided by Velika.

Quinn removed her clothing and decided against the pink one Petra had chosen. She just didn't think it was her color. Instead, she went to the black one first. She slid it on and turned to the mirror.

A gasp escaped her.

It molded to her body, showcasing her curves.

"Ms. Hogan, do you require assistance?" Furia knocked on the door.

"Um, yes." The back clasp needed buttoned.

The door opened, and Furia waltzed in.

"Oh, that is beautiful on you, my dear." The woman quickly took care of the few buttons at the back. "It complements your skin tone quite perfectly." She moved out of the way and waved to the door.

Quinn took a few shaky steps and left the room. She felt like she was in a fairy tale. She'd never been doted upon before. Velika's eyes lit up when her gaze landed on her. She gave an appreciative nod.

"Please come over here to this platform." Furia pointed to a round raised area that was positioned in front of a few mirrors that allowed her to see different angles.

Quinn stood on it and stared at herself in the mirrors.

Who was this woman?

She looked sophisticated, elegant, and beautiful.

None of these had ever described Quinn before.

"This dress is amazing," Velika murmured. She came to stand beside her.

"You're only saying it because it's black," Quinn teased. She cast her eyes down at the floor. From what she could tell, Velika only wore black.

"My mate can tell jokes," Velika grumbled.

"Black is a powerful color, it's bold, aggressive, and can be very sexy all at the same time."

Quinn met her gaze. Her breath caught in her throat at the feral look in Velika's eyes.

"She has fine cheekbones, and this short hairstyle is dashing on her," Furia noted, obviously not picking up on the sexual tension between the two of them. She was there for the sale, and Quinn was sure she would brag that she'd sold the princess's new mate a dress.

"What do you think?" Velika asked her, ignoring the saleswoman.

Quinn glanced back her reflection and liked it, but she wanted to see the white one. She would try not to get too used to this. But the white one called to her, and she just had to see it on.

"I really want to see the white," she admitted.

"Then go. Try it on." Velika nodded to the changing room.

Furia came over and undid the buttons. Quinn rushed over to the room and closed the door. She carefully took off the black dress and jiggled her way into the white one. She turned around and immediately was in love.

This was it.

What luck did she have to find the perfect dress

on the second try? She slid her hand over her hips and loved how the soft material caressed her skin. She left the room and was met by the sound of Velika's quick intake of breath.

Her heated gaze roamed Quinn's body.

Quinn's nipples beaded into tight buds. Her body came alive under this dress.

By Velika's reaction and stare, she confirmed this was the one.

Not that she was trying to please the princess, but the dress did make her feel confident and sexy.

She walked over to the row of mirrors and stood on the raised surface.

"This one is magnificent," Furia gushed, clapping her hands.

Velika stepped up behind Quinn. The warmth of her breath caressed Quinn's shoulders. Her hands ran over Quinn bare arms. She closed the gap between them. Velika leaned in, her lips brushing Quinn's neck.

"You look absolutely exquisite in this, *miere.*" She teased Quinn with her fangs, running them softly up her neck. "It will look quite divine on the floor of my sleep quarters."

Quinn shivered. She met the heated gaze of the princess in the mirror.

"I love this one," she whispered.

"Then you shall have it." Velika wrapped an arm around Quinn's waist and hauled her back to her, leaving no space between them.

Quinn had to admit they made a dashing couple.

"Thank you."

"It is my pleasure." Velika peered over her shoulder at Furia who stood by quietly. "We shall take both the black and the white one."

"Yes, Your Grace." Furia bowed.

"Come. Let's go find Petra after you change. I'm sure she's on the search for the finest accessories she can find."

Quinn went back in the room and changed out of the dress and put her clothes back on.

She inhaled sharply.

Velika's kindness, gentleness, and the apparent need to please her was unexpected. If she wasn't careful, she would develop feelings for the vampire.

"I absolutely love the market. You can always find little handmade trinkets that are so cute." Petra strolled alongside Quinn with their arms entwined as if they had been friends for years.

The market was a large area with vendors set up. The room was brimming with excitement, and she could barely hear herself over the roar of people conversing. A large crowd filled the area with individuals walking along browsing, to people who were negotiating prices.

Quinn took it all in. She was amazed. They didn't have something like this back home. Delicious scents filled the air from some of the vendors who were cooking and selling meals. Quinn's mouth watered at the lovely aroma floating by.

They browsed a few tables with Petra bargaining for a silk scarf. Quinn turned and saw Velika at the next table. She pulled away from Petra and went over to see what Velika was looking at.

"What do you think of this?" Velika held up a leather sheath of some sort.

"What is it?" she asked.

"It goes around your thigh so you can hide a

knife on you." Velika positioned it near Quinn's thigh.

"You would trust me with a knife?" Quinn asked, amazed. She hadn't thought of her little one she had hidden in her possessions. Now Velika was shopping for one for her?

"Do you know how to use one?" Velika's perfectly sculpted eyebrow rose.

"Um, no." Quinn hated to admit she didn't know how to use any weapons. She had always tried to not put herself in a predicament where she would need to defend herself. She always ensured she was home before dark and if she had to work late walked with someone so she wouldn't be out alone. She kept her old one with her, but lucky enough, she had never had to use it.

Then entered the draft, and she was thrust to live with a vampire.

"Then I shall train you." Velika turned back to the man behind the table. "How much for this?"

Velika would train her how to use a knife? She stared at the leather material. It was dark mahogany and appeared to be soft and supple. Quinn was looking forward to that. If she was to leave here, then she would need to know how to defend herself.

Suddenly, the thought of leaving had Quinn feeling nauseated.

"This is made of the finest steel that Ensfield has to offer," the man said.

Quinn blinked and concentrated on what he was showing Velika. There was a small dagger in his hand. The steel blade was double-edged with a handle made of bone that had intricate designs etched into it.

"Try it out. You'll see the craftsmanship is one of a kind."

Velika took it from him and held it out. She grasped it and flipped it over, staring at it. She motioned for Quinn to hold out her hand.

"Grip it and let me see how it looks in your hand," Velika said.

Quinn took the weapon with Velika closing her fingers around the handle. It was smooth and fit snuggly in her grasp.

Velika stood in front of her, staring down at the weapon.

"I think this will be perfect." She turned back to the man.

"I shall wrap it and the sheath up for you. This will be perfect, Your Grace." He gave a small bow and spun away from them.

"You will no longer have a need to be fearful. I shall train you to defend yourself should you ever need to." Velika cupped Quinn's cheek and stared down at her. "One way to defeat fear is to conquer it."

Quinn nodded and found herself leaning into Velika's embrace.

Yes, if she wasn't careful, she would fall for the vampire.

Velika bent down and planted a soft kiss on her lips. Quinn's lips parted, wanting more.

A commotion sounded, drawing their attention. Velika's head popped up. She glanced over to where the noise was coming from.

"Keir," Velika growled.

"Rogues." The guard appeared out of nowhere.

"Go to Petra," Velika urged. She gave a gentle push and spun away. Velika disappeared into the crowd.

Quinn searched for Petra. She was not at the table she had been at before Quinn joined Velika. She took a few steps and scanned the area looking for her.

Her gaze landed on Petra who had moved to a few tables away. Quinn walked toward her, not wanting to get lost. If Velika wanted her with her friend, then that's where she would go.

Rogue vampires nearby had to be important.

Quinn assumed, if they were rogue, they didn't conform to vampire laws. She quickened her pace.

A cry escaped her lips as firm hands grabbed her and pulled her. She stumbled and was lifted from the floor. She opened her mouth to scream, but it was covered by a foul-smelling hand.

She gagged, the contents of her stomach threatening to spill forth.

Quinn refused to be kidnapped from one vampire and taken by another. She kicked and squirmed, wasn't going to make it easy for someone to take her.

"Be still," a gravelly voice hissed in her ear.

She struggled even harder.

"Halt!" a sharp voice growled.

Quinn opened her eyes and saw one of the guards standing before her and her captor. For the life of her, she couldn't remember his name, but the deadly glint in his eyes and the sharp, long dagger in his hand was one hell of a combination.

"This isn't right!" the voice shouted. "Humans should not be mating with vampires."

"Death will be your only option if you do not drop the woman," the vampire guard snapped.

Quinn was thrown down onto the floor. She cried out as her knees scraped the stone floor. The man dashed away with the guard running off behind him.

"Quinn!" Petra shouted. A panicked look was on her face. She raced over and knelt beside Quinn. "Here, let me help you up."

Curious bystanders eyed her. Quinn shuddered at their expressions of pity.

Why didn't any of them try to help her?

Tears blurred her vision at how helpless she felt. She was going to take Velika up on the training. She was no longer in her safe little apartment in Stramford, where she could hide and remain by herself.

Here, she was going to be a target because of her vampire.

"Are you injured?" Petra's gentle hand rested on her arm.

"No. Not really." Quinn stood and wiped the tears from her face. She glanced around and caught sight of Velika heading in her direction with a murderous expression.

"What the hell happened?" Velika roared. Her

fangs were on full display, and her irises were translucent.

Quinn immediately stepped back, her heartbeat pounding in her ears.

"I don't know. I heard Fane shouting at someone, then he took off running after them," Petra said.

"I tried to go to Petra as you said, but she was farther away. When I went to her, someone snatched me up." Quinn shrank back at the rage in Velika's eyes. Maybe she shouldn't have spoken up.

"Where is he?" Velika demanded.

The other guards were surrounding them by now.

"I don't know. I will go search for them," Keir said.

"It is time for us to leave," Velika ordered. She turned to Quinn, her features softening. She stepped toward her. She reached out and took Quinn's hand. She brought it to her lips and kissed it. "I have promised you no harm would come to you, and it looks as if I am already failing."

"You haven't," Quinn whispered. She stepped closer, not liking how the patrons stared at them. She trembled, the cold chilling tendrils of fear gripping her.

She would be safer with Velika.

"Let's get you home."

They strode through the market. The sea of shoppers parted to allow them to pass through. They exited the building, and their SUVs were parked out front. Velika led Quinn and Petra to theirs, where Sabien was waiting.

"Your Grace!" a voice called out.

Velika paused at the open door and glanced in the direction her name was called. She held Quinn close to her side.

"Get inside," Velika murmured.

"No. I don't want you to leave me—"

"It will be all right. Sabien and Petra will be inside with you." Velika kissed her forehead. "It will fine. I won't be gone long."

Quinn nodded. She peeked around Velika and found Keir standing with the other guards. She entered the vehicle. Petra got in behind her and moved to the third row and took her seat.

Velika gave her a nod then shut the door.

Quinn folded her hands in her lap. Her cloak had been returned to her and offered her warmth.

Maybe leaving wasn't the best idea. If another vampire got their hands on her, there was no telling what would happen to her. She was far away from home. She knew what those vampires would do to a woman on her own.

Velika had vowed to cherish her and protect her.

But she hadn't mentioned love.

Wasn't that important? Wasn't that something she would need? What if she fell for Velika, but her love wasn't returned?

That would certainly kill her.

CHAPTER TEN

"What the hell happened out there?" Luther snapped.

Velika strode to her second-in-command. Fury and rage were mounting in her. Quinn was almost taken from right under her nose. The commotion at the market was a distraction. Rogue vampires were causing trouble at one of the vendor tables.

Naturally, she and her men had zeroed in on them. The moment they'd seen them coming, they'd taken off, scurrying away like roaches.

"They tried to take my mate," she growled.

Velika was practically seeing red at the memory of Quinn's terrified expression.

Luther grunted and walked alongside her down the hallway that led to the back of the building.

When they had arrived at the castle, she had ensured the servant, Delia, was to see to Quinn and get her comfortable in Velika's chambers. After this incident, there would be no need for Quinn to have her own room.

They headed down to the lower level of the castle where the dungeon was located. Fane had captured the vampire who had dared put his hands on her mate. The stairwell was dark, the walls stone with lit sconces shining a low light. This part of the castle still held on to the old-world charm. It wasn't meant to be fancy or elegant.

Velika's eyes adjusted. Being a nocturnal creature, she was able to see just fine in the dark. She arrived at the lower level and proceeded with Luther right behind her.

Arad appeared from another hallway with a few warriors behind him.

"Your prisoner awaits you, my princess." He gave a nod to her.

"Where?" she demanded.

"In a cell where he belongs," Arad snarled. He waved for her to follow.

They walked past empty cells. They had rooms designed for any creature. Vampire, lycan, witches or more. These rooms were used to exact justice on those who had broken the law.

As the commander in this territory, it was Velika's responsibility to hand out punishments for those who broke the law.

They arrived at the room with the only habitant in it.

Velika stepped forward and stared at the rogue through the steel bars. They were enhanced to withstand massive force. The prisoner was braced against the wall with iron shackles around his wrists. His head was down, his dark hair acting as a curtain.

Velika's fingers itched to draw her blade and bleed him until he died.

But she wanted answers.

Who would dare try to abduct her mate in public with her near? That was either bold or stupid.

"Open the door," she ordered.

A click sounded, and the bars slid to the side. She marched inside with Luther behind her. He moved off to stand along the wall. Her friend was just as pissed as she was. She could feel the anger pulsating from him.

She walked over to the vampire and stood before him. He didn't even acknowledge she was in the room.

"Your princess is in the room," Luther snapped.

The blatant disrespect was picked up by him as well. He pushed off the wall, but Velika held up her hand. She didn't need any help extracting information.

"She's not my anything," the vampire rasped.

"How about the person who will sign your death warrant is standing before you. The least you could do is look her in the eye," she dared.

He slowly raised his head, the curtain of hair moving away to show his face. Hate shone brightly in his eyes as they met Velika's.

"The mighty Velika Riskel, youngest daughter of King Niall Riskel. Ruler of the North America vampires, killer of his own kind—"

"Watch it," Velika interjected. She moved closer to him, sliding her small dagger from its sheath on her waist. She held the tip underneath his chin. "I could bleed you dry right now just for insulting my father."

The son of a bitch grinned at her.

"The fruit certainly doesn't fall far from the tree." His gaze narrowed on her.

"What is your name?" she asked. Her patience was wearing thin. Her first thought was to end him here, but then she wouldn't have information on who wanted Quinn.

"Why should I tell you? I'm a dead man." He shrugged. He stood to his full height and leaned back against the stone wall.

"We'll give you a proper burial with a stone with your name on it." Velika gave him a cynical grin with full fangs. At least he knew what his fate would be. Putting his hands on Quinn had signed his death warrant. She leaned in closer to him. They were about the same height. She gripped his hair and tugged his head to the side, exposing his neck. "You know there are ways I could extract the information I need."

Yes, she could bite him and through his blood view memories. But the only problem was a rush of nonessential memories came with it. She would have to sort through them to find what she wanted.

She wasn't as strong as her mother or father when it came to this. Her eldest sister, Hegna, had conquered this power. She, like their parents, was very powerful.

His body trembled at the mention of her taking his memories in the ways of the elders. It was an old practice that many were unable to successfully perform.

"Um, my name is Lionel. Lionel Daire," he whimpered. He grimaced and tried to look away from her.

She slid her blade across his throat, and anticipation of seeing his blood flow down his skin filled her. Her gaze flicked back to his.

"Who dare order for you to take my mate?" She knew he wasn't acting on his own. This was a suicide mission with her and her warriors nearby. He was just a pawn in the fight against her and her ruling.

"I can't tell you." He jerked his head in a hard shake.

"What harm is it going to do when you are going to die anyway? You either tell me now and have a quick, painless death, or, we'll draw out the pain and torture you, where you will beg for death." She released his hair and stepped back. She slid the dagger back into its sheath.

"Vampires mating with humans are an abomination," he ranted. He surged forward, the shackles holding him back as he frantically glanced around at the warriors standing outside the cell and Luther. "Our blood should remain pure. Humans are our food source. Not our mates. We are—"

His words were ended by Velika's fist. His head jerked back, and he fell against the wall. Her patience was up. He either told her what she needed to know, or she'd discard him.

She flew forward, crashing into him. Her fangs sank into his skin, and she was immediately rewarded with his warm blood. At the second touch of his blood on her tongue, she began pulling on his memories. His thick blood slid down her throat.

Flashes of a white church came forth. It was nighttime. A secret meeting. A naked body of a woman laid out on the table. Vampires standing around it with goblets filled with blood. One particular face was revealed. She locked in on that image.

Velika released Lionel who fell down to his knees, his arms hanging up in the air from the shackles.

She stepped back, his blood running down her chin. She wiped it away with the sleeve of her shirt.

She knew who was behind this.

Velika turned to Luther who was idly watching

the exchange. He held a knife in his hand as if waiting for her to give the order.

"Kill him," she sneered. "I want it long and drawn-out. Make him pay for laying a hand on my mate."

"Yes, Your Grace." Luther bent down in a bow at the waist. He straightened, and a devious glint appeared in his eyes.

"We will meet tomorrow to discuss our retaliation." She spun on her heel and exited the cell.

"Your Grace." Arad and the others bowed to her.

She stalked from the dungeon, Lionel's screams echoing behind her.

She had to see to her mate.

Tomorrow, she'd start planning the destruction of the rogues. But for now, she had to ensure there was no harm done to Quinn. If there was one scratch on her, there was nothing the rogues would be able do to stop her from annihilating them all.

Velika entered her living quarters and found servants preparing the room. The fire was roaring in the fireplace which would normally be welcoming, but tonight she didn't feel like sitting before it.

"Out," she ordered.

The servants rushed out as she marched into her bedroom. There was no sight of Quinn anywhere. The sound of light chatter in the bathroom drew her attention. She walked in there and found Quinn in the sunken tub with plenty of bubbles surrounding her.

Delia was kneeling on the floor by the tub, washing Quinn's hair. Delia turned, and with one look at Velika, bowed her head.

"Your Grace," Delia murmured.

"Leave us," Velika demanded.

Quinn spun around in the tub, floating in the water. Her eyes were wide as she took Velika in.

"Yes, Your Grace." Delia stood from her perch and rushed out with her head lowered.

Velika's focus was on Quinn. She barely heard the door shut behind the servant girl. Velika began disrobing, dropping her clothes in a pile on the floor. She toed off her boots, dropped her knives and daggers on the floor on top of her clothing until she was left naked. She stood with her hands on her hips, watching Quinn's reaction.

Her beautiful mate hadn't taken her eyes off her since she'd entered. Quinn rested a forearm on the edge of the tub.

"Are you okay?" Quinn asked softly.

"I should be asking you that." Velika smirked, moving over to the tub. She walked down the few stairs that put her into the warm water. With her standing, the water came to just below her breasts. She floated over to Quinn, needing to be near her.

"Just a little shaken, but physically I'm okay. He didn't harm me."

"He should have never touched you." Velika pulled Quinn to her. The water sloshed between them. A growl vibrated in her chest. The feeling of her mate in her arms, naked, was the best feeling she could ever remember experiencing.

There was nothing like it.

Quinn moved closer, pressing her breasts to Velika's.

Velika ran a hand along Quinn's cheeks. She gazed upon her mate, looking for any sign of the vampire. She turned her face and peered at her neck. Her fangs ached to sink into Quinn's soft flesh, but she knew her mate wasn't ready for it yet.

"He didn't bite me," Quinn said.

Velika brought her face back and lowered her head and claimed Quinn's lips.

Quinn gasped, allowing Velika's tongue to slip inside. Velika took her time, stroking her tongue against Quinn's. The kiss was deep and arousing. The need to have her mate grew within her.

"It will never happen again." Velika broke the kiss. She slid her hand to the base of Quinn's neck. In just a small instant she could have lost her mate. Vampires were vicious, and the rogues who had it out for her, and her family, would not hesitate to torture and bleed her mate until she no longer breathed. Velika's hands shook at the thought.

"What is it?"

"I can't lose you," Velika whispered. Her fingertips skated across Quinn's collarbone and disappeared underneath the water's surface.

"I don't understand." Quinn's voice quivered.

A moan slipped from her when Velika's hand encircled her breasts. The soft mound was the perfect size, filling Velika's hand. Velika rested her forehead on Quinn's and inhaled the sweet aroma of her mate.

"You are my other half. Fate made you for me. We are to spend all of eternity together, and the more you are around me, the more you drink from me, the more you will experience the same."

"What does it feel like?"

Velika lifted her head, meeting Quinn's curious gaze. A small smile played on her lips as she thought of all the emotions that took over her when she was near or thought of Quinn.

"It's consuming. You are my focus. The need to please you, the need to provide for you, protect you, drives everything I do." Velika's hand trailed down Quinn's torso. Quinn's soft skin was so tempting. She splayed her fingers over Quinn's ass, holding her against her. "You humans won't ever understand what it is to mate. It's different than your love. Much deeper, and it's forever."

"Not all humans can love," Quinn whispered.

They floated along together in the water. Quinn's hands had found their way onto Velika's body. She had lifted and entwined her fingers at the base of Velika's neck. She held on, allowing Velika to have full access to her body.

"But all vampires have a mate. It's part of our DNA, our makeup, and ingrained into each one of us. We just have a hard time finding them, and it was because of my father and his scientist that he discovered that the answer lay in humans. Our mates were not just vampires. They were other species, and if not for the draft, we would never have found each other."

Velika covered Quinn's mouth with hers. A snarl escaped her when Quinn pulled back.

"Velika, I've been thinking," Quinn began.

Velika stiffened, unsure of what her mate was about to say. She tightened her grip on her, holding her snug against her.

"And I've decided, I want to give this a shot. I know I'm dealing with a lot of things from my past, but I want to learn more about you and vampires. I want to give us a chance."

"Did you ever think that I wasn't going to let you give me a chance?"

"Hey," Quinn exclaimed. She playfully slapped Velika in the arm. "There's some things you are going to have to learn about me."

"And that is?" Velika raised an eyebrow.

"I can think for myself. Make decisions on my own. I've been doing it for a long time."

"That I can agree to."

"I'm learning you are very stubborn and bull-headed." Quinn's lips tipped up into a small smile.

"Determined." Velika pressed another kiss to her lips. She was pleased her mate was slowly accepting her ways. It wouldn't be long before she'd be begging for Velika to bite her. She shivered; the anticipation of tasting Quinn's blood was building.

She positioned them next to the wall. She continued to plunder Quinn's mouth while sliding her hands between them, parting Quinn's labia. A thrill shot through Velika at the sound of Quinn's deep moan.

Her fingers encircled Quinn's clit. She slowly teased and pulled at the sensitive nub, slipping her two fingers inside Quinn's warm channel. Velika held Quinn's leg that had lifted under the water. She braced her mate against the wall of the tub while she fucked her with her fingers. Quinn squirmed in place while her hips thrust on Velika's hand.

Velika buried her face in the crook of Quinn's neck. The intense urge to bite her mate was strong, but she fought it off. Instead, she ran her tongue up her mate's throat and trailed hot kisses down it with gentle nips with her fangs.

"Velika," Quinn moaned.

Velika increased the pace of her fingers. She rotated them, searching for that certain spot that would send her mate screaming. Quinn was a trembling mess under her touch.

She wanted to taste her mate on her tongue.

Velika withdrew her fingers. Quinn's eyes snapped open.

"What's wrong?" Quinn groaned.

"Nothing." Velika lifted her mate out of the water and sat her on the edge.

Quinn fell back and rested on her elbows. Velika pushed her legs open, dropping them to the side to put her beautiful pussy on display.

"Oh," Quinn quipped. Her eyes closed the second Velika's mouth covered her core.

Velika circled her clit with her tongue, drawing it into her mouth. She suckled the bundle of nerves, leaving her mate writhing on the bathroom floor. The taste of Quinn exploded on her tongue.

Quinn's hand shot out and gripped her braids.

Velika expertly stroked her mate's sensitive flesh while pushing her two fingers back inside her tight sheath. The sweet scent of her mate was enveloping her. She would gladly drown in the nectar that poured from Quinn. She set a grueling pace with her fingers. Quinn's hips bucked to meet them.

Velika concentrated on Quinn's bud, wanting to coax her climax from her.

Quinn's cries filled the air. She rotated between whimpers, cries, and chanting Velika's name.

She finally reached her tipping point. Quinn's body shook uncontrollably, her muscles tightened, and the grip on Velika's hair grew. Velika ignored the pain of her hair being tugged, willing to experience it anytime if it meant her mate was enjoying what she was doing to her.

The scream that pierced the air echoed through the bathroom. The sight of her mate's body arching off the floor as she rode the waves of her orgasm was the most beautiful sight she'd ever witnessed.

Quinn flopped back down on the floor, her chest rising and falling fast. Her mate's release coated her face, and Velika would wear it proudly. She licked her lips. The taste of Quinn was better than her favorite type of blood.

Velika brought her mate back to her and guided her into the bath.

Quinn's body rested against hers. Velika was pleased that she was able to give her mate such pleasure. She positioned Quinn in front of her with her back to her chest.

"What about you?" Quinn whispered, resting her head on Velika's shoulder.

Velika reached up and grabbed the cleaning cloth and began washing her woman.

"Don't worry about me." She ran the cleansing cloth along Quinn's arm then brought it up to her breasts. "Right now, allow me to care for you."

Quinn relaxed back without another word. A pleased, calming sense took over Velika. Her mate was safe in her arms, and she was going to keep it that way.

CHAPTER ELEVEN

Quinn inhaled Velika's scent. She nuzzled her face into the nook of her vampire's neck. She didn't know when Velika had become her vampire, but after seeing how the attempt on her life affected Velika, she was willing to claim her.

No one had ever wanted to protect her or take care of her the way Velika was.

What she had said to Velika about giving them a chance was true.

She was going to try to put aside all her prejudices regarding vampires and live in the moment.

Velika's toned body was pressed against hers.

They had moved Quinn into Velika's quarters. No longer would she have a separate area to stay. Velika had given the orders when they'd arrived home, and it had been final.

A shiver coursed through her body. She hated to admit, but she loved when Velika took control. She was a leader, and her people followed her.

She wasn't sure what time it was. The steel coverings were still down, leading Quinn to believe it was sometime during the day. She had slept on and off since they had made it to the bed.

Velika rolled over onto her back. Her eyes were still closed, and her breathing was even.

She must be still asleep.

Quinn propped herself up on her elbow and stared at her vampire. Velika's braids had come half undone, and her blonde hair was spread out on the pillow. The cover slipped down, revealing her breasts. Her deep-rose areolae and her beaded nipples were mere inches away from her.

Quinn snuggled closer to Velika. The woman had given her so much pleasure that she wanted to return the favor. She reached out and cupped the perfect breast. She slid her fingers over the nipple then covered it with her mouth. She bathed the taut bud with her tongue. She flicked it, a small moan slipping from her.

She glanced up and found Velika's clear blue eyes locked on her. She didn't say a word but allowed Quinn to continue.

Quinn guided her hand over Velika's stomach. The skin was soft to her touch, but there were well-defined muscles that some people would kill to have. Quinn shifted on the bed and braced herself above Velika. Her lips skated over to the other teat. She nipped it with her teeth, eliciting a moan from Velika.

Quinn's pulse pounded in her ears. She found herself wanting to please Velika. Her lips moved along the breast. Her tongue skimmed across the underside. Her hand held it up for her while she licked every inch of the tasty mound.

She went south, her tongue blazing a trail down Velika's torso. She traced each line of the muscles on her stomach, dipping her tongue into the slight depression of her navel.

"Quinn," Velika breathed. "My mate."

She licked down farther. Velika's thighs opened, presenting her pussy to Quinn. Her hairless mons was pink and beautiful. Quinn hadn't found one piece of hair on the vampire.

Velika's labia were rosy pink and slick with her desire. Her clit peeked out from between her lips. Quinn kissed the inner part of Velika's thigh while running her fingers through her slit.

Quinn pressed a kiss to Velika's pussy, ready to dive inside it. Her tongue snuck out, and she took her first taste.

A whimper escaped Quinn. It was so good. She needed to have more of it.

She spread her lips apart and captured Velika's clit. She suckled it, pulled it, flicked it while being rewarded with Velika's gasps and moans.

Her tongue glided through Velika's slit, gathering all her juices. She drank it all in, lapping it up. Her tongue pushed forward into Velika's core, getting more of her honey.

Quinn feasted upon Velika, unable to get enough.

Velika trembled underneath her. Quinn felt her own wetness coating her thighs. She moved up and latched on to Velika's clit, humming while she suckled it. She pushed two fingers into Velika's hot core, the muscles gripping her tight. She pumped them inside her.

She cried out as Velika lifted her and dragged her over her body. She found herself suddenly on her back with Velika lying on top of her. They mouths met in a passionate kiss.

Quinn was quickly losing control. She returned the kiss with the same fire that Velika had.

She growled when Velika broke the kiss. Her vampire reached over and opened the drawer on the nightstand beside the bed. She took out an electric massaging wand. Quinn's eyes went to the ripped round head, and she automatically licked her lips.

Velika grinned and came back to her.

"Let's have a little fun, shall we?" Velika murmured. She positioned them to where their pussies were brushing each other.

Quinn moaned, trying to rub herself against Velika.

Velika held the vibrator between them, resting it on both of them. She turned it on, and the vibrations started.

"Oh," Quinn gasped.

Velika pressed closer to her, keeping the toy between them. She thrust forward on it with Velika.

She held her lover's gaze as they moved against the toy together. The speed increased while the vibrations grew fiercer.

Quinn reached up and gripped Velika to her.

Velika's fangs were on display when she opened her mouth and cried out. Quinn gripped Velika's ass, guiding her to her.

"Harder," Quinn begged.

Velika braced herself with one hand while she kept their toy in place for them.

Quinn captured one of Velika's breasts with her mouth. She played with the hardened nipple with her tongue.

Velika increased the speed and sent a rush of sensations through Quinn. She was on the edge of her orgasm and was so close. She widened her legs to allow more of the massager to tremble against her clit.

It was too much. She couldn't hold back any longer.

Quinn threw her head back and screamed. Her climax washed over. A rush of warmth gushed from her core just as Velika reached her peak.

Velika's arm gave way, her body falling onto Quinn. A fine sheen of sweat covered both of their bodies, but Quinn didn't care. She wrapped an arm around Velika and held on to her. Velika pulled the massager from between them and tossed it on the bed. She lifted her head and gazed down into Quinn's eyes.

Yes, she was catching feelings for the vampire.

Quinn cupped Velika's cheek and brought her down. Their lips molded together in sweet, slow kiss.

If she had to belong to a vampire, she didn't want anyone else but Velika.

Velika stood next to the bed fully dressed and stared down at Quinn's sleeping form. Her mate was on her stomach, and the blanket was pulled up to her ass, leaving her back exposed. Velika stared at the soft, brown skin and didn't want to leave.

Unable to resist, she knelt on the bed and kissed the center of Quinn's shoulder blades.

A moan slipped from Quinn. She rolled over slightly.

"Velika?" Her soft voice was tantalizing.

Velika wanted to strip her clothes off and climb back in with her. They had spent all day in the bed, sleeping and fucking. The sleep Velika had gotten was the best she'd had in years.

"Sleep, *miere.*" Velika ran her hands over Quinn's short dark curls. She dropped another kiss on the back of her neck. "I shall send someone for you later."

Quinn nodded and snuggled into the bed, holding her pillow. Velika tugged the covers over Quinn. She walked from the room. Once she was out in the hall, she was met by Keir and another guard.

"My mate is to rest. When she awakens, she may go where she pleases, but under no circumstances is she to leave the grounds," Velika announced.

"Yes, Your Grace." Keir nodded.

She spun around on her heel and stalked away. She had reassigned her personal guards. They were needed to patrol around the castle. After the attack on her mate, she was not taking any chances.

The urge to consume blood filled her. She headed to the kitchen where she could grab a glass. It was nothing like getting it from the source, but she had to curb her desires. Until she completed the full mating bond with Quinn, she would need to obtain blood from another source. Once they were mated in all the ways of vampires, she would only drink from her mate.

"Your Grace." Timbi turned when she entered.

The woman greeted her with a smile and moved over to the fridge.

"Evening, Timbi." Velika stood next to the island and paused. The chef had been with her for a long time.

"How's your mate?" Timbi brought over her favorite blood type, B, in a large goblet.

The copper aroma was wonderful. She took a big gulp of it before resting the cup on the counter. A warmth filled her from the blood. Blood provided all of the nutrients and nourishment she needed.

"She is doing well." She inhaled the smells from the food Timbi was cooking. She had never been curious about food before. She wondered what Quinn's favorite things were to eat.

"I heard about what happened. She's such a sweet girl. I'd hate to see anything happen to her." Timbi leaned against the counter, a worried look on her face.

"Don't worry, Timbi. Nothing will happen to her." Velika took another sip of the thick fluid. It was warmed to a perfect temperature.

"I hear Councilwoman Iona will be hosting the party in yours and Ms. Hogan's honor."

"She is." Velika glanced down at the almost empty goblet. She lifted it and finished off her drink and placed the goblet on the counter. She pushed it over to Timbi. "My mate is still sleeping. Please ensure she is well-fed."

"I will, Your Grace. I'm getting food together for all of us now." She grinned and took the goblet.

"Thank you." Velika walked out of the kitchen. It was time she met with Luther and Arad about what she had discovered from Lionel.

She arrived at her office before them. Her footsteps echoed through the air. The sun protectors began to rise on the windows. They were automatically set to open once nighttime fell. Not that they received much sun in their part of the country. But it was still necessary for the days the sun did come from behind the thick clouds.

She headed to the window and paused to take in the beautiful darkening sky. There was mounting stress falling upon her, but it was nothing she couldn't handle. Her father would not have allowed her to take over this territory if he didn't think she was fit to oversee it.

A knock sounded at the door.

"Come in," she called out over her shoulder. Her gaze went back to the moon and the clouds slowly drifting before it.

"Your Grace," Luther spoke from behind her.

She turned to see him and Arad walking to her.

"Luther. Arad." She nodded toward them. These two were her most trusted vampires. "I trust you handled our little friend last night after I left."

"We most certainly did. He should have just cooperated with you from the start." Luther shrugged.

"You must teach me that skill of yours. The way you fillet the skin was something short of amazing." Arad chuckled.

They stopped in front of her desk, folded their hands behind their backs, and focused their attention to her.

"Sounds like you had fun." She smirked. She would normally have participated, but seeing to her mate was top priority.

"How is Ms. Hogan?" Arad asked.

"She is unharmed and doing well. I thank you for asking." Velika waved them to the chairs near them. "Please have a seat."

"I would prefer to stand—"

"Sit." She walked over to hers behind the desk. She sat in the high-backed leather chair.

"I was able to gather from the rogue's memories who ordered the capture of my mate," she began once they had settled into their chairs.

"Who?" Luther growled.

"Cain Theron."

Curses filled the room. It was well-known the vampire was against the royal family. He had been a pain in Velika's ass for years.

And now, he had signed his own death warrant.

She had dealt with him before and had not considered him a true threat. Not only did humans protest vampire and human intermingling, so did vampires.

"Consider him good as dead," Arad snarled.

"He will die by my hand," Velika ordered. "Before I was lenient on the rogues, but no more."

The rogues had been growing in numbers. Anyone who didn't side with the Riskels were considered against the crown, therefore a rogue. Cain had been a vampire who had been very outspoken against her family and their ruling.

His following was growing, and he was gaining power. He was in her territory, so he fell under Velika's jurisdiction.

Now, she would squash him and his rogues like bugs.

"In the wretched memories, there was a white church. A place where they sacrificed a woman. They meet there," she shared.

"That gives us very little to work with, but I'm sure we can build on that," Luther said.

"I have a few contacts I can reach out to and see what they know," Arad offered.

"We don't have much time. The council will be hosting a welcoming ball here at the castle soon." Velika still wished she could stop it. Her mate wasn't yet ready to be exposed to everything vampire.

"Don't worry, Your Grace. We will ensure the property is the most secured. No harm will come to your mate." Luther pounded his chest.

"Agreed. We will have the top warriors present." Arad thumped his chest as well.

It was all they could do, but if they were able to capture Cain, all the better.

"Arad, reach out to your contacts. I want to hear something by morning."

"Yes, Your Grace." He stood and bowed to her. "Anything else?"

"No, that is it for now." She nodded to the door, giving him permission to leave.

He stalked from the room, leaving her and Luther alone.

"Today, I will not be able to spar with you," she said.

"Oh?" He raised an eyebrow at her.

"I will be working with Quinn. I want to teach her to defend herself."

"That would be best." He immediately grew serious and nodded. "Hopefully she won't have to, but it would be good for her."

"That I agree. I purchased the perfect weapon for her. Something discreet and small for her to use."

"I'm happy that you have a mate, Velika," he said. He gave a sarcastic laugh. "I'm a little jealous and secretly hope my name is matched with some-one. These years have certainly been lonely."

She stared at him, not ever seeing this side of him. She had thought he was happy with life the way it was. But he was right. Their long years could be very lonely on this earth.

"Well, I will hope the goddess above will match you with a human of your own, or better yet, you stumble upon that person." Same-sex mating was very common in the paranormal world. It was only humans who tried to deem heterosexual pairings as against the norm.

"Thank you, Your Grace." He pushed up from his chair and nodded to her. "I shall begin preparing the security detail for the party. I'll let Arad take the lead on the hunt for Cain."

"That would be perfect." She leaned back and rested her boots on her desk. She could count on these two.

He left the room, and Mortas stood in the doorway.

"Your Grace. It is time for your public hearing," he announced. The older vampire was a man of few words. He was very loyal to her family and had been around with them for centuries. When she took over this castle, he was promoted to head butler to oversee the workings of the building.

Velika sighed. This was something her mother had suggested. A hearing of sorts with the royal family. Vampires from the coven could come to her with problems, and she would hear them out. She allotted two hours of her time each week for this.

"Very well, Mortas. I will be on my way."

"Yes, Your Grace."

CHAPTER TWELVE

Quinn strolled along the path in the gardens. The majestic aroma of roses filled her senses. After awakening, Delia assisted her in getting dressed, and then she was escorted to the kitchen for her meal.

Quinn was off her normal human schedule. Usually, she would be either at work or winding down at this time of the evening.

She was going to have to get used to sleeping during the day and being awake at night.

"Who oversees the planting of the flowers?" She

looked over her shoulder at Keir and Fane who were walking behind her.

They informed her that the princess had given her full rein of the house and property. She had gone exploring, and when she had stepped outside, she'd fallen in love with this area.

The fresh air was lovely. The night sky was beautiful. She glanced up and wished she could share it with Velika.

She didn't understand how after such a short time, she was already needing her. She wanted to experience discovering little things with her. Today she was dressed in a soft oversized maxi dress that fell off her shoulders. It went down to her feet that were encased in strappy sandals.

She felt like a million bucks. She'd never had so many new clothes, she didn't know what to do with herself. When she'd woken up, Delia was guiding servants in with tons of boxes with new clothes, shoes, and everything a woman needed.

It was hard to not feel like she was in a fantasy romance or something.

"There is a human gardener who is in charge of the grounds," Keir replied.

"I'd love to meet them," she said.

"I'm sure it can be arranged," Keir replied.

She came to a stone fountain with running water. There was an angel statue a few feet up in the air with water spouting from its lips. She sat on the edge and took in her surroundings.

For the castle to be as old as it was, it was in magnificent shape.

And she got to live here.

A small smile graced her lips. She had truly enjoyed her day. Timbi had ensured her belly was full of good food. She was surely going to gain some weight with the way that woman cooked.

Slight guilt filled her as she stared up at the moon. Here she was, given a great life with a woman who vowed to protect her, and her brother was still missing.

Was he looking up at the same moon?

Was he in pain?

Was he even alive?

Her vision blurred, the tears falling. She reached up and brushed them away.

"What is it, *miere*? Why are you crying?"

Quinn gasped and spun around. Velika strolled to her with concern on her face.

"It's nothing." Quinn shook her head and tried to offer a warm smile. She stood when Velika reached her.

"You mustn't lie to me, *miere*," Velika murmured. She reached out and pulled Quinn to her. She tipped up Quinn's chin and kissed each cheek.

"I'm not." She sighed. She laid a hand over Velika's heart. Just being in her presence was calming her down. "Thank you for all of the clothing and items you had delivered. You didn't have to do that."

"I do. What kind of mate would I be if I don't provide the necessary amenities?" Velika's hand brushed along her hairline and down to her neck. "Now tell me. What brings tears to your eyes?"

The vampire was extremely stubborn. She wasn't going to let up until Quinn told her why she was crying. Quinn stood up on her toes to try to kiss Velika, but the woman pressed a finger to her mouth.

"Don't try to distract me. Tell me." Velika hardened her voice slightly, standing firm in her request.

Quinn's shoulders slumped.

"I'm worried. My brother has been missing for ten years. I was never able to find him. I paid investigators to look for him, but they all came back with the same results. Nothing."

Velika stared at her without saying a word.

Quinn had never had anyone she felt close enough to share this information with. All the stress of worrying about Lane had been on her. It had only been the two of them for years.

"We were so close. When our parents died, we vowed we would never leave each other. One day he went off to work and never made it. He broke his promise."

Her voice ended on a hiccup.

Her brother had been her rock, her strength, and protector.

And he was gone, leaving her to survive in this world alone.

The floodgates opened. She leaned her forehead to Velika's chest and sobbed. The pain of losing her last family member flooded her. She'd had to be strong for so long, trying to keep everything in her life together.

It felt good to unleash it all.

Velika didn't say a word but held her.

The soft caress of her hand running down Quinn's spine provided some comfort. Quinn lost track of time and didn't know how long they had stood there. She lifted her head, taking in the wetness on Velika's leather tunic.

"I'm sorry," Quinn blurted out.

"Don't worry about my clothing. Why have you been holding this in for so long?" Velika asked. She wiped away Quinn's tears and cupped both sides of Quinn's face in her hands. "We will search for your brother and find him."

"Even if he's dead, I just want closure, but deep in my heart, I know he's alive." Quinn sniffed. This was something she believed in her heart. Lane couldn't be dead. Her elder brother was too stubborn to die.

She gripped on to Velika's hands.

Again, she wasn't sure why, but being in her vampire's presence was calming her racing heart. She trusted that Velika would keep her promise. If anyone could find Lane, Velika could. She had much more resources than Quinn did.

"There was a reason I came to find you." Velika chuckled. Her hands dropped to Quinn's shoulders.

The heat of her touch had Quinn's core clenching.

How could she possibly want this woman again? They had spent hours pleasuring each other throughout the day.

Apparently, her body didn't remember. Her nipples drew into taut little buds and pushed against the soft material of her dress.

"And what was that?" Quinn asked. She bit her lip and leaned into Velika.

"I came to collect you so we may begin your training."

"Oh?"

"Yes. As the mate to the warden of the North-west, you must be able to defend yourself." Velika took her hand and led her past the guards who had backed away to give them privacy.

Quinn didn't think she would ever become a powerful fighter such as Velika, but if she could teach her the basics, she would feel safer.

"Did humans and vampires mate before the draft?" Quinn asked. She glanced up from her book and peered at Petra.

They were in the library for Quinn's daily tutoring session. Each night, they met for an hour or two. Quinn loved hearing all about the history of vampires. Petra was very knowledgeable, and it was no wonder she was the advisor to Velika. The woman certainly knew her history.

"Of course. Vampires and humans have lived alongside each other from the beginning of time.

We revealed ourselves only to those we trusted," Petra said. She sat back in her chair and lifted her goblet to her lips.

Quinn had grown used to the scent of blood. To anyone looking at Petra, it would appear as if she were enjoying a nice glass of merlot.

"Did you have any human friends?"

"Of course." Petra shrugged. She sat her glass down on the table and leaned forward. "Some lovers. I have to say, humans enjoy the bite of a vampire in the heat of passion." She tossed a wink at Quinn.

"Did, um, Velika have human friends?" Quinn asked. She bit her lip, trying to push down the jealousy that reared its ugly head inside her. She brushed a piece of invisible lint off her long skirt, unable to meet Petra's gaze.

Petra barked out a healthy laugh.

Quinn flicked her gaze up and found Petra's cheeks flushed. She snorted, trying to inhale while she waved a hand.

"That I am not going to answer. If you want to know that you are going to have to speak with Velika." Petra chuckled. She pushed back from the chair and walked around the table, stopping next to Quinn. "Now, my curious little student. Let's move on to the history of the Riskel regime. If you are to mate with the daughter of the king, you must know the family."

Quinn settled into her chair, watching Petra turn the pages in her book. At the request of Velika, Petra had begun to teach her the history of vampirism. She had quickly learned that most of what she had known had been rumors and a pile of untruths.

And the vampires who ruled her town were not living in line with the laws of vampires. She now knew her town was run by rogues. The treatment of humans was illegal, and she promised she would do all she could to fix that.

"King Niall Riskel is an older vampire who fought and conquered. The previous ruler was one who did not have any values, and his beliefs were aligned with the old world. That was a dark period in our history."

Quinn gazed upon the page that showed a man with dark hair standing proudly dressed in armor and held a sword in his hand.

"And what of the humans? At that time were vampires known?" Quinn was soaking up all the information she could. This was much more interesting than her schooling. She had barely graduated from high school with the world practically falling apart. Had she had a class on vampirism, she would have excelled.

"There were many myths circulating about vampires. Some compared us to witches, others demons. They didn't have a clear understanding of what vampirism was. I believe my father used to tell a story of how people would go around to graves and dig up the dead and proclaim them to be vampire if their body wasn't decaying fast enough."

"What?" Quinn's eyes widened. Where did people come up with this nonsense? "But you are a living being. I've felt Velika's heartbeat."

"Of course, we are alive. We are born vampires. Yes, there are vampires who are turned. They are not full-blooded like Velika and me, but they are still vampire."

"What about children? If a human and a vampire have a child, what do they become?"

"That is complex. Dhampirs are children born from a vampire and human mating. The human genes appear to be dominant, but they have all of a vampire's strengths but none of our weaknesses."

"They can go out in daylight?"

"They are the lucky ones." Petra leaned against the table and nodded.

"What if…" Quinn bowed her head. She grew embarrassed with the question she had forming on the tip of her tongue. She wasn't sure where it came from, and she had never really thought of it before.

"What is it?" Petra asked. She must have sensed Quinn's embarrassment. She chuckled and shook her head. "Go ahead. Ask away. I promise no question is a stupid question."

"What about children for me and Velika. I'm sure as one of the princesses and a warden of the Northwest, she will want heirs. How would that work?" There were countless numbers of human children up for adoption. Would they just adopt? Were there orphaned vampire children who needed parents?

"You are thinking of children?" Velika's voice appeared behind Quinn.

She jerked around in her chair to find Velika staring at her. Quinn swallowed the lump that formed in her throat. She hadn't really started thinking of children until she had moved into the castle.

She'd had a dream the night before where she was pregnant. Her belly had been very large, and Velika was there with her, holding her in her arms.

Quinn knew, of course, that dreams could be

symbolic for practically anything, but just the image of her swollen with child had stuck with her.

Did she want kids?

Velika slowly ambled toward her. A look of wonder was on her face. She came to kneel before Quinn.

"I'll give you two some privacy." Petra backed up then spun around on her heel and walked away.

Neither Velika nor Quinn paid her any attention.

"I'm just curious how that would work," Quinn whispered.

Velika reached up and dragged a finger down her temple to her cheek. "But you've thought about having children?"

"When I was living back home, children were the last thing on my mind. There was no way I would have wanted to bring life into this world under those circumstances." Quinn had been extremely poor, barely able to pay her rent and bills. She was just living day to day back in Stramford.

That environment wasn't conducive for raising children.

"Now?" Velika asked. She cupped Quinn's face and brought it close to hers.

"How would it work?" Quinn asked.

"Be that I am the daughter of the king, I will need an heir. Our scientists are very advanced with in vitro insemination. There are plenty of sperm donors available, and they could harvest our eggs. Viable embryos would be implanted after fertilization. Success rates are almost one hundred percent."

"And then I could carry the baby to term?" Quinn asked. It was a no-brainer that she would carry any child they had. Velika couldn't go off to war pregnant. It was almost laughable to imagine a stubborn Velika trying to wield a sword with a belly the size of a basketball.

Over the past week, she was becoming more attached to Velika. Her eyes dropped down to Velika's lips. She reached out and traced them with her fingers.

Her heart rate increased. She opened her legs to allow Velika to move closer to her. Quinn leaned down and pressed her lips to Velika's. She grew bold and thrust her tongue inside Velika's mouth.

The need for Velika was growing as each day passed. A moan slipped from Quinn from the feeling of Velika's hands on her waist.

Their lips moved over each other. Their tongues

dueled in a gentle dance. The taste of Velika was divine. Quinn could never get enough of it.

Velika's hands slid underneath her skirt. They skated their way up her thighs. Velika's fingers met Quinn panties.

Her fingers pushed the small material to the side and parted Quinn's labia. A pleased rumble was emitted from Velika when her fingers were met with the proof of her desire.

"You're so wet," Velika murmured, her lips brushing Quinn's. She glided her fingers through Quinn's moist folds, gathering some of her nectar, circling back to Quinn's clit.

"Yes," Quinn hissed.

Velika wrapped a possessive arm around Quinn and brought her forward to the edge of the chair. This opened Quinn fully, allowing Velika's fingers to dive inside her core.

Quinn cried out from the wonderful sensation rushing through her body. She threaded her fingers into the loose strands of Velika's hair and slammed her mouth onto hers.

Quinn trembled from the immense pleasure of Velika's fingers. Her vampire was fucking her with her fingers, and she loved it.

"I love when you voice your pleasure," Velika

growled. She withdrew her fingers and slipped them up to Quinn's nub and rubbed it. "I love watching you shatter in my arms."

Quinn could barely breathe. She was drowning in the sweet torture of Velika working her pussy. She didn't care what she looked like with her legs spread wide while Velika had her at the edge of her orgasm.

She was overwhelmed by everything. The way Velika treated her, took care of her, provided for her, and wanted to ensure she had everything she would ever want or need.

The sex was the icing on the cake.

Her body was Velika's playground, and she would never tire of the countless orgasms.

Velika was perfect. Everything about her from her pure beauty, crystal-blue eyes, and toned body was amazing.

Quinn held on to Velika. She was going to come soon. It was obvious from the way her body trembled, her muscles tightened, and how her core pulsed.

Quinn was desperate for her release. She was growing quite addicted to them and needed Velika to give her what she craved.

Velika's fingers moved faster on her bundle of

nerves. The exquisite torture was worth it. Her vampire knew how to get her off. She pinched and tugged on Quinn's clitoris, and that was it.

Quinn detonated.

She screamed, uncaring who would hear her as she rode the waves of her release. Quinn was barely conscious when Velika lifted her slightly and lay her on the table. The books she had been previously reading were shoved off onto the floor.

"Velika," Quinn moaned. Her skirt bunched up at her waist, and her legs were pushed up into the air. The sound of her panties ripping was a distant memory. Her skirt met the same demise. Her blouse soon followed.

Velika was having her way with her body, and Quinn loved it.

Velika's tongue slid its way through her drenched slit and circled her clit. Quinn whimpered, her bud still sensitive.

Her eyes rolled into the back of her head.

Velika feasted on her, and Quinn could do nothing but hold on to her. The beautiful woman loved licking her pussy until she screamed. One orgasm was never enough. Velika always ensured Quinn had multiple climaxes each day.

"I want you to want me," Velika commanded.

Quinn glanced down at her to see a hunger like she'd never seen before in her eyes.

"I do want you," she whispered. A cry fell from her lips as Velika pushed her fingers back inside her.

"I want you to want me," Velika repeated, but only this time her words ended in a growl. Her fangs were noticeable from underneath her lip. Her fingers went deep, earning her a gasp from Quinn. Her fingers fucked her slowly at first and increased in tempo.

You will want my bite.

Quinn's eyes closed. She knew what Velika was wanting.

I'll taste your pure sweetness, and then you will consume my blood.

Was she ready for that?

Velika was keeping her promise. She was a woman of her word. She treated Quinn like she was a queen.

Maybe she could get Velika to love her.

Safety, security, and love was all a girl needed.

Right?

Velika's lips closed around her clit, and all thoughts exited Quinn's brain. She lost herself to Velika right then.

She would be happy to admit she craved the woman's touch, her mouth, and just her presence.

She needed her.

Velika was her vampire.

Her body arched off the table and, in that instant, she knew she would soon beg for that bite.

CHAPTER THIRTEEN

"Again," Velika commanded.

Quinn knelt on the mat and pushed up to stand. Velika had easily knocked her down again. No matter how many moves she tried, Velika bested her.

They had been at this for some time now. Quinn would have to admit she was getting better. She gripped her bone-handled knife. It fit perfect in her palm. She tightened her fingers on it. She hadn't felt comfortable training with it. Quinn was afraid she would injure Velika, but apparently vampires healed rapidly. She had only managed to deal out small cuts on Velika.

Her breaths were coming fast. An hour had passed since they had begun her training session. Sweat coated her skin while Velika looked as if she were out for a Sunday stroll. They were in the workout room where warriors came to train.

"Don't be frustrated. You are doing quite well for an untrained human," Velika tried to soften the blow.

"Whatever," Quinn grumbled, sliding her knife back into her thigh sheath. She wiped the moisture from her brow and focused on Velika.

"You are not going to war. Remember, I don't want you to take down a vampire. We are naturally stronger and quicker than a human."

"You just want me to be able to get away," Quinn said. This was something Velika had stressed to her. Quinn knew Velika was much stronger than her. The way the woman could pick her up and toss her was amazing. Quinn was no small woman. Since moving into the castle she had picked up more weight, thanks to Timbi.

She had thought she was thick before, now her curves were more defined.

Velika hadn't seemed to mind. It didn't keep her

from diving face-first between Quinn's thighs every morning when they went to bed. Quinn was now used to the vampires' schedule. She felt great. She thought it would be hard to get used to the life of a nocturnal being, although sometimes, Velika prowled the castle during the day.

"Close your eyes and relax," Velika commanded.

Quinn did as she was ordered. She inhaled softly. The room was silent. Velika was light on her feet, not making a sound. Quinn was sure Velika was going to try to surprise her.

She needed to anticipate the attack.

"Now open." Velika's voice was behind her.

Quinn opened her eyes and found the room cast into darkness.

Quinn spun around, unable to see. Her pulse pounded in her ears as she waited for her eyes to adjust.

"Pretend you are taking a walk on the grounds. You are in the gardens enjoying the night air." Velika's voice came from a different area.

Quinn silently turned, trying to pinpoint where Velika was.

"If I were to walk at night, there would be a little light to guide me," Quinn grumbled. She moved again, only now able to see shadows. Something dashed passed her on the right, but yet arms wrapped around her waist from behind.

She stumbled back into Velika, taking her by surprise just as she was taught. She stomped on Velika's foot, then pushed her arms against the hold. She broke through and dashed forward.

"Perfect," Velika praised.

The lights flicked on. Quinn beamed, feeling more confident.

"Your Grace," Arad called out. He came marching into the room with a serious expression. He stopped before them and pounded a fist over his heart. "There is news on Cain."

Quinn had learned Velika and her men were tracking down the vampire who had ordered her kidnapping. Velika glanced at her, and Quinn already knew she was about to send her away.

"I want to hear." Quinn stood up straight. She didn't want to be coddled any longer. She was growing stronger, and if Velika had her way, she would be kept in their private quarters forever.

"Fine." Velika took her hand, and they followed Arad through the building.

Excitement filled Quinn that Velika was

including her. They had made great strides in their relationship.

If she were going to be the mate to the warden of this territory, she was going to have to find a purpose.

They went to a lower level of the castle to an area she hadn't explored yet and entered a room filled with warriors. Quinn recognized a few of them.

Luther, the second-in-command to Velika, stood at the helm of the table.

He glanced up from a map and nodded to Velika. He arched an eyebrow to Quinn but said nothing. Velika guided her to a chair at the table while she moved over to Luther.

Quinn took in the other vampires. All were pledged to Velika. Quinn the met the gaze of one of the warriors who bowed his head to her.

Luther began to update Velika, and Quinn tuned in.

"Cain has been on the run. He's trying to dodge us and doesn't stay in one place long," Luther said.

Velika didn't like the sound of this. Why was he constantly moving around in her territory? Why not leave? He had failed his attempt in kidnapping her mate, so why stay around?

Velika knew the answer.

He was going to try again. It was the only reason why he would risk her men capturing him.

"Where was his last known location?" she asked. Velika rested her hands on the table and stared at the map. It was marked with last known positions of the deranged rogue leader.

"Vancouver."

Vancouver was a city that was overrun with vampires. Many were supporters of her family and the throne, but as with all cities, there were those who opposed her father. There hadn't been too many reports coming out of Vancouver until now.

"Our informants have shared with us that the numbers of rogues have increased. There has been a record number of human attacks in the city," Arad shared.

"Why wasn't I notified of this?" Velika tried to

keep herself from looking in Quinn's direction. Any changes in her territory should have been brought to her. It was her responsibility to handle any insurgents.

"The Vancouver station had assured me they were handling everything," Luther said. He folded his arms in front of him. "This was how our informants found out about the surge in numbers. The violence increased."

"We have a location, and I say we invade it. For the kingdom." Arad thumped his chest.

"The kingdom," the other warriors in the room followed suit, banging on their chests.

Velika stared at the map, contemplating the notion. The welcoming ball was going to be held in a week. If they raided the rogue's lair now, then they would eliminate the threat against her mate. Protecting Quinn was top priority.

"What are the numbers of rogues?" she asked.

"Last we checked, there was over a hundred just in that location," Luther replied.

She glanced at the both of them, trusting their judgement.

"And the informants you've used are reliable?" She raised an eyebrow. If they were going to swarm in on a city, she needed to make damn sure the intel was good.

"Of course." Luther nodded.

It wasn't that she was doubting Luther, it was always these unknown informants who could give information to the highest bidder.

"I know of a way you can confirm," Quinn's soft voice cut through the tense silence.

All eyes shifted to her. Confidence radiated in her eyes as she met Velika's gaze.

"And how is that?" Velika asked, curious about the input her mate had to offer.

Quinn sat up straighter. "By speaking with the humans. They will know the areas to avoid, and if it's true about an increase in violence, then they will be able to confirm it. Had a person approached me in my old town, I would have been able to tell them areas to avoid, where attacks happened and when."

Velika was impressed with the suggestion. She wouldn't have thought to speak to the humans about vampires' whereabouts. It still angered her about the way her mate had to live in fear of her life.

Well, no more.

Velika would ensure Quinn would never have to

look over her shoulder again. She wanted her to enjoy all the pleasantries the world had to offer.

"The humans won't talk with us." Arad shook his head.

Grunts went around the room. He was right. If the attacks had increased the way they were being reported, then a vampire was the last person a human would speak with.

"They'll speak with me," Quinn said.

"No," Velika growled.

"But it's your only chance to confirm where the vampires are. I'm the only person in this room who can get close to humans."

"One of us will try," Velika snapped.

"And none of you will pass for human no matter how hard you try." Quinn slowly stood. She glanced around the room. "After the war, many humans tried to stay clear of vampires. We just wanted to live in peace. But we learned the tells vampires give off. The way you walk. The way you talk. There are certain mannerisms that are recognizable as vampire."

"Then we'll find another way." Velika rested her hands on her hips. There was no way in the seven hells would she take her mate on a mission to invade a lair of vampires.

"I'm going." Quinn's jawline hardened.

Velika cursed, not sure if she liked this stubbornness in her mate.

"I'm not saying I'll run in fighting with you," Quinn said, "I will just go to gather information. I can go somewhere else that is safe while you do all the fighting."

"Whatever we decide to do, we have to move tonight," Luther said quietly. "If we wait any longer then there is a high chance he would be on the move, and it would take us days to locate them again."

"Days we don't have," Velika muttered. She stood to her full height and met the gaze of each of her men in the room. These were Luther and Arad's most trusted warriors who served under them and were completely loyal to her and her family.

"What are we doing?" Luther asked.

She stalked over to Quinn and stood before her. She hated to admit Quinn was right.

"We'll find a place for you to go to question humans. It will be a public place where I can see you, then when you have the information, we will transfer you to a secured location." Her heart was racing. She couldn't remember the last time she was not calm going into battle. Now there were more stakes on the table. This was a short-notice mission which already made it dangerous since they didn't have days or weeks to plan an attack. There were numerous areas where this could go wrong, but she had confidence in her warriors.

Instead of going into this situation with a level head, she would be distracted by having Quinn nearby.

"The best place would be a popular diner or bar," Quinn said. "Somewhere humans can congregate and will be comfortable talking amongst other humans."

Velika stared at her and tried to push down the urge to pick Quinn up and toss her over her shoulder. She wanted to take her upstairs and lock her in their bedroom with guards standing by to protect her.

Velika spun around and stared at her men.

"Cain Theron has lived too many days on this earth. It is time to rid the world of the scum who don't want to conform to our way of life," Velika said.

Growls echoed around the room.

Velika folded her hands together behind her

back. Going into battle was always a serious decision, and now, there was a damn good reason.

To protect her mate.

"There is only one ruling king in this land, and that is King Riskel. We fight to uphold the laws of vampires. We fight to protect our peace and we fight to protect my mate. Cain has tried to take her from me. That will be the worst decision he has ever made." Her fangs had descended, and she brandished them proudly. Cain Theron was a dead man. She would hunt him down and end him, bleed him dry for thinking he could lay a hand on her mate.

Quinn closed the gap between them and wrapped her arms around Velika's waist. Velika looked down at her, and even though she was scared shitless of having her mate go out on a mission with them, she was damn proud of her.

"Prepare the choppers, we leave in one hour," Velika announced. She spun on her heel and dragged Quinn behind her. If she was going to tag along with them, then she was going to have to be prepared.

"Where are we going?" Quinn asked. Her hand tightened on Velika's while she rushed to keep up with her.

"You can't go dressed like that." Velika knew that no human would trust her if she went dressed in the finer clothes that most humans didn't have access to.

They climbed the stairs and headed toward their quarters.

"What do you mean?"

They arrived at the first level and walked down the hallway toward the main part of the building. They were a little way away from their room and they had a short time to get her ready for her undercover mission.

"The humans will know that you belong to a vampire. Your clothing will be a dead giveaway, and they may not give you any information," Velika said.

Quinn glanced down at her clothing and nodded. Even though she was dressed in workout gear, it would still stand out.

"What am I supposed to wear?" she asked.

They continued, almost running through the castle.

"You'll have to wear something that you brought with you when you arrived."

They entered their private area. Quinn rushed over to the closet and returned with her tattered bag. She sat it on the bed and reached inside, pulling out items. Velika stood next to her and rested a hand on her shoulder.

"You don't have to do this," Velika murmured.

Quinn lifted what looked to be a sweatshirt and held it to her chest. Her head lowered, and she shook it.

"I have to. If I can help the people of Vancouver in any way, then I will." She sniffed. She turned her big eyes to Velika, and her once hardened heart melted. "There wasn't anyone who came to my town and helped us. I can do that for the people of Vancouver."

Velika understood the need to help one's people. She was proud of her mate who had grown confident since her arrival. Velika squeezed her shoulder and gave a nod.

"Then we will do everything we can to keep you safe. Come. Change your clothes and keep your knife on you. I don't trust anyone near you." Velika dropped a kiss on her forehead. She didn't trust herself to do anything more, for they would end up in the bed. "We'll take down this rogue lair and then when we return, we will prepare for the ball."

Quinn turned and dragged more items out of her bag.

"It won't take me long to get dressed," Quinn said.

A glint of metal snagged Velika's attention.

"What is this?" Velika picked up a small crude knife that had fallen out of the sweatshirt Quinn held.

Her mate froze and stared at the weapon.

"That was mine. It was my protection for when I lived alone." Her voice was lowered. She cast her eyes downward as if ashamed of her past.

Velika moved closer and tipped her chin up to force her gaze to hers.

"There is nothing wrong with wanting to protect oneself." She couldn't imagine the horrors Quinn had lived through. Now her mate wanted to go and help her fellow humans to make their town safer. Quinn would make a great princess.

They would do one thing at a time. First defend Vancouver and capture Cain, then they would come home and face her coven together.

Velika would introduce Quinn to the vampires that served under her, and all would be well.

CHAPTER FOURTEEN

Quinn remained silent and observed the men surrounding her and Velika. It was amazing to see how these men were fearlessly following her vampire into the unknown. Quinn may not be a person who could plan a battle attack, but she could see the risk of what they were doing.

No time to plan, research, and scout out specifics meant they were going in blind.

Quinn swallowed hard.

Vampires were hard to kill. She'd learned that in her studies with Petra.

Decapitation, sunlight, and the draining of their blood.

Quinn shivered. She prayed nothing would happen to Velika. She didn't know what she would do if something did. They hadn't completed their bond. Her blood rushed through her system at the thought of Velika sinking her teeth into her throat. She loved the sensation of those sharp fangs running alongside her throat.

What would it truly feel like to have her vampire drink from her?

The bird they were riding in was no ordinary helicopter. She had imagined something only a few people would be able to fit in. No, this was high-tech and military-grade. She had to walk up a wide loading ramp that was located at the rear. She was sure it could also haul large vehicles and other items, if need be, but tonight, it was transporting a small vampire army.

There were rows of vampires quietly waiting to get to their destination. The tension in the chopper was thick.

Quinn was seated between Velika and a window that allowed her to glance out at the night sky. She turned back to Velika's conversation when she heard her name.

"There's a bar at the edge of town that is a few miles away from the lair. Quinn can go in there," Luther said. He had a tablet in his hand and pointed to the map on the screen.

"I don't like it. I should go in there with her," Velika murmured, studying the tablet.

"And they will make you the second you enter the building." Arad shook his head.

"He's right," Luther agreed. "She'll have the communicator on her, and we'll be outside not far away."

Velika ran a hand down her face and glanced over at Quinn who offered her a tight smile. She trusted her vampire would protect her. Velika hadn't lied to her once.

The chopper jerked and shuddered for a moment. Quinn reached out and gripped her seat. Her stomach wasn't too keen on the bumpy ride. She had only flown once in her life before, and it was on a larger plane where the seats had safety belts.

"Fine, but if anything was to happen, I will burn the entire building down."

Quinn's core clenched at the growl that spilled from Velika. Quinn turned her opalescent eyes to her, and she knew Velika meant what she said.

This woman would do anything to protect her.

"And we'll be right there with you." Luther gave a nod.

Quinn reached up and felt for the small communicator Velika had outfitted her with. She wasn't too nervous to go into a human establishment as she was for the short walk she had to make alone. It was nighttime, and she was sure there were dangers in Vancouver as there were in Stramford for a woman walking alone at night.

She had her knife tucked in a sheath inside the waistband of her jeans. It was the only weapon she was to wear.

Velika touched her ear, then stood.

"We'll be landing in three minutes," Velika announced. She glanced around at the warriors who had locked their eyes on her. She was a true leader. She was decked out in her leather pants, tunic, and had weapons strapped to her. The golden strands of her hair were contained in intricate braids. She was the epitome of fierce warrior princess. "Tonight, we will fight in the name of our king. This territory is mine, and we will defend it."

Growls filled the air. The warriors were growing restless and flashed their fangs as they prepared for the mission.

"Victory is ours. Rogue blood will be spilled, and we will go home and celebrate." Velika pounded her chest. She turned, and the fierce gaze that landed on Quinn made her happy she was on the side of this vampire.

Quinn walked down the street and tried not to look spooked. She slid her hands into her sweatshirt and exhaled. The sidewalk was void of anyone, and her sights were set on the neon sign of the bar.

Being back in her old clothes felt foreign. Her life had changed so much since being matched to Velika. Wearing them tonight was a reminder of where she had come from.

The door to the bar swung open, and a couple of women exited. Their giggles filled the air, hinting at their inebriation. Quinn shook her head. In a town run by vampires, walking around drunk was extremely dangerous.

But she couldn't worry about them.

She was on a mission and needed to confirm the rogue vampires were located close by.

"If you are in trouble, don't forget to use your safe word," Velika's voice came through the comms unit that was hidden in Quinn's ear. Hearing her vampire's voice calmed her nerves. Velika was located nearby. They had coached her right before she'd left.

She was new to town and was trying to find a safe spot to settle. She would go into the bar and strike up a conversation. Velika had given her some cash because that was the only tender that wouldn't be questioned.

"I know," she murmured. She was growing a little paranoid and wasn't sure if she were truly alone on the street. Vampires could easily hide in the shadows.

They had determined that if she were in trouble and needed to be extracted, she would say a key word and Velika and her warriors would swoop in to get her.

Her word of choice, sunflower. It was one of her favorite flowers she remembered from her childhood.

"I'm here." She arrived at the door and opened it. She went inside, and immediately the aroma of stale cigarette smoke and unwashed bodies greeted her.

This was an old dive bar and would be perfect.

Quinn slowly walked in, her eyes adjusting to the dim light and thick smoke. This place wasn't too different than the bars at home. There was a nice-sized crowd, a few men shooting pool, and a few tables had patrons sitting around them. The bar had some open seats. The television had a sports game on that she was sure was a rerun. After the destruction of the country's infrastructure, some of the professional sports teams did not return.

Quinn beelined it to the counter and took a seat. The bartender, a young woman who appeared to be the same age as Quinn, ambled over to her.

"Well, you certainly are new to this part of town," the girl said with a grin.

"I am," Quinn admitted. She folded her hands in front of her and smiled.

"My name is Velvet. What can I get you?" The woman leaned her hip against the counter. Her smile didn't quite reach her eyes, but there was a curious glint in them.

"What's good?" Quinn asked.

"You got cash?" Velvet asked.

Quinn nodded.

The woman leaned over behind her and grabbed a menu. She slid it across the counter to

Quinn. "Take a look at what we got. Most of it is decent. Drink specials are on the back."

Quinn took the menu and opened it to study it. She didn't want to be eager and start asking questions right away. Humans were naturally cautious around strangers. She was going to have to gain a little trust in Velvet before she was sure the bartender gave her any information.

"I'll give you a few minutes." Velvet moved on down and struck up a conversation with a man at the end of the counter.

Quinn tried to focus on the menu to decide on what she would order. She couldn't come to a bar and not order anything. That would be suspicious.

Quinn casually glanced around and took in a few large men who appeared to be the security detail for the place. Turning back, she skimmed the flimsy paper that held all the bar had to offer.

She made her decision and flagged Velvet down.

"What can I get you?" Velvet asked. She came back to stand before Quinn.

"I'll take the wings and a Coke." She wasn't going to order more than that. The prices were a little steep, and she refused to take a ton of money from Velika. She had to remember what it was like to struggle and budget.

"Sure thang." Velvet walked away and disappeared through a set of double doors Quinn assumed was the kitchen. A few minutes later, she returned with Quinn's drink.

"Thank you." Quinn opened the straw that was next to her glass and took a healthy sip of the soda. It tasted slightly watered down, but that was common. Establishments wanted the supplies to last longer. It was a standard practice in her old diner.

Without looking, she knew the other patrons at the bar were watching her. She was comforted with knowing that should she need Velika, her and her men were not too far away. She was surprised Velika had remained quiet in her ear once she had entered the building.

"What's a pretty little thing like yourself doing in a place like this?" a gruff asked. A figure plopped down in the chair next to her.

Quinn stiffened and glanced at the man. He was filthy with streaks of dirt on his face, the teeth that remained in his mouth were yellow, and the stench of him turned her stomach. His hair was long and dark, held back in a low ponytail.

Quinn faced forward, trying to not breathe. She played with her glass and exhaled slowly.

"I just moved here and was seeking for a decent place to get some food," she replied. She prayed her answer would satisfy him.

"And you're all by yourself?" he asked.

The hairs on the back of her neck stood to attention. Women went missing every day, and Quinn was fully aware of how it would look if she were dining and lived alone.

"Are you safe?" Velika whispered fiercely in her ear.

Quinn cleared her throat, unable to answer her now.

"No. There are others with me, but I was hungry." Nervous, she glanced down toward the end of the bar and found Velvet staring at her and the newcomer.

The woman pushed off the counter where she had been speaking with another customer and ambled her way over.

"I'm fine," Quinn said.

She prayed Velika took the hint. She hadn't got the information yet, and it wouldn't do any good if vampires came storming in now to rescue her.

"Leave her alone, Cliff," Velvet said.

"I ain't doing nothing but making conversation," he grumbled. "She said she was new to town. I was just going to warn her."

"Warn me about what?" Quinn's heart skipped a beat. Was it going to be that easy to find out where the vampires were located?

"Vampires, of course," he muttered.

"Oh, well, thank you." She widened her eyes. She hoped her acting skills were up to par. "We've been trying to avoid them."

She shivered, trying to appear frightened.

"Don't worry, honey," Velvet said. She tucked her pen behind her ear. "As long as you stay away from the northern part of downtown, you will be safer."

"Oh?" Velika would be proud of her. She may not be able to wield a sword and fight like a vampire, but she was a master of manipulating humans. It came in handy when serving in a diner. It helped with tips.

"Our intel must have been wrong. We were told there wasn't much vampire activity in this city?" She reached up and covered her neck. Her hand trembled.

Velvet and Cliff were eating out of the palm of her hand.

"Sounds like you were set up. There are too many vampires running around this damn town. Take my word and get out of town. Those blood-suckers are attacking and killing people left and right." Cliff slammed his fist down on the counter.

"We have what we need," Velika's voice came through the comm. "We've confirmed the area the humans just shared with you. Good job, *miere*."

Quinn beamed on the inside. She finally felt as if she were doing something. Little did the humans in this bar know, she would be helping rid the vampires from their town.

"Oh, let me get your food. It should be up by now." Velvet pushed off the counter.

"You know what, I'll take it to go," Quinn said.

"Sure thing, hon." Velvet nodded then spun around and walked off.

"If you're leaving, I'll be happy to escort you to your friends." Cliff's eyes narrowed on her.

"Oh, that won't be necessary. They aren't far from here."

"But I insist." He patted her on her hand. "We can't be too careful around here."

"This human male is teetering on a thin line," Velika growled.

Quinn didn't have to be standing next to her to

know she was growing agitated by Cliff. If Quinn didn't lose the guy, Velika would kill him.

"Get rid of him or he's a dead man."

"It won't be a problem, sir. They know I'm here getting me something to eat."

"Then why didn't they come with you? What? Are they not hungry?"

Quinn's heart beat erratically. She wiped her hands on her pants and exhaled, trying to think of something to distract Cliff. He was growing more suspicious.

The other customers sitting at the bar were not hiding the fact they were eavesdropping.

This was bad.

This could go wrong on so many levels.

"Two of my friends are together." She wagged her eyebrows. "And they wanted some alone time, if you know what I mean, and my other friend went to go meet someone he knew. He's going to be meeting me soon. Believe me, I'm okay. I wouldn't have made it this far if I wasn't."

Cliff's murky eyes stared at her. She refused to back down. As if believing her story, he relaxed a little after what seemed to be an eternity. Velvet arrived just at that moment with her food packed away in a bag.

"Here you go, sweetie." She sat the bag down and told Quinn her total.

It didn't slip past Quinn that Velvet's hand was still resting on the bag. She may have been comforting Quinn a few minutes ago, but that didn't mean she didn't trust Quinn not to run out of the bar with her food.

Quinn reached into her pocket and pulled out a few bills to pay.

"You can keep the change," she said.

Velvet smiled and took the money off the counter. Cliff's eyes carefully watched her. Quinn slid off the stool and snatched the bag up.

She offered them both a smile. "Thanks for the warning. I'm going to share it with my friends."

"Next time, bring them along," Velvet said, pocketing the money.

Quinn turned and headed through the crowd, praying she made it out the door without any incidents. Once out on the sidewalk, she breathed a sigh of relief.

"Come to me, *miere*," Velika said.

Quinn headed down the sidewalk, clutching her bag to her. The scents coming from it were heavenly, and she couldn't wait to devour it. Her stomach grumbled, reminding her it had been a while since she'd eaten.

The hairs on the back of her neck were still standing.

Something was off.

She glanced back over her shoulder and took in a few figures strolling along the sidewalk.

Damn the city for not having too many streetlights. Unlike Velika, Quinn couldn't see that well at night. She picked up the pace, knowing she had to get around the corner and Velika and her men would be waiting.

"I think someone is following me," Quinn whispered.

She blinked, and standing on the corner was Velika.

"Pretty girl!" a familiar gruff voice called out behind her.

Quinn closed her eyes.

Cliff.

He'd followed her. She knew he hadn't trusted her.

"Keep walking, *miere*. I will handle these humans." Velika's eyes narrowed on the objects over Quinn's shoulder.

"No," Quinn pleaded. She spun around and

looked to Cliff. "I'm fine, Cliff. You don't have to escort me."

"That's a damn vampire behind you," he shouted.

He and the two other men lifted their hands. The light from the lone streetlamp near them reflected off the metal objects. He and his men were striding toward her fast.

"Move!"

Gunfire ripped through the silence of the night.

"No!" she screamed.

CHAPTER FIFTEEN

Velika dashed forward using her vampiric strength and knocked Quinn out of the way. The bullets zipped past her head. Her mate went flying against the brick building.

The humans and their guns would draw attention.

"Why am I hearing gunfire?" Luther's angered voice came through the comms.

Velika ignored him. Her rage fueled her at the thought of those humans firing their weapons and almost harming her mate.

She flew in their direction, her dagger drawn.

She arrived in front of the first one; the smell of his filth reached her nostrils. She growled, her knife easily slicing through his gun. The weapon clattered to the ground in pieces.

His shocked gaze flew to hers.

Her fist landed in his gut.

"Vampire," he gasped, falling forward onto the ground.

She twirled around, kicking out at the other male's gun and knocking it from him. Velika's body moved swiftly on the attack. The third male was just as easy to disarm. A throat punch, then a kick to the knees brought both men to the ground.

"Bitch," a voice rasped behind her.

She spun around with her dagger in her hand. It landed, pressed against the first man's throat.

"Be careful of what you say, human," she hissed. Velika brandished her fangs.

The other two men lay groaning on the ground. He glared at her with hate-filled eyes. Footsteps sounded. She glanced in the direction she'd come from to see Luther and two of his soldiers with him. She held up a hand. They halted near Quinn who had remained leaning against the building.

"We are not your enemy."

"You think we are supposed to believe you?"

The male spat. His gaze narrowed on her. "Kind of hard to believe when you have a knife at my throat."

"You attacked first," she growled. Taking his life was still on her mind. He had dared shoot at her with Quinn in the way. The fact he hadn't hit Quinn was the only reason he was still alive.

"Well, you vampires tend to have a thing for draining humans for their blood." He straightened up taller on his knees as if waiting for her to slice his neck open.

It was very tempting, but that was not why they were in Vancouver.

"Human, do you know who you are speaking with?" Luther stalked forward.

The two soldiers stood near Quinn, their weapons drawn, ready to protect her. Velika gave them an approving nod.

Luther's hardened gaze took in the three humans and the guns resting on the concrete. "You are speaking to Princess Velika Riskel, warden of the Northwest. You will respect her."

"I don't have to do nothing but survive or die."

"Don't make me choose for you." Velika stepped back, putting the weapon in its sheath. Today was not the day he would die. At least not by her hand. She eyed him and recognized his voice. "You are the male who was speaking with my mate."

"Mate?" His head whipped around to Quinn.

"Do not look at her." Velika was becoming very protective of Quinn and would not hesitate to kill anyone who looked at her wrong.

He slowly turned back around, a scowl in place.

"Let me guess. The draft?"

"It is none of your concern."

The other males stood, their fear permeating the air. Only this one in front of her wasn't afraid of her and her men.

"Stand up," Luther ordered.

The human sneered at Luther, moving to his feet.

"Why were you so insistent upon following a human female?" Velika asked. She stood with her hands resting on her waist.

"Because there was something about her. I thought she was a spy or something, and it would appear I was right."

"What is your name, human?" she asked.

"Cliff."

"Well, Cliff. We are not the vampires you think we are." She stepped closer to him. The stench of his body was grotesque. She met his gaze with a cold one of her own. "We are here to get control of the vampires running amuck here."

"And what are you going to do? Slap them on their wrists?" Cliff snorted. He glanced at his fellow comrades, chuckling. "Oh, you're killing too many humans. People are taking notice."

Velika rested her hand on hilt of her dagger. Anger at his disregard for her status filled her. There was nothing funny about the situation going on. This human didn't know how dangerous Cain and rogue vampires were. A vampire not bound by laws was the ultimate threat. Not only would they be punished for the unsanctioned human kills, but they would also suffer the consequences for attempting to steal Quinn away from her.

"These vampires here are breaking the laws set forth by the king. For this and other crimes they have committed, they will die."

Cliff sobered immediately. More of her warriors came around the corner. The two guarding Quinn were still in place. Arad must have sent them since they were taking longer than expected.

A thought suddenly came to her. She glanced over at Luther who looked as if he'd had the same idea. She wouldn't be surprised. That was why he was her second. They pretty much thought alike when it came to battle planning.

"I have an idea," she said.

Cliff's eyes widened at her expression.

"You can't have my blood." He stepped back away from her with his hand flying to his neck.

"I don't want your filthy blood," she exploded. A scowl formed on her face. She knew this might be a mistake, but it would be a great plan. "You are going to lead us to the vampires you so fear."

"What?" He moved farther away from her, but Luther was there to catch him. He struggled against Luther, but he was no match for the strong vampire soldier. He turned back to Velika. "I would be just as good as dead. You might as well kill me and get it over with."

The other humans tried to run, but Sabien and Fane were there to block their paths. The men cowered at the sight of them. There was nowhere for them to go. The street remained bare except for them.

Velika took notice of the shades and blinds slightly open. They snapped shut once she glanced in their direction. The humans in these parts were either smart or stupid.

Hiding to survive or leave their fellow man to die at the hand of a vampire. Staying inside was a smart move at this point. They would be unmatched by her and her men.

"Work with us and we will protect you." Velika didn't trust many people, and humans were right there at the top of her list. She had lived a long time on this earth and witnessed how the humans had treated each other. If they fought against each other, betrayed one another, and didn't work together, then why would she trust them? There were only so many she did trust, and that number was low.

"Like we are supposed to believe you," Cliff said.

"I find it amusing you to think you have a choice. It's been a while since I had to use my skills of compulsion, but I won't if you just do as I request," Velika breathed. A small smile crossed her lips. Her fangs peeked from underneath her lips. She knew the second Cliff caught sight of them. An uncontrolled shudder took over him. She glanced at all three humans. "Betray me, and you will wish I had given you to the other vampires."

* * *

"I don't want to separate from you," Quinn said. This didn't sit right with her. Something was off. She needed to be by Velika's side.

"It will be okay, *miere*," Velika murmured. She trailed a finger along Quinn's face. "Sabien and two guards will be with you."

Quinn glanced at the black van they were to ride in. It reminded her of the vans in movies where the main character was kidnapped. She turned back to Velika and leaned forward, resting her hands on her vampire's chest. The strength of Velika radiated underneath her fingertips.

"Promise me you will be careful." She glanced up, tears blurring her vision. She didn't care. She didn't know how she would grow used to Velika rushing off to battle. She blinked back the tears slipping down her skin.

Velika's eyes softened. She wiped the wetness from Quinn's face.

"That is a promise I can make." Velika dropped a kiss on her forehead. "I do not want you in the vehicles with the humans. I want you safe, away from them."

"Fine." Quinn nodded. She leaned up and kissed Velika's lips, then turned away. Her heartbeat thundered in her ears, but she held her head high and went over to Sabien.

He helped her in the vehicle and shut the door behind her.

Quinn didn't take her eyes off Velika's figure as she walked over to the identical van.

Within a few minutes they were driving along the streets of Vancouver. The tension was thick while they drove in silence. She stared out the window, barely seeing the scenery. She folded her hands on her lap.

Twenty minutes later, they were pulling into an abandoned warehouse district. It was pitch-black outside, and the only lights were the ones from the vehicles.

Quinn shivered, pressing her face against the window. The area screamed danger. No streetlights and plenty of shadows.

"We're almost there," Sabien announced.

There had been a little chatter on the radio from all the other vehicles. Quinn had tuned them out, but at the sound of Velika's voice, she perked up.

"Sabien, I want your van to stay back. Protect my mate at all costs," she said. Her voice may have been calm, but there was a threat hidden inside it.

If they didn't, they would be punished severely.

Even Quinn heard the unspoken promise.

"Yes, Your Grace. We will," he replied.

The other two soldiers in the van with them thumped their chests. It comforted Quinn slightly, but she would rather have Velika with her.

"Will you be able to keep tabs on Velika?" she asked.

"The line will go dead while they are infiltrating the lair." Sabien turned around and glanced at her. "We have to cut the communication to decrease distraction, but it will reconnect once they are in."

Quinn didn't like the sound of the loss of contact, but there was nothing she could do about it. She sent up a prayer and hoped all would go well.

They parked in a lot behind a building. She watched Velika and the others exit their vehicle and go inside.

"Is this it?" she asked.

"No, from what the humans shared, the building is close by. This is housing the rest of the warriors, my lady," Sabien said.

"And why can't we go in and wait there?" she asked.

"Because the princess has ordered us to take off to the chopper if anything were to go wrong."

She met his gaze in the rearview mirror.

Of course, Velika would have a backup plan for her. That vampire was always thinking of her safety.

Quinn exhaled and settled back. She didn't know how many minutes this would take, but she hoped it wouldn't be ages. This place was giving her the creeps. Goosebumps formed on her arms. She didn't know why, but she had the sense something was going to go wrong.

She had only survived as long as she had by listening to her gut. She rubbed her arms, trying to warm up herself up.

They sat in silence for a fair while. She had lost track of time.

"Shouldn't we have heard something by now?" she asked.

"Yeah." Sabien sighed.

"Patience is a virtue, my lady," the warrior sitting next to her said.

She glanced at him, but he was staring straight forward.

"And what is your name?" she asked softly.

"Ozul, my lady." He had yet to meet her eyes.

His spine was ramrod straight, his long dark hair held back in intricate braids.

"Do you have a mate, Ozul?"

"No, ma'am."

"Then you don't know what I am going through right now. I am not a warrior, I am the mate to your princess. No matter what is going on, I will worry about her when she races off to battle. Fear that she will not come back to me is sitting with me. But you, who does not have a mate, will not understand what I am going through." Her voice raised in a shriek at the end. Her chest was rising and falling as panic showed its face.

Ozul then looked at her. In the low light she could see him dropping his gaze to the floor.

"I am sorry, my lady. I meant no harm," he began. He glanced back up at her. "But you must have all the confidence in Princess Velika. She is a valiant warrior and has won many battles in her long life. She will prevail." He thumped his heart and bowed his head. "And if I were to ever have a mate as powerful as the princess, I would do what I must to remain strong."

Quinn stared at him, at a loss for words. He was right. She must remain strong. She couldn't be the weepy-eyed damsel in distress. Velika had been teaching her to protect herself, wanted her to understand vampire history so that she could be strong as a person and as the mate to the warden. Ever since arriving in Ensfield, she had grown. She was blossoming with all of the resources that were provided to her.

"Ozul," Sabien snapped.

He and the other vampire stared at him with scowls lining their faces.

"No, he speaks the truth." She held up her hand. "It is I who should apologize. This all is new for me, and he's right. I need to have the utmost trust that Velika will come back to me the victor. I will work on that so that I may be the best mate for your princess."

The van grew silent.

The radio sizzled to life.

"Get out of here," a voice growled. Static crackled, cutting off the voice.

"What did he say?" Quinn gasped.

"It was a trap," the voice cut through again.

Sabien threw the van into drive and hit the gas. The wheels screeched against the pavement. He guided the van through the parking lot and headed toward the street.

Quinn bit her lip, knowing this was what they

had planned, but she had hoped they wouldn't have to run and leave Velika behind.

What would happen to her if Velika was gone?

A force slammed into the side of the vehicle, sending it spinning in circles. Quinn screamed, trying to find something to hold on to. She was thrown to the floor. They crashed into something unseen, and the sound of crunching and tearing metal filled the air.

Quinn lifted her head, moaning from a sharp pain coursing through her body. Darkness surrounded her. She whimpered and tried to push up.

"My lady, are you injured?" Sabien's pain-filled voice cut through the air.

"I don't know." She glanced up and saw Ozul sitting still in his spot, his head hanging low in front of him.

Velika.

She had to get to her. If this was a trap, she had to help her. Running away was not going to save her mate.

"We have to go help Velika," she gasped.

Ozul raised his head and grimaced.

"No, ma'am. We have to get you to safety," Sabien said.

"Well, it certainly isn't safe here. What happened?" She crawled back into her seat.

"You're right. We need to leave." Sabien kicked at his door, trying to get it to open. "Ransly, get the princess's mate out."

The other vampire who had been sitting in the front with Sabien was able to open his door. He stumbled out and came around to the sliding door near her.

"Are you okay, Ozul?" she whispered.

"Yes, ma'am. I think a couple of ribs are broken, but I shall be fine." He gave her a nod.

The sliding door was ripped off the van. Ransly held out his hand and helped her out. Quinn stepped out and stood by herself. Sabien walked around the van and stopped in front of her.

She glanced at the van and shivered. It was mangled beyond recognition, and she wasn't sure how any of them walked away from it.

"We need to keep moving," Sabien said. He cupped her elbow and led her down the sidewalk. "I don't know who shot at us, but we don't want to stand around and wait for them to come."

Quinn almost had to run to keep up the pace.

"We need to find Velika." She tried to pull her

arm away, but he tightened his hold on her. "If it was a trap then they will need our help."

"Not happening. The princess gave me direct orders to see you to safety." He scowled.

"Wait a minute." She tore her arm away from him and turned to face them. She rested her hands on her waist, unsure where this boldness and daring behavior was coming from. "As the mate to your princess, you have to listen to me, don't you?"

"Well, yes, my lady," Ransly said.

"Then I'm commanding you to go after your princess. We need to help her."

"But we have orders," Ozul sputtered.

"And I'm giving you new ones. Let's go find Velika. I am not leaving here without her." She stomped her foot. She glanced around and took in the darkness everywhere. With no streetlights, she could barely see ten feet in front of her.

"The princess will have our balls," Sabien muttered.

"If you take me to her, I will ensure that your balls remain safe," she said softly. Vampires had no problems seeing in the dark, so she gave them her biggest puppy dog eyes she could, trying to wear them down. If they didn't help her, she would find

Velika on her own. "What kind of mate would I be if I ran off and left my mate to die?"

They stared at her for a moment, then gave in.

"You don't leave my side." Sabien pointed to her.

Quinn celebrated on the inside and gave him what she thought was her best salute.

"Yes, sir."

CHAPTER SIXTEEN

"Son of a bitch," Velika growled, dodging a fist. Her anger fueled her, sending her into a blinding rage. Her movements were flawless and swift.

The underground lair had been a trap. There had been no sign of Cain. Apparently, he had known they were coming and had run.

The coward had better hope she didn't get her hands on him.

Now, they had to fight to get out of the building. The only comforting thing was that Quinn was safe with Sabien. The message had been sent for them to head to the chopper. If she didn't make it, she had left clear instructions they were to take her mate back to the castle.

"You don't rule us," the vampire hissed.

She swung around, sending her blade deep into the belly of a vampire. They fell back against the brick wall of the empty office that had been Cain's. It was littered with a desk chair and a few tables, but there was nothing worthy of a clue as to where he had traveled to next. The only thing he had left for her was a photograph of Quinn at the market when they were shopping.

It was a sign.

He was after her mate.

Quinn snatched the dagger out and whipped it around, separating his head from his neck. The head rolled away on the floor while the body remained standing for mere seconds before falling to the floor.

"Velika!" Luther's yell had her turning and seeing another one racing toward her. They had been ambushed, and someone was going to pay.

Either the intel was incorrect, or someone had leaked Cain their plans.

The male slammed into her. She wasn't afraid

to be in close contact during a fight. This was his tragic mistake.

She thrived off being so close to her opponents. She wrapped her arms around his neck and flipped him onto the floor in front of her. He tried to break free from her hold, but she swiftly snapped his neck. The body fell to the floor, motionless. She refused to leave any survivors. They followed Cain, therefore, they were against the throne.

They had to die.

Vampires could heal practically anything. It would take some time, but he would still be alive. She bent down and severed his throat with her dagger. The serrated edge cut deep into his arteries. The blood ran out of him onto the floor.

He would be dead in minutes, having bled to death.

"Let's get the fuck out of here," she snarled. She stalked toward the door.

Luther brutally ripped the throat of the male he was fighting. The vampire fell to the floor, thrashing around as his blood flowed out around him.

Luther glanced at her, his iridescent-eyed gaze landing on her. He used his sleeve to wipe the blood from his face.

"Ladies first," he said, following behind her.

They raced down the hall and came to the main lounge and found her soldiers to be victorious. On her orders, her soldiers were to sweep the entire underground lair and kill all who put up a fight.

"What are we to do with the living?" Arad turned his focus to her. There were a few rogues kneeling on the floor in a row.

She stalked forward and stood before the three men. They glared at her with hatred in their eyes.

"I'm going to assume you know who I am," she growled. Her chest rose and fell fast. The thrill of the battle had her on an adrenaline high. Her grip tightened on the hilt of her blade. She narrowed her eyes on the one in the middle. His scowl drew her attention. She lifted her blood-coated dagger toward him. "You. Where is Cain?"

This interrogation was only going to go one way. She would get her information, then they would die.

No negations.

Arad silently moved to stand behind him, waiting for her command.

"You will never find him," the vampire spat.

Arad gripped him by his hair and sliced his throat with his sword. His eyes widened as the blood spurted out of him. Gurgling noises sounded from him, while the blood slowly seeped from his lips. He fell over onto the floor.

She moved to stand before another one. Arad shifted to stand behind him.

She paused and didn't say a word. The rushing of his blood racing through his veins could be heard. He was nervous, as he should be.

"Are you going to share with me where Cain is?" She cocked an eyebrow.

"I don't know. He doesn't tell anyone where he is going accept the ones closest to him," he cried out. "Please don't kill me. I'll tell you anything you want to know."

"Seeing how you can't tell me what I want to know, I have no use for you." She spun on her heels and walked away. "Do not leave any alive," she ordered.

"How are the others faring?" she asked. There were two other levels to this underground building.

"From the reports, we have taken control of the building. We will carry out your orders and ensure there are no survivors." Luther bowed slightly to her.

"Burn this building and the bodies still in it." She glanced around the area and took in the bodies lining the floor.

Arad and his men were walking around the room ensuring all the rogues were indeed dead.

"Yes, Your Grace." Luther turned and walked away to alert the others.

Velika headed toward the stairs and sheathed her weapon. She took the stairs two at a time. Cain Theron could run and hide now, but it would only be so long before she caught up to him, and when she did, he would beg for her mercy. Footsteps followed behind her as her soldiers ascended from the depths of the building. She arrived at the first floor where it was an old dry-cleaning business that used to be a front for illegal operations, hence the lower-level area.

Her soldiers poured out of the stairwell and headed outside. She had kept men posted outside to meet any rogues who had been lucky enough to escape the lower level.

She followed them outside and stood in the middle of the street. She was sure Luther and the others were preparing to bring this building down. She peered down the road and froze in place.

"Velika!" a familiar voice shouted.

It couldn't be.

Quinn broke free of Sabien's hold and took off

running toward her. She opened her arms just as her mate slammed into her.

"Oh God. I thought something happened to you," Quinn cried out.

"What are you doing here? Why are you not on the chopper?" Velika glared at Sabien and the two warriors she had charged to protect her mate. She had wanted her far from danger, not in the middle of it.

"I had to come make sure you are okay. I wanted to help." Quinn lifted her head and gazed up at her.

Velika took her in, and even in the dark, she could see a bruise forming on Quinn's cheek.

"Who did this to you?" she growled.

She darted her gaze back over at Sabien. He, Ozul, and Ransly stood to attention behind Quinn.

"Our van came under fire when we were leaving after we got the message. We all are a little banged up, Your Grace," Sabien said.

"Came under fire?" Velika inhaled sharply. She tightened her grip around Quinn. This was twice in one night her mate's life had been threatened.

Cain would die.

"And if the danger was in this direction, why, pray tell, are you four here? Especially when I gave orders for you to protect my mate at all costs," she snapped.

Sabien looked straight ahead. "Ms. Hogan insisted we needed to assist you."

"Don't be mad at them. The van is totaled, and I needed to help you," Quinn said. She rested a hand on Velika's sternum. "I don't want to be the mate who runs when danger strikes. I was so scared I would lose you that I wanted to be with you and help fight."

Velika gently prodded Quinn's cheek. Satisfied that she didn't see any other marks on her mate, she stood to her full height.

"They were given strict orders, *miere*. It was for a reason. Me and my men were fine," she scolded Quinn. Her mate had had only a few training sessions, and now she was ready to fight?

Velika wouldn't share the pride that filled her that her little human was wanting to protect her. Just thinking of her mate trying to fight one of those rogues sent a chill down her spine. Those vampires would have been bloodthirsty and certainly would have drained Quinn dry.

"But our van was destroyed—"

"My men are very resourceful and would have found other transportation," she cut Quinn off. Her mate could make all the excuses she wanted. She would have to speak with her men about disobeying direct orders even if it was because of her mate. Velika had half a mind to lock her mate up once they returned home. Tie her down to their bed and never let her out of it. Maybe then she would be safe. "Isn't that right, Sabien, Ozul, and Ransly." She glared at them over Quinn's shoulder.

"Yes, Your Grace," they echoed.

Luther and Arad made their way from the building.

"Is everything set?" she asked, turning to them. She kept an arm around Quinn's waist.

"We need to get a move on it," Luther said.

"This baby is about to go up in flames." Arad grinned.

"Stay on alert," Velika warned. "The van that housed my mate came under fire. There may be more rogues out here."

Luther jerked his head in a nod. She knew she wouldn't need to say anything else. Her warriors were waiting for their orders.

"Let's move out," Velika shouted. She swiveled her gaze back to Sabien, Ozul, and Ransly. "We will chat about this later."

The three of them nodded and spun on their

heels and walked away.

"I promised them you wouldn't take their balls," Quinn murmured.

"What?" Velika sputtered. She gripped Quinn by her arms. "Why would you be discussing their testicles?"

"Because they knew you would be pissed for bringing me here." Quinn widened her eyes and gave a little pout. "Don't go too hard on them. Please."

That word please and the whimper was enough to break Velika.

She could deny her mate nothing.

"Next time you make my men defy a direct order, it will be you who pays, mate." Velika dropped a hard kiss to Quinn's lips. "Now let's go."

Quinn's face was pressed against the window of the chopper. They flew over the building where Velika and her men had raided. The flames of the fire practically licked the sky. She was in awe of the bright lights, and if she closed her eyes, she was sure she sensed the heat of the blaze.

The chopper was going fast. Quinn glanced over at the rows of soldiers who were seated before her. It reminded her of the trip on the way to Vancouver. Only now, most of them were filthy with blood smatterings and there were a few empty seats.

Sorrow filled her at the remaining chairs with no warriors in them. She lowered her head with the realization those men had probably died while fighting under her mate's command.

It was eye-opening and it hit home that vampires could die.

She didn't know what had transpired in the building, but she was no dummy. Blood caked Velika's fighting leathers. It was on Quinn's clothing, too, for she hadn't seen it when she'd jumped into Velika's arms.

"What is it, *miere*?" Velika rested a hand on her thigh. She held a look of concern in her eyes.

"Some of your men didn't make it, did they?" she whispered.

"We lost a few good vampires." Velika stood from her seat. She thumped a hand over her heart. "Those men we lost were honorable and will not be forgotten."

Grunts and growls permeated the area along

with the sound of chest pounding. The soldiers all turned to Velika. Quinn took in the determined expressions that graced their faces. They would truly follow this woman anywhere.

"When we return home, we will have a ceremony and drink to the honor of men we've lost," Luther chimed in. He stood, a fierce expression on his face. "These men followed our princess in to battle to uphold the laws of vampires."

More chest thumping and grunts.

Velika took her seat after the shouts and yells quieted down. These men were passionate for their cause and for their kind.

Velika took her hand and brought it to her lips. Quinn entwined their fingers together and held on tight.

The flight back to Ensfield seemed to fly by. The sun would soon be rising, and the vampires all needed to get inside away from the harmful rays.

Before Quinn knew it, they were landing at the airfield. She held on to Velika as she guided her off the chopper and into the waiting SUVs that swiftly carried them home. They entered the castle through a secret doorway located in the back.

Quinn glanced around, trying to make out landmarks. She had walked around the back and had never seen this entrance before. It was as if it hadn't existed until they'd come upon it.

Was this magic?

Was that another thing humans didn't know about?

"Your Grace, I take it the battle went well?" Mortas greeted them once inside.

"Not as well as I was hoping." Velika huffed.

In the light, Quinn was able to take in Velika. She looked like a woman who had gone to war. Blood covered her everywhere, wisps of her hair had escaped her braids, and a few smudges of dirt were on her face.

"Is there anything I can do to serve you, Your Grace?" he asked.

"My mate and I would like to remain undisturbed. We are both tired, and I for once want to sleep the day away," Velika said.

They walked down the winding hallways of the castle until they reached a grand staircase that would lead them to their quarters.

"Yes, Your Grace. I shall send up a glass of your favorite blood and something for your mate to snack on. I'm sure you're famished." Mortas bowed his head.

Quinn's stomach chose that moment to make

itself known. The food she had gotten from the bar had been destroyed when Cliff and his cronies had tried to attack Velika.

"I would really appreciate it," she murmured. Her body was starting to ache, and she suddenly felt tired. Her knees shook and threatened to buckle. She leaned into Velika, not wanting to fall on the floor.

"*Miere*, what is it?" Velika wrapped both her arms around Quinn and took the brunt of her weight.

"I don't know," Quinn mumbled.

"Call for the healer and send her up immediately." Velika lifted Quinn into her arms and raced up the stairs.

Quinn could do nothing but hang on. Her body trembled uncontrollably. She wrapped her arm around Velika's neck and didn't let go. They arrived at the door to their suite.

Velika pushed it open and strode across the room toward the bed.

"Don't worry, *miere*. We'll get you help."

"Okay." Quinn tried to remain alert, but the darkness pulled her in, and she didn't have the strength to fight it off, so she gave in.

CHAPTER SEVENTEEN

"There is nothing wrong with her," Kismet murmured.

Velika stared at the elder vampire as if she had grown two heads.

"What do you mean there is nothing wrong with her?" She knocked back the rest of her blood and swallowed the thick, warm liquid. She sat her goblet down on the table and strode toward the bed.

Mortas had done as promised and sent up blood for her and food for Quinn. Her mate had passed out and had yet to waken. Her food was resting on a tray on the table.

"Don't use the tone of voice with me, Princess." Kismet stood from the bed with a small smile gracing her lips. She was an elder, close to the same age as Velika's father. She had been one of the healers first assigned to the royal house before coming to work for Velika.

Kismet was a powerful vampire. Her hair was fiery red and flowed down her back in waves. She had bright-blue eyes, and her skin was pale and flawless.

"She has been through much today and she's human. Her body was overloaded. I'm willing to bet the adrenaline in her had run out and she shut down. It also didn't help she was in an accident. Her body will be sore." Kismet glanced back at Quinn who was resting on the bed. She reached out and ran a finger over Quinn's smooth brown skin.

"What shall we do if she is in pain when she awakens?"

"A nice warm bath. There are oils I always recommend to be kept in the bathrooms. Use the eucalyptus oils and a few drops of peppermint. That should help ease her muscle aches."

Velika nodded, her gaze again moving to Quinn's resting form.

"She's a special one, Velika. The bond between the two of you is growing. I can sense it. Don't wait too long to claim her." Kismet didn't miss a thing. She eyed Velika with a knowing look.

"She is perfect for me." Velika moved closer to the bed, staring at Quinn with awe. She still couldn't believe fate had made this beautiful woman just for her. The need to claim her was overbearing, but Velika wanted to make sure Quinn was ready to take the next step. There was no turning back once they completed the bond.

It was forever.

"I told her I wanted her to come to me," Velika admitted. That was the only way she would be sure Quinn wanted to mate with her. She had been through troubling times, and her experience with vampires had been traumatizing. Velika would never be ashamed or hide what she was.

"I'm sure the right time is coming sooner than you think. It is very honorable you are allowing her to make the decision for the both of you." She faced Velika and gave a slight bow of her head. "Now if you don't mind, I have some warriors who need my attention."

Kismet would be busy at this time. With the warriors returning, there was always someone who would need the expertise of the healer. Setting of broken bones and sewing up deep wounds until they could heal would keep Kismet occupied.

"Please, see to my men. Thank you for coming at such short notice to check on my mate." Velika walked with Kismet through the suite to the door. She held it open for Kismet who turned to her.

"Quinn has a beautiful soul, and she would make a great mate for you. Just imagine, two princesses ruling together." Kismet's smile widened. She reached out and took Velika's hand, giving it a squeeze. "The ball is the talk of the coven. Everyone is excited and can't wait to meet her."

Velika stood and waited for Kismet to get to the stairs. Velika gave the two guards standing outside her room a nod, shutting the door. After the multiple attempts on Quinn's life tonight, she was tightening up security. They had been lax lately, but now she wasn't going to take any chances.

Velika headed back into the bedroom and found Quinn sitting on the side of the bed.

"*Miere*, you must be careful." She rushed across the room to Quinn.

"I'm fine. I don't know what happened." Quinn

smiled. There were smudges underneath her eyes, alluding to how tired she was. Kismet was right. This had been too much for her mate. "Who were you speaking with?"

"The healer, Kismet. I had her come and check in on you." Her stubborn mate insisted on standing. Velika stood before her and took her hands in hers, ready to catch her if she fell. "She just thinks it was too much excitement for you."

"I may have to agree with her. The second we returned, my body began shutting down." Quinn chuckled. She winced a little and pressed a hand to her side. "I would love to have a soak to get clean."

"Come. We both need to get cleaned." Velika assisted her mate to the bathroom.

Quinn moved slowly and tried to brave the pain. They entered the room, with Velika making Quinn sit in the chair by the door. Instead of calling for one of the servants to draw the bath, Velika did it herself.

She was a warrior princess who had plotted out plenty of military attacks. She could figure out how to get a bath together for her mate.

The oversized tub was soon filled with warm water and bubbles. She added some of the oils that were kept on the counter. She thought back to all of the baths the servants had prepared for her and she now realized why she always felt invigorated afterwards.

Kismet's oils.

"You do that very well. Maybe I'll hire you to bathe me every night." Quinn winked at her. Even though she was tired, her spunkiness was beginning to shine through.

Velika's lips curled up into a rare smile.

"It would be a job I'd be honored to have." She stood from her kneeling position by the tub and made her way over to Quinn. She helped her up and began disrobing Quinn. Once her clothes were in a neat pile on the floor, Velika removed her fighting leathers. She grimaced at the amount of blood caked on both of their clothing. She didn't mind hers, but she never wanted Quinn anywhere near fighting again.

They entered the bath, Quinn groaning aloud. Her deep husky sound had arousal shooting through Velika down to her core.

But this was not the time to be thinking of sex.

Her mate was sore and slightly injured from her ordeal in the van.

Velika eased down into the water, floating

behind Quinn. She wrapped her arms around her and brought her back against her.

"This feels so good," Quinn murmured. She leaned her head back on Velika's shoulder.

Velika reached for the washing cloth and dipped it into the water and used it to wipe Quinn's face and slide it across her shoulders.

"Yes, I might have to hire you."

Velika chuckled and took her time bathing her mate. They floated around the water together in a comfortable silence. Velika washed Quinn from the top of her head, down to her small dainty feet. The bond forming between them was making her want to care for this woman.

Put her needs before her own.

And ultimately ensure she was pleased. Not just sexually, but in every way possible known in the universe.

Sliding her hands over Quinn's curvy frame was absolute torture. Her mate's body was beautiful from her perky full breasts, down to her soft stomach to her wide hips. She ached to lave her tongue along every inch of her mate.

"My turn," Quinn murmured. She twirled around in the water and faced Velika with a playful expression. Her skin practically glowed from the warmth of the water and the oils soaking into their skin.

Velika caught Quinn's hands before they could reach her.

"No. You need to rest. Sit over here." Velika guided her over to the built-in seat. Quinn gave a cute little pout of her lips. It was hard to resist kissing them, but Velika knew if she did, then things would get out of hand.

She floated away from Quinn and reached up and began undoing her braids. Quinn watched Velika's every move. Heat radiated from her eyes. She had grown since arriving at the castle. The fear she had harbored was no longer there. Instead, there was a woman who had gained a confidence she hadn't had before, and had a heart of gold.

Velika was proud of her mate.

And to think she had been resistant to the prospect of a mate. Fate had certainly known what it was doing when it had paired Velika with Quinn. No one else would do for her. She would gladly spend the rest of her long life with this woman.

Once her hair was free, she dipped beneath the water's surface, allowing the dirt and grit to float off her. She opened her eyes and took in Quinn's brown legs. She swam the couple of strokes to get to

Quinn. She ran her hands up Quinn's legs, breaking through the surface again.

Quinn's giggles filled the air. It was a sound that Velika wanted to hear every day. There was a day when her mate hadn't laughed. The longer they had spent around each other, the more relaxed and trusting her mate became. Velika drew closer to her, unable to stay away from her. She kissed Quinn's lips then swam away again.

"Hey," Quinn called out.

Velika washed the remaining blood and grime from her body, moving back over to Quinn.

"This bath would have been better had you allowed me to help you."

"And we wouldn't have gotten clean." Velika snorted and shook her head.

"We would have eventually." Quinn shrugged.

Velika snagged her hand and guided her off the chair and into the middle of the tub. Her small mate wrapped her arms around Velika's waist.

Velika stared down into Quinn's eyes, sensing the need to claim her human growing. Her gums burned and stretched from her fangs breaking through. The scent of her mate had her feeling euphoric. She inhaled it and nuzzled her face into the crook of Quinn's neck. She slid her tongue down the soft column of Quinn's throat.

She could hear the blood flowing through Quinn's veins. It was calling to her.

Just one taste.

Quinn's soft breasts brushed hers. A moan slipped from Quinn. Their legs were entwined with each other. They floated along in the water, holding on to each other.

"Velika…" Quinn's husky voice sent a ripple of desire through Velika. Her fingers threaded into Velika's hair. She tugged on the strands.

Velika lifted her head and kissed across Quinn's jawline and ended at her mouth.

Their lips merged into a deep, passionate kiss. Quinn pulled Velika closer with a whimper escaping her. They reached the edge of the tub. Velika kept Quinn pressed to the wall while deepening the kiss. She rubbed her body on Quinn's, loving the feeling of her softer form against her more leaner one.

Quinn tore her mouth from Velika. Her breaths were coming fast as she stared up into Velika's eyes.

"I want you," Quinn breathed.

Velika grew still. She slid her hand down Quinn's waist and her thigh. Her legs had wrapped themselves around Velika's waist while they floated through the water.

Her heart swelled. Velika had been waiting for the moment where her mate was ready for them to complete the bond.

"Are you sure?" Velika whispered, excited at the thought she would finally get her first taste of Quinn's true essence. She cupped Quinn's cheeks, brushing her thumb over her soft skin. "Sealing the bond between two mates is forever. You will always be bound to me and I to you. The aging process will slow drastically, and you will be by my side for all eternity."

"I understand completely. I don't want to be apart from you, and if this is what I have to do to be at your side forever, then do it." Quinn exposed her neck to Velika.

A rumble escaped Velika. She was captivated from the sight of the plump artery pulsating.

The sound of the blood rushing through Quinn's artery was deafening.

"Just think. If we find your brother, you will not age and he will grow old and die," Velika rasped. She needed to ensure Quinn understood everything. She had put feelers out trying to track down Quinn's brother. She would not rest until they received some information that would give her mate closure. Whether he was dead or alive.

"It's been so long that my hope to find him alive is dwindling. Just to see him at least once would be a dream come true." Quinn's brown eyes widened, and Velika vowed that she'd scour the world looking for any hint of her mate's brother. "I can't live in the past. I want to think of the future and prepare for that, and to do that, we must complete the bond so we can start our lives together."

Velika lifted Quinn and carried her out of the tub. This was the moment she had been waiting for.

It was time she finally claimed her mate.

"Where are we going?" Quinn whispered.

When Velika had lifted her from the tub, she had thought her vampire would have just carried her over to the bed, laid her down, and had her wicked way with her then bit her, fed her blood, and then all would have been completed.

But that wasn't the way it apparently went.

Velika had carried her in the room, assisted her into a silk robe, and then dressed herself in one.

After making a quick call, she then carted them off through the castle with their guards in tow.

They began descending a winding stone staircase that led to a lower level of the castle Quinn had not explored. The walls were cold, made of large boulders. Sconces with embers lined the walls, giving them some light.

Taking in the decor, she felt as if she had been whisked back into the seventh century. The lower they went, the narrower the width of the stairs became.

A shiver passed through Quinn. Her budded nipples pressed against the silk material. She bit back a moan, the soft material teasing her. She leaned into Velika and tightened her grip on her hand. Wherever they were going, she prayed they were close.

"This is a surprise," Velika responded. "I've been waiting to share this with you from the moment you arrived."

Quinn's heart fluttered in amazement. Velika had been planning something for her?

Her fierce warrior princess had a heart underneath that hardened exterior after all. They arrived at the base of the stairs and continued down the creepy hall. There were no signs of decay, mold, or rot. The air was fresh, and Quinn figured this part of the castle had to have undergone restoration.

They arrived at a set of massive metal doors. The guards walked ahead and opened them.

"You don't need to wait here." Velika paused and turned to them.

"Your Grace?" They glanced at each other with confusion on their faces. They focused back on their mistress, obviously not willing to defy her orders.

"This is a special night for my mate and me. Stand guard at the entrance at the top of the stairs. Aside from Lady Kismet, no one is to enter."

"Yes, Your Grace." They bowed and spun on their heel, marching briskly away.

"Come, *miere*." Velika cupped Quinn's face.

She moved to enter the room, but Quinn stopped her.

"What does that mean? You've been calling me that, but I don't know what it means."

"It's a term of endearment," Velika admitted.

Quinn was fascinated by Velika's embarrassed expression that fluttered across her face. She narrowed her eyes on Quinn and closed the gap between them. The material of their robes was thin enough they might as well not have anything on at all.

"It means honey. Your taste is one that I will always crave. Your body is the sweetest I've ever tasted, and I'm sure it is just as tasty as I'm sure honey is."

Quinn's heart melted. She leaned against Velika. Her body was still in a constant state of arousal since they had left the tub.

"Come." Velika tugged her behind her.

They entered the room, and Quinn gasped. Nothing would have ever prepared her for this.

Hundreds, if not thousands of candles lined the floor surrounding a massive round bed. It stood high from the floor with a canopy with draperies that flowed from the ceiling to the floor. They were tied back to allow Quinn to see the bed fully. Next to the bed was an oak nightstand with a vintage rotary dial phone.

The room was simple in design with archaic stone walls. An alabaster rug ran along the path to the bed. Another path led from the bed to the wall where an oversized fireplace was featured with a blazing fire in it.

There were faux windows with thick tapestries lining them to give the room a homey feel. Paintings were scattered around the room that appeared old, but there was one that caught her eye. It was that of a naked woman lying on a bed with a man biting her neck. Her expression was one of extreme pleasure.

"What is this room?" she asked.

They walked along the soft rug and stopped next to the bed. Velika turned to her with a heated look in her eyes.

"This, *miere*, is the claiming room." She reached out and took Quinn's other hand and brought it up to her lips, pressing a kiss to the back of it. "This is where we will seal the mating bond."

"But why would we need Lady Kismet?" Quinn moved closer to Velika. The desire for her vampire rose inside her. She wasn't sure if this was her reacting to Velika or the forming bond between them. She leaned in and nuzzled her face into the crook of Velika's neck. She breathed in her womanly scent.

"As a human, I'm not taking any chances with you. I want Kismet here just in case you need assistance."

"Why? What can happen to me?" Quinn looked up at her. She trusted Velika, and if she felt she needed the healer near, then she wasn't going to argue. Her hands moved and idly played with the tie to Velika's robe.

"My blood is powerful. I am a daughter of the king who was the son of a king, who was also the son of a king. We have a strong, pure vampire line, and the reaction could be a little unpleasant."

"Will I turn into a vampire?"

"No." Velika shook her head. She ran a finger up Quinn's throat, her attention locked on it. Her fangs peeked from underneath her lips.

The sight of them sent a wave of arousal through Quinn.

"That would only happen if I were to take too much blood from you which I will try my damnedest not to do."

Velika covered Quinn's mouth in a slow and sensual kiss. Quinn wanted to remember everything about this moment. This was where she was going to take the plunge and join her soul with Velika. Velika's soft lips grew more demanding, the kiss now turning harder and brutal.

Quinn tightened her grip on the ties of Velika's robe. She groaned when Velika pulled back. They were breathing heavily together as they stared at each other.

"Do you trust me, Quinn?" Velika asked.

"Yes."

CHAPTER EIGHTEEN

Quinn held still while Velika untied her robe. Velika slid it off her shoulders and allowed the material to fall to the floor. She stood proud, feeling confident as Velika took her in.

It was romantic that Velika would have a special room for them to claim each other. She understood this was a big deal for vampires. It was like a wedding between two people, only there would be no witnesses.

"Fate has willed the two of us together," Velika whispered.

She reached over to the table and picked up a small dagger Quinn hadn't realized sat next to the old telephone. She held her breath watching Velika lift the knife and prick her finger. A large drop of blood formed on the tip.

She pressed the finger to Quinn's forehead. "We shall thank the fates for the bond that has formed between us."

Quinn shivered. The warmth of Velika's blood seeped through her skin. Her heart raced, but there was no fear inside her.

She trusted Velika completely.

"We shall forever be joined together." Velika pressed the same finger to Quinn's lips, coating them with her vital fluid. The scent of copper filled Quinn's nostrils. "Through our bond, you shall live throughout time standing by my side."

Quinn's eyes fluttered closed. Velika trailed her finger down Quinn's throat and to her sternum, to her navel. Her body shuddered from the intimate touch. She then drew it up to Quinn's heart.

She opened her eyes and glanced down at herself. There was a bright-red trail of blood on her skin.

"Your heart shall dance the same beat as mine." Velika's voice grew husky.

In the candlelight, Quinn could make out the prismatic color of Velika's eyes. She didn't know why, but the blood coating her skin was tingling her skin. Her breath caught in her throat as she watched Velika close the gap between them.

Velika moved her to the bed and assisted her on top of it. Quinn stretched out in the middle of it, watching Velika remove her robe.

Her flawless skin was pale in the candlelight, her toned muscles were highlighted. Her long blonde hair hung down over her shoulders. She stalked around the bed, her body moving like a predator after its prey.

Only Quinn didn't fear Velika.

The need for this vampire was coursing through her body. The skin underneath the blood on her skin was heating up. Her skin felt flushed, her body becoming painfully aroused.

Velika knelt on the bed and crawled across it to her.

"You are a gift. One that I shall treasure for all time," Velika murmured. She moved to Quinn's side and assisted her to a seating position. She curled her arm behind Quinn's back to help keep her up.

Quinn automatically turned her face away, presenting her throat to Velika.

A rumble sounded from Velika's chest.

Quinn gazed upon the hundreds of candles burning. She was relaxed, waiting for her vampire to seal the bond between them. A calming sense of being filled her.

This was her destiny.

This was her future.

They were to have an eternity together.

"I vow to protect you." Velika's fingers slid to her throat. Soon her tongue followed, bathing her skin. Her warm breath skated across Quinn skin, sending chills down Quinn's spine. "To honor you."

The sharps points of Velika's fangs slowly scraped her. Quinn whimpered. Moisture collected at the apex of her thighs.

She wanted the bite.

Needed it like she needed air to breathe.

"To please you." Velika's hand cupped the back of Quinn's neck and held her in place.

"Velika," Quinn moaned. Her body was wildly trembling. It was no longer under her control. She arched her back, thrusting her breasts into the air while offering up her neck. "Bite me. I'm yours."

The words were uttered from her lips without conscious thought.

Velika lifted her farther, her fangs sinking deeply into Quinn's neck with a sharp pain that was short-lived.

Quinn froze, unable to breathe.

Her heart beat erratically. A gasp escaped her while Velika drank from her. The tugging on her neck brought her to the edge of her climax. The flames of the candles flickered as if a wave of air rushed through the room.

Velika released her and raised her head. Blood coated her lips and her fangs. She brought her wrist to her lips and bit herself. Blood flowed freely down her wrist.

"Drink, *miere*," Velika whispered, presenting it to Quinn.

Quinn opened her mouth and covered Velika's wound. There was no hesitation at all. The copper-tinged fluid flooded her mouth. Her eyes met Velika's while she took her first swallow.

A warmth filled her from the inside. An electrical current rushed through her body. She released Velika's wrist and cried out as the heat inside her grew.

Velika nuzzled her face into the crook of

Quinn's neck again. Her teeth sank again into her sensitive flesh.

Quinn's eyes fluttered shut at the sense of euphoria. She turned her head away more to offer herself to Velika. Her body writhed on the silky bedsheets while her lover took what she needed from her.

Velika lifted her head and drew Quinn's toward her. She lowered her head and covered Quinn's mouth with hers. Quinn's mouth opened immediately for her. Their kiss was deep and full of passion. It was unlike any other they had shared before. This was one full of dominance, Velika letting her know who she belonged to. Velika's tongue stroked hers, demanding more from Quinn.

Quinn submitted, all the emotions swirling around in her with the realization that now, she belonged somewhere. She didn't have to fear anything for she knew that her vampire would always be by her side.

Her body felt sticky from their blood coating their skin, but Quinn didn't care. It seemed to enhance the moment between them. Sharing their life's essence with each other sealed them to each other. Quinn felt a snap in her chest. She knew without asking that they were now tied to each other forever.

If she listened close enough, she could hear Velika's heart racing away. It beat in tandem with Quinn's.

Velika released her lips and trailed kisses on her body. She moved down to Quinn's breasts, bathing them with her tongue. Her nipples were ultra-sensitive, and Quinn cried out. She tried to relax back against the bed but was unable to. Her body was strung tight, and she needed her release.

Velika teased her, paying close attention to her nipples then continuing her journey south. Quinn spread her legs wide for Velika as she moved to lie between them.

Quinn's breath caught in her throat when Velika's finger skimmed her slit. She returned to Quinn's clit and pinched it. Quinn's hips thrust forward automatically.

"This will always be mine." Velika murmured. She coated her fingers in Quinn's juices that flowed from her.

Anticipation overtook Quinn while Velika continued to explore her pussy with her fingers. Velika pushed two fingers inside her slick opening. Quinn moaned, her muscles clenching down around Velika. Her thumb stroked Quinn's clit, applying pressure to the sensitive nub. Each movement of her finger brought Quinn closer to the edge of her orgasm.

She exhaled sharply at the piercing pain at the juncture of her thighs.

Velika's bite.

It sent her spiraling out of control. Her climax rushed to her, pushing her over the edge of ecstasy.

This time, she screamed, unable to withstand the pleasure barreling through her. The force of it took every ounce of energy that was left in her body.

Velika groaned, drawing much of her blood from her.

Quinn's body grew weak. Her arms fell to her side of the bed. Velika raised her head, and their eyes connected. Velika's blazed with hunger for Quinn.

Quinn watched Velika crawl over her and rested her body on Quinn's. Their breasts were pressed against each other, and their legs were entwined together. Velika bit her wrist again, blood dripping on Quinn's chest.

"Drink, my mate. We are now bonded. Do you feel it?" She placed her wrist to Quinn's lips.

Quinn was barely able to lift her head, but she opened her mouth, and the thick copper fluid rushed inside and down her throat.

Again, heat flared inside her.

This time it was different. It was scalding hot, and it radiated throughout her limbs.

She didn't dare tear her eyes away from Velika's. She took from her just as she had done, swallowing every ounce of her blood that was offered.

Her eyes widened at the sudden rush of adrenaline that filled her. Quinn's heart sped up, beating entirely too fast. Her breaths were coming in pants.

She didn't know what was happening to her, but whatever it was, it was consuming her.

She threw her head back and screamed. It echoed through the room and was louder than she ever thought she could do. She barely recognized the sound coming from her. Her body trembled uncontrollably, but Velika held her down against the mattress with her weight.

Quinn clawed at the mattress underneath her. The pain was becoming too much to bear. The heat was like liquid lava racing through her veins.

Was this what Velika had been worried about?

"It's okay, *miere*. Let it work," Velika murmured.

"It's okay. It's the change your body has to experience."

Tears formed in Quinn's eyes and fell, running back into her hair. Velika held her while the pain and tremors worked their way through her body. Quinn didn't know how long they lay on the bed until finally the pain dissipated and the tremors ceased.

Quinn opened her eyes and found Velika staring at her with a proud look.

Quinn could not move a muscle. Her body was like putty lying on the mattress.

"Am I supposed to be this weak?" Quinn muttered. She wasn't sure if her words slurred, but she could barely move her lips.

Velika shifted to lie next to her and tugged her into her arms. She wrapped them around Quinn, pulling her to her where there was no room between them.

"It's going to take time for your body to acclimate to not aging as it has done before." Velika kissed the tip of Quinn's nose.

"Oh." That was all she could muster in response.

"But don't worry, *miere*," Velika continued. "You

are mine, and I will always have you by my side and will protect you. Rest."

Quinn snuggled into Velika's hold and couldn't help but think how perfect this night had turned out to be. She was now bonded to her vampire for all eternity. There was no turning back, and quite frankly, she didn't want to.

S he was hers forever.

Velika stared down at the passed-out Quinn. Her mate had weathered the storm of her body accepting the bond. She would be weak for a while, but that was fine. Velika wasn't leaving her side. The protective urge was even stronger now that they were bonded together. Their souls would forever be entwined.

Nothing could separate them besides death.

Velika snarled at the thought of someone taking Quinn from her.

She took in her naked mate. Their blood coated their skin, and it was a wonderful sight to behold. Velika licked her lips at the memory of her mate's blood flowing into her mouth. It was the sweetest blood she had ever tasted, and she was now addicted to it.

She wanted more but had to remember that she couldn't take too much. A smear of blood was resting on Quinn's bottom lip. She leaned down and licked the dried droplet from where it rested.

Quinn's supple body was pressed against hers. She loved the feeling of the soft curves. It was a direct contrast to hers being hardened by lean muscle. They were like night and day, but they were perfect together. Her mate was a gem, and she would cherish her forever.

She would not be able to stay away from her mate. She loved everything about her and her body.

Velika gently braced Quinn back on the pillows. She wanted to inspect her neck and look at her bite marks. She turned Quinn's head and took in the wonderful sight. She would heal, but the mark would remain. It was the mating mark, and any person who saw it would know that this woman was claimed.

Any vampire who tried to drink from her would answer to Velika and suffer the grave consequences.

Leaning down, she kissed the wounds. She licked around them where there was some blood still oozing out. Her saliva had healing components in it and would help seal the wound and prevent it from continuously bleeding.

She moaned from the taste of her mate's blood exploding on her tongue. She continued to lick the area while her hand traveled Quinn's voluptuous mounds. Her breasts were one of Velika's favorite features. She played with the nipples, content to just lie in the bed, licking her mate's bloody while doing so.

A knock sounded at the door. She growled, not wanting to be disturbed, but she had given permission for Kismet to come.

She was sure the healer wanted to check on them and ensure Velika hadn't taken too much blood from Quinn. Velika arranged the blankets around them so she could cover up Quinn's naked body.

"You may enter," she called out. Velika automatically moved closer to Quinn, resting a hand on her stomach. Even though they were in the bed together, she still had to touch her.

The door opened, and Kismet peeked her head inside.

"Is it safe for me to enter?" the older woman joked.

"Only for you," Velika replied.

"Of course, I am alone. I know all too well how protective vampires after they have claimed their mate." Kismet closed the door behind her and made her way to the bed. She held the edges of her long skirt in her hand to keep them from brushing one of the candle flames.

The room was a traditional claiming room fit for a king. Velika had had it spruced up once she had felt the tug to bond with Quinn. She had wanted the night they bonded to be a special one, something they would remember hundreds of years from now.

Looking down at Quinn, Velika knew she would never forget this night.

"So how is she doing?" Kismet asked. She stood next to the bed, waiting for permission to touch Quinn.

Velika appreciated the healer understanding the importance of boundaries immediately after a mating.

Kismet nodded to Quinn. "May I?"

"She said she was weak," Velika admitted. She watched as Kismet turned Quinn's head to take in her wounds.

"Is this only place you bit her?" she asked.

Velika shook her head and moved the cover to

the side to show where she had bitten Quinn on her inner thigh. It had been the perfect spot. Right next to her mate's pussy. The scent of her arousal had been so strong that Velika hadn't even thought twice about sinking her fangs into her thigh.

She bit back a groan at the memory of her fingers thrusting inside Quinn's wet pussy as she'd drunk from her.

"The wounds should heal quite nicely. I'm worried about how much blood you took from her." Kismet stood up straight and narrowed her eyes on Velika. "She's going to need plenty of rest and fluids. I'm going to have Timbi make up some of my special brew that will help with her low energy and strength. I'll have her send it up when she gets up."

"Thank you." Velika moved the blanket back over Quinn. She eyed the healer, ready for her to leave. Now that she had done her proof-of-life check, there was no reason for her to stay.

"Don't drink from her again tonight. The sun is coming up. Get your rest, Princess."

"I will. Now leave us." Velika reached up and smoothed a finger up Quinn's face.

"I am, only because I am done with my exam." Kismet huffed. She began making her way along the path toward the door. She paused and turned back to Velika. "Congratulations, Your Grace. Everyone at the ball is going to want to meet your mate."

She left the room, closing the door softly behind her. Velika sighed, not wanting to attend the ball, but they were obligated to. She scowled, thinking of all the plans Iona had sent to her to sign off on. She had tried to stay out of it. Iona preferred to plan the damn thing anyway. It was going to be at the castle in two days' time. Afterward, Velika would start back on the search for Cain.

The entire coven would be in attendance, and she had just got word that her parents and sisters would be making an appearance. Everyone was going to want to meet their new princess.

She gathered Quinn to her and kissed her plump lips.

Her mate was not used to a life of luxury or the politics of vampirian court. They were going to want to know everything about Quinn.

Hell, Velika had been around them her entire life and she couldn't stand it.

Velika had come to better understand her mate's background where she was dirt poor, trying to make ends meet and living every day with fear that she would be attacked by a vampire and killed.

That was no longer her life.

She just hoped Quinn realized that now, she was to be addressed as Princess Quinn of Ensfield, mate of the warden of the Northwest.

No longer was she Quinn Hogan of Stramford.

A lonely human.

Now she was royalty.

CHAPTER NINETEEN

"You are breathtaking, Your Grace," Delia murmured. She put the finish touches on Quinn's makeup.

Quinn stared at her reflection in the mirror, barely recognizing herself. She had never been one to use makeup before. In her old life she had no use for it.

Delia had highlighted her best features. Her eyes. They appeared a golden brown in the lighting. Smoky dark eyeshadow and ruby-red lips completed the look.

"Are you sure that's me?" she asked.

"I'm quite sure." Delia chuckled. "I just accented your best features, but you are beautiful."

"Thank you." Quinn nervously played with the ties of her robe. It had been a couple of days since she had woken up from her post-mating slumber. She slid her hand up to her neck and felt the small wounds there. They were scabbed over and no longer painful to the touch.

Turning her head to the side, she saw Velika's mark. It was still bruised and dark, but it was apparent what it was.

The mark of a vampire.

According to Velika, with her carrying this mark, no one who was sane would touch her.

Tonight was the ball.

Prominent members of the coven were scheduled to arrive at the castle. To say Quinn was nervous was an understatement.

She was downright terrified.

This party was being held in her honor.

She was uncomfortable with the thought of all eyes on her. She would be the main attraction. Quinn was sure all the vampires would want to see who the human was who had been matched with their princess.

Would they silently hate her?

Want her gone because she was not one of them?

Humans were considered food to vampires. This was what she had been taught from the time she understood that not every person she came in to contact with was human.

Velika promised it would be fine. Vampires who were loyal to Velika and her family were going to want to meet the new member of the royal family. No matter how many times Velika had assured her it would be okay, something in the pit of Quinn's stomach was warning her.

"Time to get you dressed, Your Grace." Delia stored away the makeup and brushes. She offered Quinn an excited smile.

The ball had been the talk of the castle. It had been a while since they'd had such a large event, and the building had been bustling with the staff preparing for the big night.

"Where is Velika?" she asked. Quinn stood from the vanity and followed Delia over to the bed where she had a beautiful dress laid out waiting.

"The princess is meeting with the head of security."

Of course she was. Velika had been more protective of Quinn ever since their mating. Quinn closed her eyes and inhaled. She could sense Velika's heartbeat with hers. Ever since that powerful phenomenon that ripped its way through her body, she sensed things no human should be able to.

It was as if they were tethered to each other.

And they were.

For the rest of her years, she would have to drink small amounts of Velika's blood to enforce the immortality. She would now forever appear the same age of thirty-five. That wasn't a bad deal. She had already appeared younger than her age. Many mistook her for mid-twenties.

A snort escaped her with the thought that one day she would be two hundred and only look in her twenties. Too bad humanity couldn't bottle it up. Those who could afford it would spend their money to try to capture youth in a bottle.

"This dress is lovely," Delia murmured, running her hand over it. She turned her wide eyes to Quinn. "This is a top designer. The princess has great taste."

Clothing designers didn't mean anything to Quinn. She had never had the opportunity to follow any trends. All of her clothing had been hand-me-downs or purchased at thrift stores. She wouldn't recognize the name even if Delia shared it with her.

"I actually picked this one out when we went shopping." Quinn's gaze fell to the white lace dress. It was a daring outfit, and she didn't know if she had the confidence to wear it. She was a thick woman and did not have a model's body. But the memory of the heat in Velika's eyes when she'd walked out of the dressing room that day had her straightening to her full height. Velika was all that mattered.

"Then it is you who has exquisite taste." A teasing glint appeared in Delia's eyes.

Quinn's cheeks warmed.

"Come. You can only be fashionably late to your party." Delia motioned for her to remove the robe.

Quinn's heart raced at the thought of imagining Velika's reaction to seeing her in the dress tonight. The woman was certainly spoiling her. Anything Quinn desired, Velika provided.

Delia helped her into the soft material. Quinn officially felt like a princess. She walked over to the floor-length mirror and paused.

Who is this woman?

Quinn felt amazed at her reflection. The person staring back at her was royalty, feminine, beautiful, and sexy all rolled into one.

The white lace was a direct contrast to her honey-brown skin. The two straps resting on her shoulders were completely transparent. The material flowed over her breasts with flowers sewn into the material to cover her areolae and nipples. The full shape of her breasts were revealed by the deep V that stopped at the waistline. The skirt was sheer, the color of her skin visible. Flowers and vines were embroidered into the material.

It was the most revealing outfit she had ever worn. She was completely naked underneath it. Quinn stood to her full height.

She was beautiful.

She was mated to a princess.

The proof was on her neck. With this dress and her short hairstyle, everyone would be able to see Velika's mark. That thought had emotions swirling inside her. She wanted everyone to know she belonged to Velika.

"Here, Your Grace. Your shoes." Delia held up a pair of heels.

Quinn balked at the sight of them. They were white and pretty, but they had about a four-inch heel on them.

"Delia, I've never worn heels before. I will break

my neck in those." She shook her head and took a step back.

"Oh." Delia looked to the closet and dashed over to it, disappearing inside. Within seconds she flew out of it with a pair of white ballerina flats. "How about these?"

"Those will do." Quinn chuckled. It wouldn't make a great first impression if she fell flat on her face in front of everyone. She slipped her feet into the comfortable flats and beamed. She twirled back around to stare at herself again.

It was unbelievable that a short while ago she was a poor human living in a small town, trying to survive.

Because of fate, she was now living in a castle. She was royalty.

This was her destiny.

A small smile played on her lips.

She had come a long way.

"You are absolutely beautiful." Velika's voice sounded behind her.

Quinn blinked and took in the image of her mate walking toward her in the mirror. She spun around with a smile. Her heart skipped a beat at the sight of Velika.

Her hair was pulled back in two braids with the

rest falling to her shoulders. She was dressed in black leathers, but these appeared to be ceremonial ones. The royal emblem was brandished over her left breast. Twin daggers rested in sheaths on each side of her waist. Her feet were encased in matching boots with a heel, putting her even taller next to Quinn. She had smoky dark makeup around her eyes that enhanced the blueness of them, with lip gloss shimmering on her pink lips.

But Velika didn't need much makeup.

Quinn's mouth watered at the sight of her vampire as she stalked to her.

"Velika," Quinn whispered.

Velika offered one of her rare smiles that lightened her face. Her heated gaze roamed Quinn's form.

"You are missing a few things," Velika announced. She held her hand out to Delia who slipped a long dark velvet case into it. She opened it and pulled out a bracelet.

"Are those real diamonds?" Quinn gasped.

Velika held up the wide bracelet that held rows of diamonds on them.

"They are." Velika took her wrist and secured the jewelry onto her.

Quinn lifted it to stare at the gorgeous piece.

She had never seen anything so beautiful and expensive. It fit tight around her wrist but gave a little slack as she moved.

"And we have the earrings to match." Velika leaned forward and inserted the earrings in her holes.

Quinn closed her eyes, trying to will back the tears that threatened to spill. She had gotten her ears pierced a long time ago for fun but rarely wore earrings.

Quinn inhaled Velika's familiar scent, and immediately her body responded. She leaned into Velika, uncaring Delia was standing close by. It was an automatic action. Anytime Velika was near her, she felt the desire to touch her, be close to her.

"Now, the outfit is complete." Velika stood back and took her in. A look of pride crossed her face. "This was my grandmother's. She willed it to me a long time ago."

Quinn turned around and stepped closer to mirror so she could take in the large diamonds hanging from her ears. She brought her wrist up and stared at herself. If this had belonged to Velika's grandmother, then it was an old piece. It meant a lot to her that Velika had gifted something that obviously held meaning to her.

Velika came to stand behind her and wrapped an arm around her waist, bringing her back against her.

They made a striking couple.

"Everyone will be jealous of my beautiful mate," Velika murmured into her ear. She nipped Quinn's ear with her fangs.

It sent a rush of arousal through Quinn's body. Velika inhaled sharply. Her eyes connected with Quinn's in the mirror. A knowing look appeared in her eyes. She'd scented Quinn's arousal.

"Save that for later, mate."

Velika released Quinn and held out her hand. Quinn slipped hers inside immediately.

"Come. It is time to introduce you."

Butterflies fluttered in Quinn's stomach. She paid them no mind. If Velika was at her side, then everything was going to be fine.

She ignored that tiny voice of doubt in the back of her head.

Quinn's grip on her hand was crushing, but she tolerated it. Velika sensed her little mate was nervous. Tonight was important. It would be their introduction as a mated couple.

Velika glanced over at the mark on Quinn's neck. It was healing nicely, but her mate would always bear her mark. It would warn any vampires from her. Anyone who dared to drink from her would die by Velika's hand.

No questions would be needed.

They would sign their death warrant if they were to sip from her mate.

They walked down the hall toward the stairwell where everyone was waiting. Members of the coven from far and wide had arrived. Her parents and sisters were still not present. But Velika was sure they were all going to make a grand entrance. It had been a long time since she had been with her family, and she was proud she would get to introduce them to her mate.

She was going to get a lot of shit from her mother who wouldn't hesitate on bragging how she was right in what she had done.

The proof was the mating mark on Quinn's neck.

Velika was woman enough to admit to her mother that she had been right.

Sabien and Keir strode behind them. With the amount of guests in the castle, she was not taking any chances with her mate's security. They had caught word of the protestors outside on the edge of the property. They of course were against the thought of a human with a vampire. They never wanted to hear how the humans were treated well. They just didn't want the blending of species.

There was plenty of guards patrolling the grounds. If the humans were peaceful, they could stand with their signs and protest all they wanted.

They reached the top of the staircase.

Quinn's slight gasp caught her attention.

"Breathe, mate. They are just here to meet you." Velika turned and kissed Quinn's forehead. She knew all eyes were on them. She could feel it. There were members from the council, local coven members, and representatives from the other kingdoms in attendance. There were hundreds present to meet the first mate of the royal princesses. News had reached far that the first of the king's daughters had mated.

"It's so many people," Quinn whispered.

"And they will be jealous of us." Velika grinned. Her mate would be the most beautiful woman in the room. Velika was proud of the person her mate was becoming. She was emerging out of her shell. Velika saw great things when she looked into Quinn's eyes. She tipped Quinn's chin up and kissed her lips.

Quinn blinked, and she gave a nod.

"Come."

They began to descend the stairs.

Velika held her head up high. The curved staircase ended in the middle of the room. The decor was nicely done. Iona had spared no expense. The windows were outfitted with dark drapes, and the lighting was low, giving the room an intimate feel. Tables were scattered along the room with black tablecloths with centerpieces on them.

Servants went around the room with goblets of the freshest blood they had to offer.

There was a low chatter that ceased the second they hit the last stair.

Quinn's grip on her hand tightened.

Iona was the first to arrive to them. She bowed in a low curtsey to Velika and Quinn.

"Your Graces," Iona murmured, standing to her

full height, her gaze falling to Quinn's neck. She was in a red dress with a long flowing skirt. Her hair was pulled up in a bun on the top of her head with tendrils escaping. The councilwoman gave a slight nod to Velika. She turned to face the room. "May I introduce to you Princesses Velika and Quinn Riskel, wardens of the Northwest."

Quinn's eyes flew to her. Velika gave her a comforting smile. Her mate was now officially introduced to vampire court as a princess.

These were her subjects, just as they were Velika's.

Applause rang out for a few minutes while the vampires stood to give their respect. Velika put her arm around Quinn and held her close. Her people would respect the draft and that fate had everything to do with their relationship.

Fate should never be challenged.

Finally, the roar of the room died down. Velika nodded to a few people whom she recognized.

"Let's mingle, shall we?"

"Don't leave my side." Quinn sniffed.

They would have to do the respectable act of working the room to greet those who had come from near and far. It would be expected for Quinn to meet some of the dignitaries from the other kingdoms as well as the council. It was going to be a long night, but Velika would ensure her mate was well compensated later.

Velika had almost cast her servant, Delia, from the room the moment she had scented Quinn's arousal. It had taken everything she had not to rip the sexy dress off her mate. Quinn's voluptuous body filled out the dress perfectly. The shade of her skin was highlighted by the dress's color and the lace. It had been the perfect choice.

"*Miere*, let me officially introduce you to members of the council." She guided Quinn over to where Niles and Tobias were standing with their mates.

Their conversation ceased the second they arrived. Velika quickly introduced the group to Quinn.

"It is a pleasure to finally meet the woman who was destined for our princess." Niles took Quinn's hand and bowed his head to her.

"Thank you. It is nice to meet you as well." Quinn gave him a nod and took back her hand.

Velika didn't miss how she stepped closer to her. The maneuver was small, but the meaning behind it went a long way. Her human was seeking her protection, and Velika was thrilled by the act.

"Yes, we have been waiting to meet you," Tobias chimed in. He narrowed his gaze on Quinn and gave her the once-over.

Velika bit back a growl at his look. Her mate was stunning in the dress, and Tobias knew it.

"It was within due time," Velika grunted. Her responsibility was to Quinn, and she didn't care if the council was waiting to meet her. "We were getting to know each other."

"Ah, I'm sure that was the case." Niles shot Tobias a glare who completely ignored him. "We are sure you know what is best, Your Grace."

"That I do." Velika cupped Quinn's elbow and steered her away.

"That was odd," Quinn breathed.

"And those are the council members who are always a thorn in my side," Velika muttered. She and the council rarely saw eye to eye. They were for the good of the people while Velika was for the good of her entire region.

"Velika, darling. How are you?" A tall leggy redhead stopped in front of Velika.

Velika bit back a curse.

"Trista. I'm well, and you?" Velika scowled. Having one of her former lovers present at her ball to introduce her mate was not what she was expecting. Trista and Velika's relationship was of the physical nature only. When Velika had wanted to scratch an itch, Trista was one of the many women Velika could have called upon.

"I'm missing you." Trista pouted her ruby-red lips. She moved in closer to lean her voluptuous body against Velika's but was stopped by a short brown-skinned female shooting daggers from her eyes.

"Excuse me." Quinn cleared her throat and slid in place next to Velika with her arm wrapped around her. She held out her hand with the bracelet on it. "I'm Quinn, Velika's mate. And you are?"

Velika bit back a smile at the jealousy raging through her mate. Quinn was usually shy, but apparently the mating bond was giving her not only confidence but boldness as well.

"I'm Trista. I'm a good friend of your mate." Trista gifted her a conniving smile and shook Quinn's hand. She glanced over at Velika, not hiding any of her desires in her eyes. "We know each other very well. I'm sure she's spoken of me."

"Not a once. Why would I do that?" Velika seethed, trying to push her anger down. How dare Trista come and try to insert herself where she had no business.

"No, *my mate* has kept me very busy." Quinn offered her a big killer-watt smile. She innocently turned her head just in the right way.

Trista's gaze fell to the mating mark on Quinn's neck. Velika held back a snort. Her little human was exerting her place. If they didn't have to make their presence known, she would cart Quinn back up to their bedroom.

It didn't matter how many lovers Velika had in the past. They all ceased to exist in Velika's mind now she was mated.

"Oh, I'm sure she has." Trista stood to her full height, disappointment in her eyes.

"Please excuse us. We have others to speak with," Velika warned. She glared at Trista. If she tried anything else, Velika would personally throw her ass out the front door.

"Yes, of course. It was nice to meet you, Your Grace." Trista gave a slight bow of her head, but Velika didn't miss the hint of anger radiating from her eyes.

Quinn pressed closer to Velika as she led her away.

"Any more of your old girlfriends here waiting to make their presence known?" Quinn asked, her voice low. She kept her eyes averted when she asked the question.

"She didn't mean anything to me. None of them did," Velika murmured, her lips brushing Quinn's ear. She felt the tremor of her mate's body. "I promise I will prove this to you the second we are alone again."

Quinn eyed her, a small smile playing on her lips. "Promise?"

"I find I am making more promises now than ever before," Velika muttered. She grew amused at how far she had come. The need to please her mate in every way was strong. Velika would never look at another woman again. Fate had designed her mate to provide everything she would need in a partner.

"Princess."

She turned and saw one of the dignitaries from South America waving her down. She took Quinn by the hand and headed in his direction.

Velika and Quinn moved around the room slowly. She repeatedly introduced Quinn, stopping at everyone who was vying for their attention. It would do Quinn good to see that all vampires were not how they were in her small town. These who stepped foot in her castle were ones who should be following vampire law.

"It is lovely to meet you," Indigo Wells, a prominent vampire historian, gushed. She was one of the curators of the library in Ensfield. It was well-known that Indigo's family had been very involved in documenting the history of their race. "You must stop by the library sometime."

"That sounds wonderful. I have been reading up on as much as I can. I've had a wonderful teacher," Quinn said.

Velika glanced around the room. Where was Petra? She should be here. The moment she moved her head, she caught sight her friend speaking with the dignitary from the Asian kingdom. Petra gave her a nod, swiveling back to the gentleman she was speaking with.

Quinn was deep into a conversation with Indigo. Velika was happy that it appeared Quinn was hitting it off with the woman. From the reports from Petra, Quinn was enjoying her research. It was helping her learn more about their race, and if she was to lead at Velika's side, she would need to understand them.

"Have you heard of word on the arrival of my parents or sisters?" Velika leaned over and asked Sabien.

"No, Your Grace. Let me ask for you." He

stepped away and spoke quietly into his comms in his ear. He returned moments later. "They shall be arriving within the hour."

Velika gave a satisfied nod. She wasn't sure what held up her family, but she was anxious to introduce Quinn to them.

"Your Grace." Arad came striding up to her with two warriors in tow. The expression on his face was grim.

"What is it?"

"You are needed in your office. We have important word on that special item you had us look into." He tilted his head in a knowing way, and Velika instantly knew of what he spoke.

She hated to leave Quinn now, but this hopefully wouldn't take long. She turned back to Quinn and rested a hand on the small of her back.

"*Miere*, I am being called away for a brief moment," she murmured in Quinn's ear.

Quinn's eyes widened as she faced Velika. Her gaze flicked to Arad and his men. She jerked her head in a nod.

"Don't be long." A soft smile played on her lips, but her eyes said it all. She was putting up a brave front, but her eyes were plagued with shadows.

"I will not. I promise. Sabien and Keir will not

leave your side," she said. She glared at her men. "Will you?"

"No, Your Grace," Keir and Sabien echoed. They stood straight and clicked their heels together.

Velika kissed Quinn's temple. She spun around and headed off with Arad.

CHAPTER TWENTY

"This had better be some damn good news to pull me away from my mate," Velika growled the second she burst through the doors of her office.

Arad was hot on her tail. She strode across the room, taking in the lone figure waiting for her by the fireplace in a chair. A couple of guards waited along with him, posted by the wall.

"Leave us," she commanded.

They thumped their fists on their chests then exited the room, leaving her, Arad, and her guest.

"Your Grace." Draven Leander stood from his

chair. He put down his goblet on the table next to the chair he had been sitting in and gave her a slight bow. "Arad."

"Draven," Arad replied stiffly.

"I'm glad you have made yourself comfortable while waiting on my arrival." She stopped a few feet from him. Draven was a loyal vampire who had a way of extracting information when it was needed.

When Quinn had spoken of her missing brother, Velika had sent word to Draven. She had given him all the information they had on Quinn's elder sibling. Her mate was saddened by the disappearance of her last family member. Velika didn't know what she would do if something happened to either of her sisters.

Yes, she did.

She'd go on a hunting spree until the people responsible paid dearly for taking her sisters.

But Quinn wasn't like her. She wasn't a powerful vampire who had limitless resources. Her mate had tried her best to find him, but she'd constantly arrived at a dead end.

Now she was mated to Velika, that would not be the case.

Draven was a lone vampire who was extremely loyal to Velika. It was Velika who had saved his village over a hundred years ago from a rogue army. In doing so, she had rescued his parents from burning by sunlight. Since then, he had pledged himself to Velika.

"Congratulations on the mating. I was here drinking in your and your mate's honor." Draven grinned. He was a tall son of a bitch, with wide shoulders and long dark hair that was currently tied back away from his face. He was dressed in dark clothing and a long leather jacket that stopped at his ankles. His big fist pounded on his chest over his heart. "It's good to see you by the way."

"It's good to see your ugly mug, too." Velika shook her head. How could she forget about his crazy personality? He may be a jokester, but when provoked, he was a deadly assassin. But that wasn't why she'd hired him. She needed information. She folded her arms in front of her and sighed. "Well, do you have good news for me to share with my mate or do you not have anything to share but came here to drink my good blood?"

Draven threw his head back and barked a hearty laugh.

"Always straight to the point. You don't even want to ask me how my life has been? How many years has it been since we've seen each other?"

"It's been six months, Draven." Velika rolled her eyes.

"Oh, yeah. I seem to have forgotten about that. Must be me getting older." He wagged his eyebrows playfully.

"Will you tell me what you've found out," she growled, growing impatient.

"Fine." He reached inside his jacket and produced a manilla folder. His smile disappeared, and he grew serious. Draven was very good at what he did. He could find a needle in a haystack blindfolded. "The human you have been searching for, Lane Hogan, is very much alive."

"Are you shitting me?" She snatched the envelope from him and tore it open. A photograph and some standard paperwork fell out. There were pages of private investigator documentations of their findings, along with records of payments from Quinn Hogan and even a death certificate certifying one Lane Hogan to be officially dead.

"No, Your Grace. It would appear the human investigators had been right and did well enough to leave him alone."

"What is that supposed to mean? If he has a death certificate, how is he alive?" The moment she asked the question, she knew the answer.

"Lane Hogan was captured by vampires. He was kept for years as a chattel by rogues, passed along as a bargaining chip. He was deep in the underground vampire world. It was no wonder any of the investigators found out what they did. They tried to warn your mate off from her brother. They didn't want to garner any attention to them."

"And you have no problem diving deep, do you?" Velika rested her hands on her hips. She sensed he wasn't done with the story. There was always more when it came to Draven.

"Not at all, but that is not where Mr. Hogan's story ends. He was found and saved by another vampire. One who discovered him when he was on his death bed. One night, his owner drained him to within an inch of his life and left him for dead."

Velika's anger was rising. As much as she tried to get Quinn to see there were good vampires, something like this came to light. How would she explain the events of her brother's disappearance?

"What happened then?" she asked through gritted teeth. She was already set to leave this castle and hunt down the perpetrators who had harmed her mate's brother. They all deserved to die.

"Five years ago, a vampire was out late at night, walking along her property, and discovered a human left for dead. She had two choices. Let him die or turn him." Draven paused, looking between Arad and Velika.

"Just get on with the story," Arad snapped.

"She must have seen something in him because she turned him that night. Lane Hogan gained a second chance at life. He has dedicated his life to that vampire who turned him. She had healed him, gave him a new strength he didn't have before."

"Where is he now?" she asked.

"Aren't you going to ask me who the vampire was first?" Draven's lips curled up into a devilish grin.

"Fine, I'll play your games. Who was the vampire who saved him?" Velika would contact the person to see what she would have to do to get a hold of Lane. If he was still alive, why had he not gone to check on his sister? Why didn't he save her from the terrors of their former life?

"It was none other than your sister, Princess Lethia."

Velika froze. Her sister had her mate's brother?

"He's with Lethia?"

"And he's on his way here tonight with her. He healed and trained hard and now is on her personal guard detail. He will be escorting the princess and should be arriving anytime."

Velika turned to Arad. This was good news.

"Go send word that the second Lethia steps foot on the property, she is to be brought to me."

"Yes, Your Grace." Arad nodded and spun on his heel and left the room.

"Did I do good?" Draven reached for his goblet and finished off his drink.

"You just don't know how good you've done." She walked over to her desk and pulled open the first drawer. She reached in and took out enough to not only pay him for his services but to tip him handsomely. "This is great news, and I can't wait to share with my mate. She is going to be extremely happy."

*V*elika won't be long.

She's going to return soon.

Quinn kept chanting to herself. She continued walking through the room. She swallowed hard, still unable to believe how she had acted when that Trista bitch had tried to slide up to her mate.

Velika was hers. She didn't know where this jealous streak had come from, but she didn't like the thought of another woman touching her mate.

Velika had promised that none of the other women meant anything, and from what Quinn had read, vampires mated for life. She was confident Velika was faithful to her, but it was the other woman who had driven her to see red. Quinn wasn't a violent person, but the second the woman tried to press herself to Velika, she was ready to rip her red hair from her head.

"Your Grace. Would you like wine?" a voice asked beside her.

She glanced over at the servant who held a tray in their hand. A lone wine glass on it. Everyone else was drinking blood, so she was sure as one of the only humans in the room, it was meant for her.

"Thank you." She reached for it and smiled at the young man.

He nodded and walked away. She took a hefty sip of it, trying to use it to calm her nerves down. She began walking again, a fake smile plastered to her face. The wine glass gave her something to hold on to and to do something with her hands.

Sabien and Keir were not too far behind her. Curious, she stepped out into the hallway, music floating from the other room next door. Her heart-beat pounded loudly in her ears. She stopped at the door and glanced inside. A gasp escaped her lips.

"Your Grace, I don't think you will want to go in there," Keri said, standing next to her.

The sight before her had her frozen in place. In this room the lights were kept low. It was a smaller room with a nice-sized gathering inside. The music in here was opposite of the classical music playing in the main room. Here it was more upbeat, and harder. A woman danced on the table while men and women stood around her. She was topless and only had a thong that was in the process of coming off. She tossed it off and fell into the splits on the table. Whistles flew around as she flipped over and gyrated her hips.

At another table, a human female sat in a chair while another woman openly fed from her. A man stood next to her, waiting for his turn. The human woman's expression was one of ecstasy. Her lips were curved up in a smile as the vampire drank from her.

"What is this room?" Quinn asked.

"It is for entertainment." Sabien gently tugged on her arm. "You should go back to the other room."

"There are other rooms like this going on right now?" she asked.

Sabien and Keir glanced at each other then turned back to her. They gave her a nod.

Quinn quickly finished the wine and sat the empty glass down on the edge of the nearest table. Her gaze flew around the room, taking in the habitants. Everyone appeared to be enjoying themselves. She had never seen such a sight before. This was a side of vampirism she wasn't sure she would want to be a part of. She was no prude, but the things going on in here were making her blush.

"This is our way, Your Grace," Keir hesitated in answering. "I assure you that none of the humans are being forced to do anything they don't want to do."

Quinn backed away. She swallowed hard. This was why she needed Velika with her. She should have explained to her that there would be other activities going on in the castle as part of their celebration.

"Well, I guess if they consent and aren't being forced, then it should be okay," she said slowly. Her brain was still trying to process what she had seen. She still had the memory of Velika feeding from her and remembered the euphoric feeling she'd experienced.

She couldn't wait for the next time. It made her proud that when her mate needed blood, she would be turning to Quinn. Her core clenched in anticipation of her mate's fangs sinking into her flesh.

"I want to see the other rooms." She faced Keir and Sabien. "I want to know what else is going on here."

"But, Your Grace—"

"Please?" She widened her eyes and prayed the trick worked. "You will be right by my side as Velika requested."

"One other room." Sabien rolled his eyes, waving for her to follow. "Come."

He guided her down the hall where another room had the same setup. Human women and men were the star of the entertainment and offered up their blood while in the midst of sexual acts. The scent of blood and sex filled the room.

Her gaze strayed to the corner where a naked male was bent over a table with another one behind him. The vampire's pants were down round his ankles while he was brutally fucking the human. The human's moans and cries grew louder. A female vampire sat in a chair at the table, calmly drinking blood from the human's wrist.

Quinn tore her eyes from the throuple. Heat gathered in her core. Again, she wondered where Velika was. She had promised to not be gone long.

Her gaze landed on a table where a woman was laid out like a main course. She was naked, her legs open wide with a female feasting on her pussy. Two other women were standing around the human and were feeding from her wrists. The woman's body writhed on the table. Her cries also filled the air.

Quinn's breaths were coming fast now. She could barely tear her gaze from them. She moved over closer, taking in the scene. The woman's eyes flew open and locked with Quinn's. Her lips curved up into a smile as if to welcome another to their group.

Yes, this human was completely enjoying herself. If she were held captive, would she be smiling?

Quinn had heard of humans wanting to be bitten by vampires. Now that she'd had her own personal experience, she could see why.

The vampire located between her legs brought the woman to climax. Her body arched off the table. Her hoarse scream was drowned out by the music. The vampire chose that moment to strike, sinking her fangs in the crease of the woman's thigh.

Quinn jerked, remembering Velika feeding from her in the same spot. The spot where her mate's fangs had sunk throbbed right now. Her core clenched. She reached up and caressed her mating bite mark unconsciously.

She needed to leave this room and find her mate.

"Now will you please return to the other room?" Sabien asked. He stood next to her and motioned to the door.

"Please. Let's go." She trailed behind Keir who led the way.

They exited the room and headed back down the hall. Quinn prayed her body would calm down soon. She wasn't sure why, but she was aroused by watching the acts in that last room. She bit her lip and followed Keir to the main room.

If Velika could scent her arousal, she was sure any other vampire within a mile radius could see how turned on she was from observing the acts in the last room.

They entered the ballroom, and she breathed a sigh of relief. She walked past Keir and looked around. She didn't know anyone. She had caught sight of Petra earlier, but she had disappeared.

She was on her own until Velika returned.

Exhaling, she circulated the room again. She nodded and smiled to everyone she passed.

"Who said the royal family had to participate in that wretched draft?" A woman sneered. She rolled her eyes and took a hefty sip of her blood.

Quinn paused, unsure she was really hearing someone speak ill of the draft in the castle. She was aware there were people on both sides who opposed the draft. She was just shocked someone would be openly speaking out against it here since the king was the one who had instituted the draft.

"Like we would ever accept a human as the mate of royalty." The man with her snorted.

Quinn stood to her full height and walked in front of them so they could see her.

"Hello." She smiled softly, deciding to kill them with kindness. She was sure that even vampires were like humans. They would say one thing to your face and then wait until your back was turned to show their true colors. "My name is Quinn—"

"We know who you are," the woman barked. She leaned in closer, keeping her voice down. "You don't belong here. You are human. Go back to where you came from."

"Minerva," the male said. He tugged the vampire by her arm. He offered a phony smile. "Please forgive my mate. She's a little delusional at the moment. Hasn't had much rest."

"I know exactly what I'm saying. None of us want you here." Minerva narrowed her gaze on Quinn. "Take it from me, it's better you leave now. The revolt will happen."

"Back away from the princess." Sabien stepped in. He narrowed his hard gaze on the couple. "Is there a problem?"

Minerva straightened to her full height and brushed her hands on her skirt. She flicked her gaze to Quinn then turned her focus on Sabien.

"No, there is no problem. I just wanted to let Ms. Hogan—"

"Princess Quinn is how you are to address her." Sabien snarled. "Show her some respect. She is the mate to your princess."

"We don't mean to offend," the man said.

Quinn was in disbelief that they could be so vile out in the open. If they felt that way, how many others did but weren't bold enough to say?

"I think it is time for you to leave." Keir

grabbed both of them by their arms and dragged them away. Two other guards converged on them and assisted him in removing them from the room.

"Don't listen to a damn thing they said," Sabien said.

"Is there somewhere I can get some air?" she asked. Suddenly she was feeling suffocated. She needed to breathe in fresh air.

"Sure. Follow me." He guided her through the crowd to a private balcony. There was no one on it. The moon was high.

"Can I have a moment to myself?" she asked.

"I am not to leave your side," he growled.

"You can stand in the doorway. I just need to breathe. All of this is too much." She sniffed and held up a hand. "I just need a little space. Just a few minutes."

He paused for a moment, releasing a curse. He ran a hand over his face.

"Do not leave from here. I will be watching you from the door." Her gaze flicked to the staircase that descended to the gardens.

She jerked her head in a nod. He spun around and went back inside, leaving her alone. She exhaled and turned, walking over to the stone wall. She just needed time to herself. The music was slightly muffled from the ball. The party was still going strong.

Quinn looked up to the moon and stared at it. Disbelief at what she had just heard filled her. Just as she'd known, not everyone was going to accept her. She dare not tell Velika. If she did, her mate would be going after each vampire who agreed with the crazed couple.

But what were they talking about a revolt? She didn't want to be the reason a line was drawn between Velika's people. She couldn't handle another war.

Not even one just between vampires.

Now that she was mated to one, she had a reason for the vampires not to go to war. She cared for Velika, hell, she was in love with the tough vampire.

She knew Velika cared for her in her own way. They were mates. She was driven by the distinct need to claim her mate. Quinn, a human, didn't have that. She'd felt drawn to Velika at first, but now they were mated, she had the craving to be around Velika.

But did Velika love her?

Quinn wasn't sure why, but she wanted to hear those words come from Velika's mouth. She couldn't help it. She was human and craved love.

She loved Velika.

There, she'd admitted it. She would share this with her vampire. She was going to have to explain human's emotions and feelings. Maybe one day Velika would love her.

"Humans," a voice in the distance said. "How dare she flaunt a human as her princess, her mate?"

Quinn's hand bunched into a fist. More people were against her being here?

Tears blinded her. She stayed where she was so she could try to get a glance of who was talking.

"Lower your voice. I heard they just tossed Minerva and Tomasi out for speaking ill to the new princess," another male said.

They were walking along a path that led to the gardens. Two male vampires dressed in long robes and their hair pulled back from their faces. She didn't recognize them as anyone she had spoken with in the ball.

"They are lucky they didn't end up in the dungeon. Velika would surely tear their tongues from their mouths."

"Vampires aren't going to stand for a human as the mate to the warden. Velika is going to have her hands full. I hope she's ready for this fight," the second one said.

Quinn closed her eyes. Did everyone feel the same as they did? She was going to have to alert Velika. This was something her mate would need to know about. If vampires were going to band together to fight her mate because of her, she needed to let Velika know.

A lone tear slid down her check.

The memory of her plotting her escape from this place surfaced. She laughed. Now she was in love with her vampire and didn't want to leave. Things had certainly changed in a short time. Now she understood why humans never came back around after they became acclimated to life as the mate of a vampire.

"Your Grace. Are you all right?" Sabien stepped out onto the patio and walked toward her.

"I'm fine. Just give me a few more minutes." She glanced in the direction the males had disappeared.

"Don't listen to those asshats," Sabien said. He moved to stand next to her and stared at the moon. "It doesn't matter who Princess Velika mated, no one would be happy. Had you been vampire, then they would have claimed she should only mate with other royals."

"You heard what they said?" She looked over at him.

He gave a nod and shrugged.

"Do you feel the same? That Velika should have just mated a vampire? I didn't have a choice. It was the damn draft."

"I believe in fate, and that is all that matters. The draft was built off of fate. The two of you were meant to be together, and that is all I care about." He leaned against the railing and folded his arms in front of him. He was a good man and was completely loyal to Velika. He stared at her momentarily. "You make my princess happy. I've never seen her like this so I know you are the one. Any warrior who upholds the crest of the Riskel family will lay down our lives to protect you, Princess."

Quinn brushed the tears from her cheeks and smiled.

"Thank you, Sabien. That means so much—" Her words ended on a shriek.

A sword burst through Sabien's chest. His eyes widened in shock. He reached up to grip it, falling to his knees.

"Run," he whispered.

She spun around and ran right into a hard chest. Dark figures climbed up the balcony with low chuckles filling the air. A thump on the ground sounded by her feet, but she dared not turn around to see. Without looking, she was sure it was Sabien.

"Well, well, well. They just made this too easy for us," a deep baritone voice snarled.

Her gaze climbed upward and was met by a menacing glare. This man—no, vampire—grinned, showcasing his massive fangs.

A sharp pain landed at the back of Quinn's head, then everything went black.

CHAPTER TWENTY-ONE

"Now that this one problem is solved, after the party, we can now focus back on Cain," Velika announced.

She and Arad walked out of her office and headed back to the party. Draven had left only moments before, wanting to join in on the festivities.

"We've reached out to all of our sources trying to track him down," Arad replied.

"Good. I want to broaden the search. There is no telling where the son of bitch could be."

The music grew louder as they got closer.

She couldn't wait to tell her mate the good news. As soon as her sister arrived, they would arrange a meeting between the long-lost siblings. Quinn was going to be ecstatic her brother was alive and well.

There had to be a good reason why Lane hadn't sought Quinn out. Velika was itching to hear what would keep him away from protecting his younger sister.

"Your Grace." Ozul stood to attention. He was posted at the entrance to the ball with another guard.

She gave him a nod and entered the crowded room.

She had lost track of time and hoped she hadn't been gone too long. She had promised Quinn she would only be away for a short while. She hated breaking promises, even if it was a little one. She wanted Quinn to always know she could trust her.

She scanned the sea of people and didn't catch sight of Quinn.

"Your Grace. I take it you and your mate are enjoying the party?" Iona glided over to Velika's side. A wide smile was on her lips. She held the hand of a young male, who appeared to be human.

"I had to step away for a moment for business. Have you seen Princess Quinn?" Velika asked.

Iona's eyebrows shot up. She gave a shake of her head. "No, Your Grace. I haven't seen her since the two of you first arrived." She drew the male to her and rubbed her nose against his ear. Her gaze turned back to Velika. "On second thought, I did see her leave a while ago and go down the hall with those two guards behind her."

Iona shrugged and sauntered away with her plaything in tow.

Velika's breath caught in her throat. Quinn had probably discovered there was more to the party than the gathering in this room. Velika hadn't had a chance to explain to her mate the other festivities that went along with a party such as this.

Vampires would be vampires.

They were very sexual in nature, desired fresh blood from the human volunteers, and most times, the two went together.

She was sure Quinn would have been concerned for any human who was present.

"Please tell me my mate did not venture into one of the playrooms," she uttered, closing her eyes briefly. She was going to have a lot of explaining to do.

She opened her eyes, and Keir was in her line of sight, headed toward her. She instantly tensed at his hard expression.

"I wish I could tell you that, Your Grace." He arrived in front of her. "But unfortunately, she made us take her."

"Shit," Velika cursed.

"She went into two rooms, Your Grace," he admitted. "After she went into the first one, she demanded we show her what was going on in another one. Sabien made her promise only those two and we had to come back here."

"Well, where is she?" Velika asked. She glanced around and still didn't see any signs of her mate.

"There was an altercation that I had to handle," he said.

"What altercation?" she growled. Something happened while she was away from her mate. Where the hell was Quinn?

"A couple of extremist were here and spouting about the revolution bullshit," he spat.

Just great. That was all she needed. Vampires who were against the mating with humans verbally attacking her mate.

A scowl formed on Keir's face. "I ensured they were escorted off the property."

"Who the hell let them in?" she demanded. If they said anything to upset her mate, she would put them in the dungeon and cut their fucking tongues out.

"Don't worry about it, Your Grace. It is handled for now. I personally ensured the couple were thrown out of the building. Sabien had stayed behind with the princess."

Something wasn't sitting right with Velika. In all of her years of experience as a well-trained warrior, she sensed something was wrong. Her gut had never let her down before.

Quinn was in danger.

Velika tried to test out the bond link between them, but she couldn't sense anything. They connection was just starting to form. The more time that passed since their mating, the stronger the link would be.

"I don't like the feeling I'm getting. Something is wrong." Her hand went to the dagger at her side. The feel of her palm around the handle comforted her slightly. They were starting to gain attention. "Gather your men, spread out and find her and Sabien."

Velika kept her face neutral, not wanting to alarm anyone. She walked through the crowd and paused at her name being called.

Luther waved at her from the entrance. She quickly made her way to him.

"What is it?" she demanded to know.

"Your sister, Lethia, has arrived." He was dressed in his official ceremonial leathers, just as all the warriors fanned out around the building. He narrowed his eyes on her. "What is wrong?"

"Quinn. She's missing." Velika kept her voice low.

He cupped her elbow and guided her out into the hallway, away from the crowd. They moved far enough out of earshot of anyone trying to eavesdrop.

"What do you mean she's missing?" he asked.

"As in, no one has seen her or Sabien for some time," she growled, ready to tear the whole damn castle apart to find her.

"Your sister is waiting in the formal sitting room, Your Grace. What do you want us to do with her?" he asked.

"Fuck." She couldn't keep her sister waiting. Velika spun on her heel and headed in the direction of her sister. This wasn't the reunion she was wanting, but it would have to do. "We can't keep her waiting. I've already ordered a full manhunt of my mate. No one leaves the grounds until she's found."

Luther stalked alongside her, speaking low into his comms. Velika had never experienced nervousness like this before, and now she didn't like it.

They arrived at the door of the sitting room. She paused for a moment. She hadn't seen her elder sister in a while, and she was sure Lethia would be pissed for being swept into a room to await her arrival.

"How long until my parents and Hegna arrive?" she asked.

"Within the hour," Luther replied.

Velika gripped the handle of the door and tore it open. She entered the room to find her sister seated in one of the high-backed chairs facing the door. This was the room to receive guests who visited the castle. The decor was simple and pleasant.

Lethia's personal guard detail was posted around the room, armed to the teeth to protect the warden of the Northeast.

Lethia, like Velika, was blonde, tall, and toned with hard muscles. She was the middle child and five years Velika's junior. She, unlike her sisters, enjoyed the wealth that came along with being royalty. She had an eye for fashion and was dressed in a long sweeping black dress with a high split that showcased her long legs. Her hair was left down, flowing around her shoulders.

But it didn't fool Velika.

Lethia was a trained warrior and always had weapons stashed on her body. She may love to play dress-up, but she was just as deadly as her sisters.

"It's about time my little sister arrived," Lethia seethed. Her bright-blue eyes narrowed on Velika. She held a goblet. At least the servants had come and provided a warm drink for her sister. "Do you want to tell me why I am corralled in this room and not joining the festivities to celebrate my sister's mating?"

"Hello to you, dear sister. As I'm sure you've assumed, the reason why I had you escorted here was because of an important matter I need to discuss with you." Velika ambled over to her sister. It was damn good to see her, but too bad their reunion was going to be interrupted by the little detail of her mate being missing.

"Seriously? You sound like Hegna and dear old Dad." Lethia snorted. She took a gulp of her blood and turned her attention back to Velika. "What could you possibly want to discuss at a time like this? We should be in the great hall mingling with your guests and maybe finding a human snack to enjoy in your honor." She grinned, showcasing her pearly-white fangs.

Velika's gaze roamed the room. She took in her sister's security, and her gaze landed on one individual.

He was tall, broad-shouldered, had honey-brown skin, short hair, and eyes that were eerily familiar.

This was Quinn's brother.

"Him." She pointed to the guard standing closest to her sister.

His eyes widened in surprise, as did Lethia's.

"What?" Lethia sputtered. She sat her goblet down on the table next to her and stood. "What would you want with him?"

"Is your name Lane Hogan?" Velika asked. She took a few steps toward him and stopped.

He met her gaze with a curious one of his own.

"That would be me." His voice was a deep baritone. He was dressed in fighting leathers with the family crest embroidered on it. Each warden was assigned a color to signify their house. Velika's was red, while Lethia's was blue. "May I speak freely, Your Grace?"

He glanced at Lethia who nodded.

"Of course, you can, Lane," her sister replied.

"How do you know me? We have never met to my recollection. I have a superb memory and would definitely remember the sister of my princess." He stood to his full height.

It didn't take much to see he didn't trust anyone. Knowing his background, Velika understood where he was coming from. Had she been in his shoes, she would be the same way.

"Stand down, Lane. It would appear that we are now family. My mate is your sister," she announced to a stunned room.

"My...my sister?" He swallowed hard and blinked a few times, glancing over at Lethia then turning his full attention to Velika. He took a step forward, a worried expression on his face. "Quinn. She's here?"

"She has been for a while. We were matched together through the draft," Velika explained. The anger she had first felt when finding out he was alive dispersed. She did not know the reason he would have chosen to distance himself from Quinn, but she was all ears now. "She's been searching for you ever since you disappeared."

A pained expression crossed his face. He shook his head and ran a hand along his jawline.

"I had hoped she would give up, get on with her life. I don't want her to know all of the details of what happened to me."

Velika's eyes met her sister's. Lethia held up a hand, and Velika knew not to push him.

"Whatever you want to tell her is up to you, but she deserves to know something. She loves you so much."

"I know." He took a few steps away and paused. His shoulders slumped. "I failed her. I was supposed to be her protector, but instead I—"

His voice cut off. He took a few deep breaths and walked over to the window. He didn't say anything for a moment.

"I will speak with my sister. You are right. She is owed an explanation. I've thought of her constantly, praying she was safe. You don't know what we've been through as children and growing up after our parents were killed in the war. I didn't want to go back to her like this." He grimaced and motioned to himself. "My sister was deathly afraid of vampires. Where we lived, they hunted humans down as if they were prey."

"You are stronger now." Lethia moved to his

side. She laid a hand on his arm, breaking him from whatever memories he was experiencing. "You have a second chance at life now. If your sister loves you as much as you think, she would have accepted you."

Something passed between the two of them. Velika could see her sister cared for Lane. He turned to face Velika.

"It will not be up to me to explain your absence. Just know that she will be extremely happy to know you are alive. She never gave up hope," Velika said softly.

The haunted look in his eyes gave way to things that she could only imagine. She was just glad the Hogan siblings were going to have a happy reunion.

"Where is my sister?" he asked. "I would like to speak with her now."

"I've sent my men to go get her." She folded her hands together behind her back. Her jaw tightened. They had better bring her mate to her fast. Knowing Quinn, she had seen one or two rooms and her curiosity probably got to her. The woman was a sponge for knowledge, learning as much as she could.

Luther placed his hand to his ear and moved away, speaking into the comms.

"We're in the formal siting room," he murmured. His gaze flew to Velika's.

The pit of her stomach dropped. She cursed the decision to not wear one tonight. It was to be a happy occasion to celebrate, and tonight was spiraling out of control.

"What are you not telling us?" Lethia asked suspiciously.

Her sister was damn good at reading her.

Velika hesitated on sharing with them, but since Lane was here, she didn't want to start a relationship with her new brother-in-law on the wrong foot.

"I had to leave Quinn's side for a moment for a brief business meeting." Her gaze turned to Lane. "It was about you. I had taken over searching for you because there was something my mate was desperate to know: were you dead or alive? My informant had just shared with me your whereabouts. When I returned to the great hall, she was nowhere in sight."

"And you think something is afoot?" Lethia interjected.

"Then why are you here? Shouldn't you be out searching for her?" Lane growled, his fangs peeking through underneath his lip.

Luther growled, too, coming to stand next to

Velika. She held up her hand to him. Fighting amongst them would not solve anything.

"My men are doing that now. I can't be in two places at once." She ignored the tone in his voice. It matched the level of rage brewing inside her.

Velika paused.

There was the sensation of a faint heartbeat racing.

Quinn was scared.

It was the bond. Velika sensed Quinn's emotions, and they were coming through strong.

The door of the room flew open. Velika spun around, her hand going to her dagger.

Arad stalked through the door with a few men behind him. Velika tensed at his fierce scowl. The warriors he brought with him were armed and ready to go to war.

Lethia came to stand by Velika's side.

Velika knew before he opened his mouth, her mate was gone.

"Your Grace." He stopped in front of her and gave a short bow to her sister then her. "I've come with news. We found Sabien injured on the balcony. A sword through the back, and there is no sign of Princess Quinn. We have searched the property and have come back empty-handed."

Velika's grip on the handle tightened.

She knew she shouldn't have left her mate's side.

A growl behind her sounded. It was Lane. Lethia held up a hand, signaling to him.

"We have the footage from outside the castle, Your Grace." Arad swiped the screen of the tablet he was holding. He paused and glanced at her. "I'm not sure you want—"

"Show me." She held out her hand. She needed to see what had happened to Quinn and who she would need to kill. Velika took the tablet and saw the outside patio of the castle. It was off from the great hall. It was a little nook that provided privacy for anyone who wanted to enjoy the outdoors. She tapped on the screen and hit the 'play' button.

Lethia, Lane, and Luther all gathered around her to watch.

Quinn was standing alone, her face lifted to the moon. She wiped her cheeks and leaned against the railing. Was she crying? Quinn's attention was drawn to something below in the gardens. Moments later, Sabien came out and joined her. There wasn't audio for them to hear what was said. Their conversation was cut briefly by the silent attack.

Velika's grip on the tablet tightened. She watched her mate be surrounded by figures dressed in black while Sabien lay at her feet. Quinn was hit from behind, and her body crumpled to the ground.

The figure who stood before Quinn glanced into the camera.

Cain Theron.

"He's mine," Velika sneered.

Luther and Arad nodded.

"Find them. I don't care what you have to do, who you have to kill," she said. "I want to know where Cain has taken my mate."

"You have my men at your disposal," Lethia said. Her blue eyes turned polychromatic, her expression that of a fierce warrior. "We will get your mate back. I will notify Father and Hegna that they are coming into a hot situation."

The rogue vampire wanted a war, and he was going to get his wish.

CHAPTER TWENTY-TWO

Quinn groaned. Her head pulsed with an ache that radiated from her eyes to the base of her neck. She didn't remember drinking so much wine at the party. She turned over, but the pain intensified for a brief moment before dissipating.

Where was she?

She turned over and froze. She was on something hard and cold, and it was certainly not the comfortable mattress she slept on every night next to Velika. Her eyes fluttered open, and she froze in place.

She was staring at an unfamiliar ceiling. Her gaze swept the area, and she bit back a whimper. It was all coming back to her.

The ball.

Speaking with Sabien on the balcony.

She gasped, remembering the sword piercing his chest, then the men who'd appeared around her.

Quinn rolled to the side and pushed up. She was still dressed in her white gown, but it was filthy. She took in the small room that appeared to be a jail cell. There were three other cells that were empty.

The cell next to her reeked of a horrid stench. She gagged, her stomach threatening to empty its contents. She didn't know what was on the floor of the other cell, but it was dark and murky, and if she didn't know any better, she would say it was blood.

Lots of it. She jerked up to her feet and moved to the far end of her cell. She frantically looked around to see if there was anything she could use for a weapon.

Nothing.

Her body trembled while she crept along the wall to the bars. She kept her eyes on the single door against the far wall that must be the exit. She bit her lip to keep from crying. This was not the time to be weak. She had to be strong and figure out a way to get out of here.

Velika had to be going crazy with worry. She was sure her vampire was aware she was missing by now. Quinn gripped the bars. She quietly made her way to the cell's door. She pulled on it, but it didn't budge.

Voices sounded off in the distance. She rushed back to her corner, trying to make herself smaller. She knelt, unsure of who was about to come through the doors.

The only face she remembered before everything went dark was that of the vampire with large fangs.

She braced herself when the door opened. Two large males in dark clothing burst into the room. Their gaze landed on her.

"Well, it would appear sleeping beauty is now awake." The first one snickered. His long blond hair was drawn back away from his face.

"Good, I didn't feel like dragging her ass to see the boss." The other had short greasy black hair.

Blondie opened the door. He grinned, brandishing his fangs while ambling over to her.

"Leave me be," she yelled. She tried to fight his hold but she was no match for the strong vampire.

"No use in fighting." He snickered and yanked her arm, sending her falling forward onto her knees in front of him.

"Look at her. Already knowing her position." The black-haired one snorted. He stood in the cell's doorway and leaned against the bars. A cynical smile spread across his face. He palmed his crotch and leered at her.

"I would love to try her out." Blondie chuckled. He reached out and gripped her face in his hands. "Why don't you open those pretty lips of yours, human. Treat me and Dozier good, and I'm sure the boss will go easy on you."

"No," she cried out. She pulled free from his hold and fell back on her bottom. She tried to scramble away, but he stepped onto her dress.

Their laughter filled the air. Her heart pounded as fear took over.

It was her worse nightmare come true.

She flipped over and tried to crawl away, but he snagged her leg and dragged her back to him. She screamed, but it was pointless. The other one was enjoying her struggle. Blondie flipped her over and straddled her. Quinn fought with all her might to buck him off her, but he was too strong for her.

"Keep it up. Fight all you want and get that

blood of yours pumping." He grinned, went for the front other dress, and tore it open, the delicate lace no match for him.

Tears blinded her. She squeezed her eyes and continued fighting him. If she had to die trying to ward him off, she would. The feeling of his hard member pressing against her had another sob welling up inside her.

"Leave me be. My mate—"

"Won't be able to save you, bitch," he sneered. He drew away and backhanded her.

The sting from the blow snatched her breath. He continued tearing her dress down the center until it was completely open. Her body fell back against the concrete floor. She blinked, trying to catch her breath.

"Horace!" a sharp bark sounded from the door.

The vampire on top of her paused and rotated to look at the person who'd called him.

"Don't touch her," the male growled.

"I just want a little taste. It won't take me long," Horace insisted.

"I'm sure that is something all your lady friends want to hear," the person replied sarcastically.

Horace sputtered. He turned back around and narrowed his eyes on her. She whimpered, thankful the person had come at the time they had.

"You better be lucky, bitch. I want a taste of you and I'm going to get it," he threatened. He pushed off the floor and stood.

Quinn scooted back away from him, trying to hold the tattered remains of her dress together to make herself decent.

The vampire standing in the doorway had on a business suit. His brown hair was cut close to his head. His pitiful gaze landed on her.

"Get her and let's go. He's waiting on you," the newcomer said.

Horace moved to her side and grabbed her arm. She cried out at the crushing grip.

"Move," Horace growled.

Dozier stepped aside to allow them to exit the cell. He walked behind him as they left the jail room.

Quinn's body was moving on autopilot. Her body trembled uncontrollably. She tightened the hold on her dress, trying to not expose herself, but it was pointless.

They continued down a darkened hall. If it hadn't been for Horace, she would not have been able to make her way. She could barely see a few feet in front of her. The suit led the way up a short staircase.

If she had to guess who the boss was, it was the same person who had orchestrated the failed attempt on her before. She swallowed hard for she knew who it was.

Cain Theron.

The rogue vampire leader. He was against everything Velika and her family stood for, and now Quinn was in his grasp. She tried not to allow her fear to control her. She knew what happened to humans in the hands of bad vampires. She had tried to avoid vampires like these but here she was.

She sent up a prayer to fate, or to any god who would listen, that Velika would find her.

Quinn stumbled but righted herself with the help of Horace almost pulling her arm out of the socket.

"This way," he grunted.

They entered a room that was barren except for a desk and a few chairs. Horace guided her over to the chair positioned in the middle of the area. He pressed her down to sit, relaxing her arm. He and Dozier moved to stand behind her.

Quinn blinked to allow her eyes to adjust from

the darkness to the light. Several floor lamps were positioned, giving them a little light.

Quinn's gaze settled on the vampire sitting on the edge of the desk staring at her. The suit went over to stand beside this man. He whispered something in his ear. Whatever it was, the other man didn't appreciate it.

"You dare put your hands on my property?" The vampire pushed off the desk and stood.

He moved closer to her, and she bit back a gasp. It was the man from the balcony.

This was the boss man.

This was Cain.

"She's a human. Who cares?" Horace replied. He cleared his throat, and nervousness could be heard.

She kept her eyes forward, not wanting to draw any attention to herself.

"Who cares?" Cain hissed. He dashed forward quicker than her eyes could track.

A loud crash sounded behind her. She cringed from the noises of a scuffle and a scream.

The trembling in her limbs increased. She gripped the opening of her dress and focused on her feet.

"For all the trouble we went through to get this

human, I gave specific orders for her not to be touched," Cain roared. He strode back around to stand in front of her.

She eyed his black boots, sensing his gaze on her.

"Do you know who I am?" he asked.

She jerked her head in a nod. The sound of Horace's pain-filled moan reached her. She tried to ignore it as best as she could.

"Who am I?"

"Cain. Cain Theron," she whispered. She didn't hesitate in answering. Her face was throbbing from the hit Horace had landed on her.

"Good. Then you know this isn't personal. You are just collateral damage." He walked away from her and headed toward the suit who held out a handkerchief to him. He wiped the blood off his hands then tossed it on the desk and turned back to her.

"Velika will kill you," Quinn vowed. She didn't know where this boldness came from, but it was right on time. She was as good as dead, so she might as well state the obvious. She didn't know if she would be alive to witness it, but this was one thing she was sure of.

Her mate would seek vengeance.

"You think so?" He smirked. He slowly made his way back to her. "Velika Riskel would have to find me first."

Cain stopped in front of her. His eyes narrowed on the bracelet on her wrist. She moved her other arm to cover it.

"That would be a nice parting gift." He yanked on her arm, going after the bracelet.

Quinn screeched, fighting against him. This was a gift from her mate, and she'd be damned if she'd just turn it over. That bracelet had been in Velika's family for ages. She leaned down and bit his hand.

"You bitch."

Her head flew back from the strength of his hit. The chair tipped over and crashed to the floor.

Her face throbbed from the pain. She rolled over off the chair, her head resting on the floor. Her mouth filled with a copper substance. She spat out the blood and groaned. Her face was on fire. Without looking or feeling, she sensed her cheek swelling.

"Get up, bitch. If I didn't need you as bait, I'd drain you dry now," Cain snapped.

He pulled her to her feet while Dozier righted the chair. He pushed her back into it and this time worked the bracelet off her wrist. She sniffled, watching him toss it to the man in the suit.

"The Riskel family has ruled entirely too long. The future they are trying to achieve is going to ruin vampires. We shouldn't be mating with humans. Your kind is our food."

Quinn stared at him without saying a word. He paced in front of her.

"What does that have to do with me?" she muttered. She froze, not realizing the words had actually left her mouth.

He spun around and glared at her.

"You are the problem. They forced you into the draft then carted you off to Velika. By the looks of your neck, she's mated you." He sneered. "That is an abomination. If she were worth anything, she would have done you the favor and drained you."

Velika wouldn't have done that. She was a true believer in fate, and they were meant to be together. Quinn stared at Cain and realized he was delusional. If vampires didn't look to humans for mates, then what were they to do? Go through their long life without someone to share it with?

She now comprehended what vampires were doing. Was it the right way? No, but she understood that desperate need to find the one to travel this lonely life's journey with.

"She's going to step down from her position as the warden. The vampires of this area have long tolerated her, and it is time she and her family gave up the throne." He was yelling by now.

Quinn gathered the material of her dress and held it tight. She glanced around, and there was nowhere for her to go. Even if she tried to make a run for it, they would be on her before she even got to the door.

She wouldn't be able to outrun them, nor would she be able to overpower them.

"Get Velika on the phone," Cain ordered.

The suit pulled a cellphone from the inside pocket of his jacket. He held it up to his ear and spoke softly. He froze, his gaze landing on Cain.

"Well?" he asked.

"The princess is indisposed at the moment," the suit said.

"Vasile, if you do not get the princess on the fucking phone, I will shove that damn device up your ass!" Cain shouted.

Vasile's eyes widened. He dialed the number again and put the phone up to his ear. He reached up and undid the top button of his shirt. He spoke into the phone and again paused, glancing at Cain.

"Sir, she's not available at the castle," Vasile said.

"Where the hell is she?" Cain spun around and zeroed in on Quinn. "Does the princess have a cellphone?"

Quinn paused and thought about it. In the short time she'd been with her mate, she had never seen her with one. Velika was well over two hundred years old, and Quinn doubted the woman used a cellular device.

"Not that I'm aware of," Quinn whispered.

"Son of a bitch." Cain stalked over to an empty chair and kicked it. The chair flew across the room and slammed into the wall, breaking into pieces. He paused and glanced back over at Quinn. "I bet she's out looking for you. The mate of the great Velika Riskel was kidnapped right under her nose, but too bad she won't find you."

Alarms blared overhead. The noise was deafening, and Quinn grimaced.

"What the hell is that?" Cain shouted. He walked around the desk and tapped on a button on the keyboard. He glanced at the monitor and cursed. His gaze whipped to hers.

Relief filled her.

Velika was here.

"How the hell did they find us?" Vasile asked. A worried look fell onto his face. He moved to stand beside Cain and yanked open a drawer, withdrawing a gun.

"Well, looks like we go to plan B." Cain straightened to his full height. "Dozier, gather the men. We are about to take out some royal vampires tonight. I want them dead, and I want Velika's head on a spike."

"Yes, sir." Dozier jogged out of the room.

Cain hurried to her and hauled her to her feet. She made the mistake of turning and caught sight of Horace lying deathly still on the floor. Her stomach did a little flip-flop at the sight of blood circling his body. Not that she was sad for what had happened to him. He'd got what he deserved.

Cain dragged her down a hall. A faint rumble vibrated the building. It grew louder as they continued on until a loud roar pierced the air. The building shook from an explosion, tossing Quinn against the wall.

"Come on," Cain growled.

The sound of fighting reached them. They rounded the corner and were met with chaos. They must be in an old police station. The bullpen was overrun with vampires fighting vampires. Bodies careened into old desks and tables. Quinn took in swords slashing through the air and the distant sound of gunfire.

"This way." Cain spun around and tugged her behind him. He came to a sudden halt with her almost crashing into his back.

"Going somewhere?" a familiar voice asked.

Quinn swayed on her feet. She stepped to the side so she could see who was before him.

Luther.

Quinn smiled.

Yes, Velika was here.

"Cain!" a harsh voice roared his name.

Luther grinned and jerked his head in the direction behind them.

Cain released a curse. He spun around and grabbed Quinn to him. He pulled a knife from somewhere and held it to her throat. Quinn grew still. The edge of the knife was extremely sharp. In that quick second, he had managed to prick her. A warm trail of blood slid down her neck.

She blinked a few times and took in the form dressed in fighting leathers headed toward them.

She would know that walk anywhere. There was another familiar figure next to her mate.

Quinn blinked again and was in disbelief.

Was that…Lane?

He looked bigger, more filled out, and was he dressed as a vampirian warrior?

What the hell was going on?

"Release her and your death will be swift and painless," Velika warned. She pointed a bloody dagger at Cain.

This was the Velika Quinn had never seen before. The woman was fully enraged, and seeing how she had come for her, Quinn realized she was completely in love with Velika.

"It won't take much for me to slit her throat," Cain threatened.

He pressed the edge of the knife into Quinn's skin deeper. She whimpered, the burning of her flesh being sliced spreading through her. A trail of blood slithered along skin.

"Look around you. There is no way for you to make it out of here. Your men are all dead," Velika snapped.

Quinn held her head as still as she could. She took in the number of dead bodies lying on the floor. The only ones standing were those dressed in the same warrior uniforms as Velika's men, only her brother's was red.

Apparently, the rogues were no match for the trained royal soldiers.

Quinn's eyes met Lane's. He tossed her a wink, and she bit her lip. That was a move he had done for her since they were children. Whenever something had her down in the dumps, a wink was his way of telling her everything would be fine.

"Stay back," Cain hollered. He gripped her small curls tight in his hand and held her head back farther to expose her throat.

Her heart raced at the sensation of the knife still pressing to her skin. She closed her eyes, waiting for the tearing of her flesh from him dragging the knife across her throat.

"You wanted me, come fight me, Cain. Why kill a human?" Velika taunted him.

"Because she's your mate," he spat. "How do you believe in a fabricated test? No one has the right to pretend they are fated. These humans are our food, not mates."

"Release her now," Lane ordered.

Excitement filled Quinn that her brother was standing a few feet from her. In his hand rested a short sword. It dripped blood on the floor. If this was the moment she was to die, she would go to Heaven a happy woman. She had fallen in love and got to experience a little piece of heaven right here, and her brother was alive and looked well.

She closed her eyes again and waited for it all to be ended.

"You don't deserve power. You don't deserve to call yourself the warden. You—"

His words were cut short. The hold he had on her grew slack. Quinn opened her eyes and out of the corner of her eye saw something protruding from his eye socket.

A knife.

His hand with the knife slipped away from her neck.

"Quinn. Come," Lane called out.

She didn't hesitate to run to her brother. She slammed into him hard, wrapping her arms around his waist. Sobs erupted from her.

He was real and in the flesh.

She rested her forehead on his chest and allowed all the tears to flow. She lifted her head and stared into eyes that were identical to hers.

"Hey, sis. Close your eyes." He pressed her face to his chest.

The knife to his eye socket wouldn't kill Cain.

To kill a vampire, one would have to separate the head from their body or sever their heart out of their chest. She shivered, not wanting to know which method Velika used.

"It is done." Velika arrived at their side.

Quinn pulled away from her brother and jumped into Velika's arms. The amount of blood sprayed on Velika hinted she had gone down the route of taking Cain's head off his shoulders. At the moment, Quinn didn't care if she got blood on her. She was already filthy, and all that mattered was that she was back in Velika's arms.

"I knew you would come for me," she whispered. Velika's arms tightened around her. She buried her face into the crook of Quinn's neck and kissed her claiming mark.

Velika pulled away slightly and took in Quinn's face.

"He didn't deserve a swift death," Velika growled. She tipped Quinn's face to the side.

Quinn grimaced, afraid to know what she looked like. She was sure her face was turning a horrible black and blue.

"If I could bring him back alive, I would just so I could draw out that next death."

"I'm okay," Quinn whispered. "He took the

bracelet you gave me. It was with Vasile. The man in the suit."

She felt guilty that something so beautiful and sentimental to Velika was gone.

"Don't worry. We'll find him and get it back." Velika motioned to Luther who jogged over to them. "Find my mate's bracelet. It's with a man named Vasile."

Quinn gave Luther a description of him. She prayed they would find it.

"We'll find it, Your Grace." Luther bowed his head to Quinn and left them.

"I can't believe you are here." Quinn glanced over at Lane.

He stepped closer to them. He reached out and gently caressed the back of his hand to her throbbing cheek.

"We have so much to discuss."

His deep-timbred voice washed over her. She hadn't heard it in so long that she couldn't help but think she was dreaming.

"Are you really here or am I hallucinating?"

"I'm here, little sis. Believe me, I'm not going anywhere." He winked at her again and leaned over to press a kiss to her forehead.

She closed her eyes, completely over the moon.

Her brother was alive!

"Let's get my mate home," Velika said. She glanced over at Lane. "You are welcome to stay as a guest. You're family."

"It would be an honor," Lane said. "I'm sure Lethia will allow me to take some time off so I may reconnect with my sister."

"She won't have a choice if I have any say." Velika dropped a soft kiss to Quinn's swollen lips.

Quinn sighed, leaning against Velika, feeling as if she had come home. There was so much she wanted to say to her, but this was not the place to do it.

"Please get me out of here." Quinn turned to Velika.

"You don't need to tell me twice, *miere*."

CHAPTER TWENTY-THREE

"I said I'm fine," Quinn repeated for at least the fifth time since they had arrived back at the castle.

Velika had whisked her up to their private quarters the second they'd stepped foot in the building.

Quinn's heart swelled so much with love for this woman. Velika had stripped the rest of the dress from her and carefully bathed the both of them, getting all of the blood and dirt from them. It would appear her vampire was always having to care for her. After their bath, Velika dressed them in their matching silk royal robes.

She now had Quinn propped up in a chair, assessing her face again. One side of her face was puffy, hot to touch and sore. Her eye was barely open, and her lips were swollen to double their normal plump size.

The fury in Velika's eyes almost made Quinn glad her mate couldn't raise the dead. Cain would be dead multiple times over in the most inhumane way that Velika would be able to think of. Quinn shivered with the notion of how deadly her vampire was.

"How did you find me so quickly?" Quinn asked.

Cain had been certain that Velika wouldn't have found him.

"The bracelet. I had a tracking beacon installed on it," Velika admitted. "I just had a feeling someone was going to try something. That's why I had security upped as high as I did, but I still didn't want to take any chances."

"Was it really your grandmother's bracelet, or were you just saying that?"

"It really was. The two earrings that matched it were diamonds removed from the bracelet, and we were able to insert fake diamonds that were actual tracking devices. I had a momentarily lapse in my memory when I panicked and forgot about it."

It was a brilliant plan. Quinn wasn't even mad at all. It just showed how serious Velika was at wanting to protect her. Quinn had been warned that her life would be in danger just because she was the mate of the princess.

"I would call for the healer, but I already know what Kismet would say," Velika murmured. She grimaced and kneeled on the floor in front of Quinn. "I am so sorry, *miere*. I failed to protect you as I have promised."

She took Quinn's hands and bent her head down and rested her forehead on them. Quinn sat in stunned silence. This was the most vulnerable she had ever seen Velika. She was normally strong, stubborn, and fierce.

"It wasn't your fault. You had business to attend to and you can't be with me every second. Sabien was—oh! Sabien. How is he?" Quinn moved to jump up from the chair, but Velika pushed her back down.

"He is fine and resting. He shall be healed up and back to normal in a day or so," Velika said.

Quinn nodded, relief filling her. Thank goodness for vampires being fast healers.

"Can I visit him soon?" she asked.

"Of course. From what I've heard, he was worried about you." A small smile graced Velika's lips. She kissed Quinn's fingers.

The simple move made Quinn feel safe and loved. She wasn't sure if Velika was capable of love, but the little things she did showed it.

"It would seem my men are just as smitten with you as I am," Velika said.

"He's a good man and loyal to you," Quinn said.

"They sense the type of person you are and that you will make a great leader beside me." Velika's blue eyes darkened. She entwined their fingers together and held on to Quinn tight. "You are strong, intelligent, and have a big heart. I am proud the fates have given you to me."

"Velika," Quinn breathed.

Her words were cut off by Velika kissing her in the softest way possible. Her lips were slightly pained, but it was worth it. She reached up and cupped Velika's face when she pulled back from her. There were so many things that she wanted to share with her. She understood life was short, no matter how many years one was granted on this earth. She had to tell Velika what was on her heart.

"I know you believe in fate and everything happens for a reason, but I just want to tell you that I'm in love with you."

The room was silent. Velika stared at her. Quinn's heart beat faster. She cleared her throat and trailed her fingers down Velika's cheek and to the neckline of the robe.

"You've made me feel things I didn't know I could, and the way you care for me, it's made me fall for you."

"You love me?" Velika's voice was hoarse. She studied Quinn's eyes as if seeking the truth in them.

"I do."

"I'm glad to hear that. I was worried you wouldn't be able to accept me and my people. I've been in love with you from the moment I first scented you."

Quinn flushed, a giggle escaping her. She wrapped her arms around Velika and held on tight. Velika nuzzled her face in the crook of her neck, kissing the mating mark. It sent a ripple of desire through Quinn.

She was overwhelmed by the emotions swirling around in her. Velika loved her. Hearing the words brought tears to her eyes.

Velika pulled back and caressed her uninjured cheek.

"Why the tears?"

"I'm so happy. Everything is perfect." She sniffed. She leaned forward and kissed Velika's lips. "I have everything I've ever wanted now."

"Good." Velika's gaze dropped to her swollen cheek and lips. "Come. Let me help my mate heal."

She aided Quinn to her feet and guided her from the bathroom and into their bedroom. Velika removed their robes and assisted Quinn into the bed. She slid in beside her and brought her close, angling them against the pillow with Quinn's back to her.

The feeling of her mate's naked body next to hers sent waves of desire through Quinn. Ever since they had completed their bond, she was always hyperaware of Velika the moment they were near each other.

Velika shifted away briefly, then brought her arm around Quinn. Blood trailed down her arm from fresh puncture wounds.

"You need to drink, *miere*. My blood will help heal you, just as it does for me," she whispered.

Quinn rested her head and brought Velika's wrist to her. Had someone mentioned to her months ago she would be drinking vampire blood, she would have called them crazy.

Now, she covered the small holes with her lips with no problem. She suckled the sanguineous fluid and swallowed.

She moaned from the taste of it.

Her eyes closed as she basked in receiving the healing powers of her mate's essence. Velika dragged her other hand down Quinn's breasts, teasing her perky nipples. She pinched them, eliciting a gasp from Quinn.

"Keep drinking, *miere*," Velika whispered in her ear.

Quinn licked her forearm where the trail of blood had flowed, returning to the puncture site.

It was amazing how she was already feeling her facial swelling decreasing. The aches were lessening.

Velika's hand traveled down her stomach and snaked between her legs. Quinn widened them to allow her mate to have what she was seeking.

Velika parted Quinn's slick folds and circled her clitoris.

Quinn was unable to hold still. Her hips thrust forward of their own accord to meet Velika's talented fingers. She moved them down and inserted two of them deep inside Quinn's wet core.

Quinn held on to Velika's arm tighter while she continued to drink. Velika fucked her with her fingers. It felt so good to have them inside her. Velika's thumb brushed her clit, sending waves of ecstasy through her.

Quinn released Velika's wrist. She ignored the trail of blood dribbling down her chin. She turned her head and offered her mouth to her mate. Velika crushed her lips to hers. There was no longer pain.

Quinn shuddered as Velika's fingers pounded into her. Her hips rocked back and forth in rhythm with her lover.

The kiss deepened, Velika controlling every part of it. Quinn shifted her body to face Velika's who slipped her fingers from Quinn's warm sheath and focused on her clit again.

Wanting to bring her mate pleasure at the same time, Quinn pushed her hand between Velika's legs, demanding entry. She found Velika's swollen nub and rubbed it with her fingers.

They pressed together as close as possible, pleasuring each other.

Their cries filled the air.

Quinn quickened the pace of her fingers, loving the sounds of Velika's gasps and groans. The lust for her mate grew even more.

Quinn was hanging on by a thread and was so close to climax.

"Quinn," Velika moaned. Her strong vampire lover was writhing alongside her in the throes of passion. Quinn loved that she could bring such pleasure to her mate. She pinched Velika's clit, sending her into a hard orgasm.

Velika rolled them over to where she was on top of Quinn, her hand still braced between her legs. She applied more pressure to Quinn's nub, and her body detonated. She threw her head back, a scream leaving her lips.

At that moment, Velika sank her fangs into the same spot of Quinn's claiming mark.

This orgasm was one of the hardest Quinn had ever experienced. Her body trembled out of control as she rode the waves of her release. She was completely consumed by the sensations coursing through her body.

Finally, she came crashing back down from her euphoric journey. Velika rested on top her, now licking the side of her neck.

Velika lifted her head and stared down at Quinn. Blood was smeared on her lips and face.

Quinn was head over heels in love with her vampire. She guided Velika's head down and kissed her. She wrapped her arms around her and never wanted to let her go.

* * *

"What if they don't like me?" Quinn murmured.

Velika glanced over at her mate and smiled. Her small human always cared what people thought of her.

"Don't worry. My family will love you."

They had finally come up for air the next night. Quinn's injuries were almost healed. Velika's powerful pure-born vampiric blood was the perfect cure for her. The swelling and bruising were almost gone.

They were on their way to the family room where her family was waiting. Her parents and other sister had arrived sometime after they had left to go after Quinn. She had refused to allow anyone in their room once they'd returned home. The mating bond had her feverishly wanting to care for her mate first.

Quinn was beautiful, dressed in a long plum silky wrap dress that flowed around her ankles. Her feet were encased in sandals. Her brown skin was flawless and was highlighted by the color of her dress.

Her mate had talked her into not wearing leather. Apparently, it was driving her crazy. So, Quinn picked out a dark pair of leggings and a long white tunic for her to wear. Her hair was left to flow down her shoulders. Her mate insisted she kept it down.

Tonight's gathering was for family only.

Keir and Fane trailed behind Quinn and Velika. After the recent events, Velika was not going to let her mate out of her sight for a while.

They arrived at the entrance for the family room. Royal guards were posted outside.

"Princesses." Both bowed and opened the double doors.

Velika squeezed Quinn's hand and escorted her into the room. The doors shut behind them. Conversation ceased, and all eyes turned to them. The king and queen were sitting together on the settee, while her sisters were standing near the fireplace speaking with Lane.

Quinn's audible swallow was the only sound.

"It's about time." Mira, the queen, stood from her chair. Her lips spread into a wide grin. "Come here, you two."

Her mother's excited laugh broke the momentary pause. Laughter filled the room as the queen practically bounced on her heels. Velika's father rose from her chair, rolling his eyes at his wife.

Velika tugged on Quinn and brought her to stand in front of the king and queen.

"Mom. Dad. May I finally introduce you to my mate, Quinn," Velika announced proudly. She stood tall and glanced over at Quinn.

"It's a pleasure to meet you." Quinn dipped down in a curtsey.

"Oh, you don't have to do that." Mira dashed forward and pulled Quinn into a hard hug. "Welcome, my dear. I have prayed that fate would intervene and bring my daughter her mate."

Quinn laughed and returned the hug. She stepped back from the queen and turned to Niall, who was patiently waiting.

"Hello, sir." Quinn stretched out her hand, but the king brought her in for a hug as well.

"There is no formality when we are amongst family," the king said. He barked a laugh and released Quinn.

He and Mira stole her attention and asked her a million questions.

Lethia and Hegna walked over to her. They

shared hugs, and of course her sister teased her about her clothing. It had been a while since all three of them had been together, and it felt good to see her sisters in person instead of via holograph.

The three sisters resembled each other. Only Hegna had dark hair like their father.

"Well, it looks like Mother's meddling has paid off for you." Hegna snorted. She folded her arms in front of her chest. The eldest Riskel sister appeared skeptical of the mating draft.

"It has. But don't forget she's entered the both of you in the draft also." Velika chuckled.

"I'm praying fate wouldn't want to stick me with anyone," Hegna said. She was very similar to Velika. She always voiced she'd rather be alone. There was too much work in insuring vampires were secured. "I'm better off alone."

Velika bit back a smile, remembering saying the same thing.

"I don't think it will be too bad," Lethia said, her gaze shifting over to Quinn. Lane had joined the royal couple. "It would be nice to have someone to come home to."

"What's up with you and Lane?" Velika asked.

The sisters never bit their tongues while together. They were close, and even though they didn't see one another as much as they would want to, they loved each other fiercely. There wasn't anything Velika wouldn't do for her sisters, and she knew the feeling was mutual.

"Nothing. We are just good friends. I've learned a lot from him since we've met." Lethia turned back to them. "He's the brother I've never had."

Velika nodded. She knew the feeling. Her relationship with Luther was the same.

"Well, I hope fate decides to bless the two of you soon," Velika teased.

"Fuck off," Hegna muttered.

Only Lethia appeared to be okay with knowing her time could come where a mate would be presented to her.

"I can't tell you two how much my life has changed since Quinn came," Velika admitted. She glanced over at her mate and felt the pull of the bond. She sensed the happiness in her mate.

"About Lane. He asked if he could stay for a while, and I left the choice up to him," Lethia said. She pushed her blonde hair behind her ear. "He is not a prisoner, and he can make the decision to stay with you and join your guard if you will have him, or he can return to my detail."

"That is honorable of you." Velika took her sister's hand in hers and squeezed.

Mortas entered with a tray of goblets and one glass of wine for Quinn. Velika's blood would be the only one that her mate would consume. A chill slid down her spine thinking of her mate suckling on her wrist and drinking from her. She pushed the thought down before she scooped up Quinn and took her off to some other room to have her way with her.

"As you've requested, ma'am." He began circulating around the room.

"Thank you, Mortas." She motioned for her sister to join the others. Once they all had their cups in hand, Velika tugged Quinn to her. "I believe a toast is in order to celebrate the extension of our family."

She motioned her glass to Quinn and Lane. She was thrilled to have her family here and to see that her parents and sisters had indeed accepted her mate.

"To family and love." Velika raised her glass.

"Hear, hear."

"I still can't believe you are here," Quinn gushed.

She and Lane wanted some time away from the others to have their private talk. They walked along the lightly lit path in the gardens. The moon was high in a sky that was decorated with small twinkling stars.

It was a perfect day.

She had a mate who loved her, and she'd got her brother back.

"You don't mind that I'm one of them now?" he asked.

They strolled along together with her arm entwined with his.

"No. I'm just happy to have my brother back." She glanced up at him with a wide smile. It was true. It didn't matter that he was no longer human. She was just glad he was alive and well. There were some shadows hidden in his eyes, and she was sure there was more to the story that he wanted to share with her.

"Lethia has given me the option of either joining your house or staying with hers," he said.

Quinn's heart raced. She would love to be able

to see her brother every day, but this wasn't a choice she would be able to make for him.

"What do you want to do?" she asked. Lethia's castle was in Maine. It was all the way on the other side of the country.

"I'm torn. She saved me. Brought me back from the brink of death and has given me so much." He glanced down at her with a sad smile on his lips. "She knows you are important to me and when she found me, I was murmuring your name."

Quinn's eyes blurred with tears. She sensed he had gone to hell and back in those years he'd been missing. How bad, she would never know unless he shared it with her. She wasn't going to push him to divulge his trauma. She would wait until he was ready.

"Oh, Lane." She sniffled, trying to hold back the waterworks.

"But now that I see you have survived, you are strong, beautiful, and are mated to an honorable vampire, I don't think I'm needed in the capacity as before."

"What are you saying?" she asked, confused.

"I was your protector. My sole purpose when we were growing up was to keep you safe. You have that now."

She nodded, understanding where he was coming from. Velika would provide any and everything she would ever need.

"And now that we are in a better place, it's time for us to live our own paths," she said.

They paused and turned to face each other. He gave her a nod.

"We may be across the country from each other, but know there isn't a moment I won't drop what I'm doing to fly to you." He reached out and cupped her cheek.

She smiled, the tears flowing down her face. She leaned into him and rested her forehead against his chest.

"You know I love you, sis."

"And I you." She lifted her head and didn't feel sorrow at all.

He was right.

It was time for them to live out their destinies. They both would live long lives and would always be a part of each other's.

"So how does it feel to be a vampire?" she asked, breaking the tension.

He barked a laugh and took her hand back in his. They strolled along the path.

"It's not too different. I thought I would miss eating food, but I don't even have a taste for it."

"Have you, um, you know…" She couldn't ask.

"Hunted? Bitten and drank from a human?"

She jerked her head in a nod.

"Yeah. It was hard at first, but then the thirst took over. As a newly turned vampire, the need for blood is overwhelming. Lethia taught me everything I needed to know. Now, I'm able to control myself and drink the majority of blood that is provided from glasses." He grinned, showcasing his sharp fangs.

She took in the word majority and didn't even want to ask the other ways he'd drunk blood. Her face warmed at the thought and her personal experience.

That wasn't a conversation she wanted to have with her elder brother.

She lost track of how long they had stayed in the gardens. They had found a bench to sit on and continued their conversation. Quinn caught him up on her life after he had disappeared.

They finally fell into a comfortable silence. Lane glanced over his shoulder and pulled her to her feet.

"Looks like your mate is here for you."

Velika was standing near the bush, patiently waiting.

"I didn't mean to intrude," Velika said.

"Don't worry about it," Lane said. He wrapped an arm around Quinn's shoulder and gave her a squeeze. "I've made my decision on where I will stay and I'm thankful for the opportunity to be with my sister, but I think staying with Lethia will be best."

Velika's gaze flicked to Quinn who nodded. She smiled, proud of her brother.

"We have agreed to stay in contact and visit as much as our time will allow," Quinn said.

"As long as the decision was yours and you are happy with it." Velika's features softened as a smile claimed her face.

"We are," Quinn said. She turned and wrapped Lane up in a crushing hug. "Don't stay away too long."

"I won't."

She backed away from him, and even in the low light, she caught his wink. He gave Velika a nod and brushed past her, leaving the two of them alone.

"Are you okay?" Velika asked.

Quinn moved over to her and stopped before her. "Yeah, I am. I don't think I've ever been this happy." She closed the gap between them and raised herself on her toes.

Velika covered her lips with hers in a chaste kiss.

"Thank you for everything," Quinn said.

"It is my pleasure, *miere.*"

EPILOGUE

Velika couldn't tear her eyes off the strap-on cock entering her mate. Quinn rested on her hands and knees on their bed while rocking back to meet Velika stroke for stroke.

"Oh!" Quinn cried out. Her soft brown skin was coated with a fine sheen of sweat. Her hair, much longer now, was swept off to the side, exposing her mating mark.

Velika reached out and gripped her shoulder while thrusting her hips faster, sending the fake cock deeper inside Quinn.

Quinn's cries grew louder.

"Play with your clit," Velika ordered. She wanted her mate to scream to the high heavens when she reached her climax.

It had been almost a year since the fateful night when Quinn had been captured by Cain and his men. Life since then had been perfect. Quinn and Lane's relationship was close, as it had been before his disappearance. The siblings spoke on the phone multiple times a week and had been to visit each other at least every other month.

Quinn had fallen into her position as a princess with all the grace of a royal as if she'd been one her entire life.

Her mission was to soothe the relationships between humans and vampires. She started off on the small scale with Ensfield. So far, so good. There was now open communication between the humans and Quinn. She would soon move on to other towns and cities they governed. The humans trusted she would keep their best interests at heart.

Velika couldn't be prouder of her mate. Together, they would rule their territory as a fair place to live for vampires and humans.

The rogue vampires had backed off. Due to the massacre and the killing of their leader, they were left with low numbers and no one bold enough to step up into power. Whoever did would have to deal with Velika, and so far, no one was brave or crazy enough to fill Cain's shoes.

"Velika," Quinn cried out.

Velika had learned that her mate was very sexual creature. Maybe it was the bond between them, but there wasn't a day they weren't bringing each other pleasure. Quinn's fingers dug into the bedding, signaling her release was near.

The scent of their lovemaking filled the air. Velika loved the aroma of her mate's arousal. She could always pick up when her mate was thinking erotic thoughts. It drove her crazy.

Velika thrust harder and faster, getting caught up in the sounds her mate was making. Velika reached down and coated her fingers with Quinn's juices. Her pussy stretched out around the cock. It was a beautiful sight to behold.

Velika's body was drawn tight. She was sure she was close to climaxing just from watching her strap-on dive deep into her mate.

Wanting to give Quinn all the pleasure she could handle, Velika pushed her coated finger into the dark rim of Quinn's ass. The puckered hole resisted at first but then opened to allow her to push her finger inside the taut channel.

"Velika!" Quinn cried out. Her muscles clamped down tight around Velika's finger. Quinn's body trembled uncontrollably while she coursed through her release. She fell forward onto the bed.

Velika grinned watching her mate curl up onto her side. Another moan escaped her as she rested back onto the bed. Velika removed the strap-on from her body and tossed it over onto the bed. She lay down next to her mate and took in her afterglow and the satisfied smile on her lips.

She brought Quinn flush against her body. Her hand instinctively went to Quinn's large, rounded belly.

"I love when you scream my name." Velika nibbled on Quinn's ear.

"Our child will definitely know their mothers' names by the time he or she is born." Quinn opened her eyes and met Velika's gaze. She rested her hand on top of Velika's.

Velika had learned she could never tell her mate no. When the subject was broached about children, she found herself ecstatic Quinn was ready so soon to start their family. The in vitro process didn't take long. Quinn had conceived immediately.

Their child would be born a dhampir. It would have all the strengths of humans and vampires.

The child should even be able to withstand sunlight and would be the first royal of his or her kind.

"That is good. I heard babies who hear their parents speaking all the time are born extremely intelligent," Velika said.

Quinn chuckled and lifted to rest on her elbow. She reached out and cupped Velika's bare breast.

"Is that so?" she asked with an innocent look. She leaned down and captured Velika's nipple between her lips. Her tongue teased Velika's beaded bud.

"That's what I've read." Velika groaned. She had been doing intensive research on the rearing of children. She had no experience with them and wanted to be the best mother she could be. She decided to tackle her education of kids like she would an enemy. Plenty of research.

Quinn shimmied her way down Velika's body to where she knelt between Velika's thighs. She pushed Velika's legs apart and eyed her pussy. She licked her lips and took one long swipe of Velika's slit with her tongue.

"And that is why I love you so much." Quinn winked at her then covered her pussy with her mouth again.

Velika's heart thumped erratically at the sight of her beautiful mate devouring her.

Fate had chosen the right person for her, and she would never stop thanking the fates for sending Quinn to her.

"Not as much as I love you, *miere*."

THE END

FROM THE AUTHOR

Dear Reader,

Thank you for taking the time to read my book! This was a fun story. I loved writing Quinn and Velika's story. This story became more than I thought it would be. The words kept flowing and I let them tell their tale. Vampires are one of my favorite creatures to write about and I was happy to be able to do so.

I hope you enjoyed this romance story. If you would like for me to continue this series, please let me know when you leave a review!

Happy reading,
Ariel Marie

The Nightstar Shifters

A FF WOLF SHIFTER ROMANCE SERIES

No wolf can resist the call to mate.

Strong female wolves are in search of their mate. The desire is strong for these women who long to find the one person meant for them.

They are fierce and determined, putting their trust in fate.

If you love lesbian wolf shifter romance filled with action and adventure, then you will love the Nightstar Shifters series.

Start the series today!

ABOUT THE AUTHOR

Ariel Marie is an author who loves the paranormal, action and hot steamy romance. She combines all three in each and every one of her stories. For as long as she can remember, she has loved vampires, shifters and every creature you can think of. This even rolls over into her favorite movies. She loves a good action packed thriller! Throw a touch of the supernatural world in it and she's hooked!

She grew up in Cleveland, Ohio where she currently resides with her husband and three beautiful children.

For more information:
www.thearielmarie.com

ABOUT THE AUTHOR

The Nightstar Shifters

Sailing With Her Wolf

Protecting Her Wolf

Sealed With A Bite

Hers to Claim

Wanted by the Wolf

The Immortal Reign series

Deadly Kiss

Blackclaw Alphas (Reverse Harem Series)

Fate of Four

Bearing Her Fate (TBD)

The Midnight Coven Brand

Forever Desired

Wicked Shadows

Paranormal Erotic Box Sets

Vampire Destiny (An Erotic Vampire Box Set)

Moon Valley Shifters Box Set (F/F Shifters)

The Dragon Curse Series (Ménage MFF Erotic Series)

The Dark Shadows Series

Princess

Toma

Phaelyn

Teague

Adrian

Nicu

Sassy Ever After World

Her Warrior Dragon

Her Fierce Dragon

Her Guardian Dragon (TBD)

Stand Alone Books

Dani's Return

A Faery's Kiss

Tiger Haven

Searching For His Mate

A Tiger's Gift

Stone Heart (The Gargoyle Protectors)

Saving Penny

A Beary Christmas

Howl for Me

Birthright

Return to Darkness

Red and the Alpha

Made in the USA
Columbia, SC
13 September 2022